S0-AAE-133

CANDLELIGHT REGENCIES

627   THE PAISLEY BUTTERFLY. *Phyllis Taylor Pianka*

631   MAKESHIFT MISTRESS. *Amanda Mack*

632   RESCUED BY LOVE. *Joan Vincent*

633   A MARRIAGEABLE ASSET. *Ruth Gerber*

637   THE BRASH AMERICAN. *Samantha Lester*

638   A SEASON OF SURPRISES. *Rebecca Ashley*

639   THE ENTERPRISING MINX. *Marian Lorraine*

643   A HARMLESS RUSE. *Alexandra Lord*

644   THE GYPSY HEIRESS. *Laura London*

645   THE INNOCENT HEART. *Nina Pykare*

649   LORD SATAN'S BRIDE. *Anne Stuart*

650   THE CURIOUS ROGUE. *Joan Vincent*

651   THE RELUCTANT DUKE. *Philippa Castle*

655   LOVE'S TEMPEST. *Elinor Larkin*

656   MISS HUNGERFORD'S HANDSOME HERO. *Noel Vreeland Carter*

657   REBEL IN LOVE. *Veronica Howard*

660   TILLY. *Jennie Tremaine*

661   COMPROMISED LOVE. *Anne Hillary*

662   BRIDE OF VENGEANCE. *Rose Marie Abbott*

665   LADY THIEF. *Kay Hooper*

666   THE BELLE OF BATH. *Dorothy Mack*

667   THE FAINT-HEARTED FELON. *Pauline Pryor*

670   TORIA. *Margaret MacWilliams*

671   OH, WHAT A TANGLED WEB. *Joyce Lee*

672   THE VISCOUNT'S WITCH. *Edith de Paul*

675   LOVE PLAYS A PART. *Nina Pykare*

676   RENDEZVOUS AT GRAMERCY. *Constance Ravenlock*

677   A WILLFUL WIDOW. *Rebecca Ashley*

680   MISS CLARINGDON'S CONDITION. *Laureen Kwock*

681   THE IMPOVERISHED HEIRESS. *Diana Burke*

682   THE UNSUITABLE LOVERS. *Phoebe Matthews*

685   SUSIE. *Jennie Tremaine*

686   THE INNOCENT ADULTERESS. *Dee Stuart*

687   LADY NELL. *Sandra Mireles*

690   BOLD VENTURE. *Colleen Moore*

691   A MERRY CHASE. *Ruby Frankel*

692   A SUITABLE MARRIAGE. *Marlaine Kyle*

694   AN IMMODEST PROPOSAL. *Dena Rhee*

695   THE ARROGANT ARISTOCRAT. *Rebecca Ashley*

696   HEATHER WILD. *Phyllis Taylor Pianka*

A CONVENIENT BRIDE

Betty L. Henrichs

A CANDLELIGHT REGENCY SPECIAL

Published by
Dell Publishing Co., Inc.
1 Dag Hammarskjold Plaza
New York, New York 10017

Dell ® TM 681510, Dell Publishing Co., Inc.

ISBN: 0–440–11472–1

Printed in the United States of America
First printing—February 1982

CHAPTER ONE

Penelope had an arm load of fragrant roses and was about to enter the dining room when she heard Constance Buxley's whining voice. "Why do we have to have her at the ball, Mama? Why?" Constance dabbed at her eyes with a scrap of lace. "She will put us to the blush, you know she will. Why do I have to present my friends to the vicar's daughter? I don't understand why she has to be here at all!" she sniffled.

Penelope's heart thudded uncomfortably when she realized they were talking about her. She shrank back against the wall of the manor house. What could she do? She couldn't enter the room, and if she moved away, they would see her and think she had been eavesdropping. She was trapped. Each word bit into her like a chill sword.

"I vow you are acting like a selfish child," Lady Buxley admonished. "You know very well it was our Christian duty to give her lodgings when the good vicar died. Everyone will think us most generous for giving the poor child a home, even though she isn't quite . . . mmm quite . . ."

"Quite used to 'polite' society you mean," snapped Constance. "She isn't of our class, Mama. She has no social graces and her clothes are positively medieval! She reminds me of a drab little mouse. What will our friends think?"

Lady Buxley crossed the room to inspect the silver on the sideboard. "I must agree she is a problem, but I really don't perceive what we can do about it now. She has to stay here until we can find her a position as a governess or paid companion, so we are at a stand." Constance started to protest, but her mother stilled her. "Please remember, she is a Stanwood, and her mother was a Lancaster. Her heritage is acceptable, if you overlook the fact that her father was but a local vicar. We had best make everyone aware of her lineage, then when we explain her circumstances they will understand. It is hardly a sin not to be plump in one's pockets."

An angry blush spread across Penelope's face. "Nothing but a local vicar . . ." The words tore at her. How dare anyone reduce her father's dedicated work of a lifetime to those few words? Maybe she had not mixed in the society her birth entitled her to, maybe she wasn't well dressed or conversant with gentry balls; still they had no right to sneer at her parents or her upbringing!

She brushed an angry tear away as Constance pleaded, "But, Mama, the marquis of Ashford will be here with all of his friends." Penelope could hear a note of awe creep into her voice. "I saw him last year and he is so handsome, Mama. You know he is of the haut ton. I want him to find favor with me. He might even fix his interest."

"Well, I am not sure the squire and I would fancy that! It would certainly be a splendid match," Lady Buxley conceded, "and your papa would be pleased to see our two lands march together, but the marquis has rather a . . . hmm . . . distasteful reputation."

"Do you mean he's a rake!" Constance's eyes sparkled. "I've never met a rake before."

"Hush!" commanded her mother sternly. "Such words on the lips of a young lady are unbecoming. Rake indeed! Pray, let us hear no more of it. You ought not even to know of such things!"

"But, Mama . . ."

"No, I want to hear no more!" Lady Buxley insisted.

"We are honored the marquis has agreed to grace our hunt and ball. We shall not speak again of his . . . mmm . . . life-style."

"All right," Constance sulked. "But we still haven't decided what to do with Penelope. She ought not to attend. Cleona told me Beau Brummell is one of his lordship's good friends. You must realize what that means. If the marquis tells everyone we are rude rustics, my season in London will be ruined!"

At the mention of Mr. Brummell's name, Lady Buxley blanched. It certainly would never do to have the famous arbiter of taste in the ton think them provincial. It could lead to one of his infamous set-downs. Yes, Constance was correct, something had to be done about Miss Stanwood. It would never do for her to make an appearance. They could not risk putting a foot wrong before the season began. With a sigh she commented, "I do wish we had thought of this sooner. The dress the village seamstress made for her is passably acceptable, I suppose, but she is bound to embarrass us with her simple vicarage ways."

"What is best to do, Mama? The fox hunt and ball are tomorrow."

"I'm aware of that, but we just can't lock her in the scullery."

There was a rap at the door and the butler entered. "Yes, Jarvis, what is it?"

"Sorry to bother you, milady, but Cook wishes a word with you. 'Tis about the trout. It hasn't arrived, and she wishes to have your permission to substitute hare."

"No, pheasant would be better. Have the gameskeeper attend to it. I will alter the menu accordingly. Come, Constance, it is time for your final fitting."

"But, Mama!"

Lady Buxley glanced at Jarvis and back at her daughter

with a warning frown. "The matter we discussed will be attended to. I daresay there will be no problem."

When the room was untenanted, Penelope slipped between the double doors and quickly arranged the roses in the vermeil centerpiece, then sped back outside. Tears stung her soft hazel eyes as she hurried to the grape arbor. Then, safe from prying eyes, she let them fall. Finally, with a determined sniffle, she raised her head and willed the tears to cease. One last tear trickled down, but she quickly wiped it away with a corner of her faded muslin skirt.

"Oh, Papa," she sighed, "why did you have to leave me alone like this!" She had asked herself that question time and time again since his death, and yet all the while she knew the answer. Her parents' marriage had been a true love match, not like the arranged marriages of the ton, and once her mother was gone, so was her father's will to live. Week by week she had watched him fade away, until he joined his beloved wife once more. Now she was left with no one.

Memories of her happy childhood growing up at the vicarage helped ease her sorrow, but those memories could not help her with the future. What was she going to do? Since Penelope had come to live at Buxley Manor, she had simply drifted from day to day. Thoughts of the future were too painful to endure. She blotted them from her mind. But Lady Buxley's words had jolted her into an awareness of her precarious position. Obviously her presence was causing problems for Squire and Lady Buxley. What was she to do? Where could she go?

Be a governess? The idea made Penelope sad. To raise the children of others, and never to have any of her own, would be intolerable. She desperately wanted a family. The tears began to gather. She tried to blink them back, yet they continued to fill her eyes until another thought, a horrible thought, drove them away. She shivered. What if . . . She had trouble forming the thought in her mind. Penelope shivered once more. What if the master of the house took familiarities? Rumors of such things had even penetrated the staid life at the vicarage. She pulled her knees up and hugged them close. If not a governess, what then? Could she endure being a paid companion? Would that not be worse? How horrid to be at the beck and whim of some old woman in her dotage. Penelope gazed sadly into space. Either would be a living death. What was she to do?

For a moment her thoughts lingered gently on the elusive image of an imaginary husband. Penelope had seen him many times in her dreams. His image was so clear to her. He was tall and strong, but his arms felt gentle when he held her and . . . She pulled herself up sharply. Oh, what was the use of dreams! This was not to be for her. Who would want a wife without a dowry? Or one that looked like, what had Constance called her . . . oh, yes, "a drab little mouse"?

With a determined shake of her head Penelope stood up and smoothed her rumpled skirt. Dwelling on the past or the uncertain future was useless. Better be concerned with the present. And the present was the fox hunt and ball scheduled for tomorrow. It was patently clear she ought not to attend, so while she walked slowly back toward the manor house she fashioned an excuse.

Lady Buxley had requested that she arrange the flowers for the party, so Penelope gathered more roses, daisies, and lilies before entering the dining room again. She was at work in the salon when her ladyship located her. Lady Buxley cleared her throat uncomfortably, but before she could speak, Penelope said, "Ma'am, I'm glad you have come, for I want to discuss a problem with you. It is about the festivities tomorrow."

For an instant Lady Buxley looked nonplussed, but she quickly recovered her composure and inquired, "Yes, Penelope. What about tomorrow?"

Penelope swallowed back a wave of shame and continued, "I want you to know that I am very thankful for your hospitality. I don't know what I would have done after Papa died if you and the squire had not opened your home to me. I don't wish to seem ungrateful, yet I beg to be excused from the hunt and ball. Papa's death is too close for me to enjoy any merrymaking."

The look of startled relief that flashed across Lady Buxley's face made Penelope lower her eyes. She was embarrassed that her presence was the cause of so much obvious discomfort. Her ladyship's voice soothed, "M'dear, I perfectly understand. We all feel the loss of the good vicar, and I'm sure you most of all." Lady Buxley patted her hand. "Think no more of it. I will inform Constance of your decision. She will be most distressed you can not attend," she lied, "but I shall endeavor to explain it all to her." She glanced around the salon. "Your flower arrangements in here are lovely. Please attend to the ones in the ballroom before you retire."

With a sigh Penelope headed outside again. Already the life of a penniless drudge was beginning. The future was indeed bleak.

The next morning Penelope was awakened early by the sound of scurrying footmen and maids preparing for the big day. She made her way quietly down the back stairs to the kitchen. A scene of utter chaos greeted her. Scullery maids were darting to and fro under the direction of the frazzled cook, and footmen were running in and out carrying loads of silver to be laid on the tables. Penelope picked her way gingerly through the turmoil and approached the cook, who turned with a startled expression. "Miss Stanwood, what are you doin' in m'kitchen. 'Tis not a fit place for a lady."

"Rosie, I'm no stranger to a kitchen. I spent many happy hours in ours at the vicarage. Mama always said that in order to run a house properly a lady must learn how to do all manner of things before she is fit to direct others."

"Humph, I'm not much holdin' with those modern ideas. I feel a lady should leave the cookin' to those of us who know better."

Penelope laughed. "Probably so, but I'm not here to supervise or get in the way. I know everyone is busy so I thought I ought to come and fetch my own breakfast this morning."

The cook looked at her sternly. "No lady is goin' to serve herself in my house as long as I'm in charge. You go to the mornin' room, and I'll have your breakfast brought, right and proper."

When Penelope was gone, the cook murmured to herself, "That poor, poor little child! What's she goin' to do? She's the sweetest little lady, so kind and thoughtful. It fair makes my heart bleed for her when I think of her future. 'Tis not fair," she sighed, "for some people who are all spoiled and the like to have so much, and that child so little."

She stared for a minute then turned and snapped at one of the scullery maids, "Well, don't stand there gawkin'! Go and take Miss Stanwood her breakfast. Scat!"

After Penelope had eaten her meal, she made one last walk through the room to check on the flower arrangements. Here and there a few of the blooms had drooped. She pulled them out and added fresh ones. Her tour done, she turned and was slowly climbing the stairs when she encountered Constance. This time, since she knew Penelope would not attend the party, she condescended to be gracious. She pivoted on the landing while displaying her new riding habit. "What do you think? Didn't it turn out just smashing!"

Privately Penelope thought the choice of color was wrong. Constance had a very pale complexion with a smattering of freckles, but she had insisted on a light pink habit. Lady Buxley had tried to dissuade her, but as always Constance forced her way. The color was not becoming.

Before Penelope could phrase an appropriately noncommittal reply, Constance rushed on, "Mama told me you have chosen not to join us for the hunt and ball. How terribly sad!" she fibbed. "You shall miss all the excitement. The marquis of Ashford will attend, plus Lord and Lady Shellingham, and the viscount of Harrington. But naturally I understand your reluctance to go into society so soon after your father's death." With a wave of her hand she dismissed Penelope. "I must be off. The guests shall be here soon."

When she reached the bottom of the stairs, she turned and called up to Penelope, "I know you don't wish to be present, but why don't you stay at the top of the stairs and watch the notables arrive." With a toss of her head she bragged, "You might see the marquis of Ashford fix his interest. After all, our lands would make a nice addition to his estate."

Penelope had no intention of staying to watch the guests arrive. Yet, when the first chimes sounded, she found herself at the banister. One peek at this marquis of Ashford could not hurt, she tried to reassure herself. Soon even such close contact as this with "polite" society would be over. Governesses and paid companions were not often allowed to mix with members of the ton, even at a distance. Why not stay and at least glimpse how others lived?

Guest after guest from the local gentry was announced

by Jarvis's ponderous tones, but not the noted marquis. Squire and Lady Buxley tried to draw their friends toward the salon, but most remained milling expectantly around the great entry hall. Finally, the sound of a coach and four could be heard arriving at the door. A hush fell over the guests as each strained to see. Lady Buxley pushed her way through the crowd in order to be near the door. She pulled Constance to her side and brushed an imaginary speck of lint from her habit. The chimes rang. A liveried footman swung the door wide and two men entered.

Jarvis's formal introductions were unnecessary. Penelope sensed instantly which was the marquis of Ashford. No wonder Constance was all aflutter. Even if he were not one of the most eligible bachelors in the ton, he would attract feminine interest simply by his commanding presence and devilish good looks. With his title and vast estates, Penelope knew why his appeal was so positively devastating! He towered over his companion. She guessed he must stand a shade over six feet. He was dressed for the hunt in a red velvet jacket that accentuated his darkly handsome features. His burnished chestnut hair was brushed à la Brutus. It handsomely set off his black eyes and aristocratic forehead. Penelope had to force her eyes away to spare a glance for his companion. The man on his left, who Jarvis announced as James Graham, viscount of Harrington, cut a pleasing-enough figure, yet next to his lordship he faded into obscurity. Without conscious thought her eyes were drawn back to the marquis.

How weak he makes other men seem, she thought, with his firm jawline and powerful shoulders. He exerts no effort, yet he dominates the scene. As he turned toward the gushing Lady Buxley, Penelope suddenly felt a pang of remembrance. His profile seemed familiar. That was not possible. Still, the vague feeling persisted till the action below drove it from her mind.

Constance was being introduced to the two men by Lady Buxley. Penelope couldn't hear the words being exchanged. But, as an uninvolved observer, she could read the meaning of the various expressions, and they told a tale of their own. Constance, who thought herself an incomparable, was using every wile to attract the marquis's attention. Yet, as he bowed gallantly over her offered hand, Penelope saw first a flicker of disdain and then boredom mar his features. How often he must have played this scene before, she mused. No wonder he is weary of the courting game. Since he made his first debut, she was sure every matchmaking mama in the ton had thrown her daughter at him in hopes that he might be caught. Penelope cringed as she saw Constance simper up at him. She is acting the hen-witted fool, thought Penelope. She is so intent on her coquetry she doesn't even realize his indifference. Lady Buxley is certainly not helping the situation either. Why must she be so blatant in her attempt to draw the viscount of Harrington and the other guests away so that Constance and the marquis can be alone? Penelope glanced at his lordship and perceived that he had missed nothing of the maneuver. There was a new cynical twist to his apparently sincere smile. What would it take to wipe that expression away, she wondered.

She knew the answer as two more people arrived. Jarvis's words echoed through the great hall as he announced, "Lord and Lady Shellingham." The marquis turned, the look of boredom gone. His eyes glittered as he bowed over Lady Shellingham's elegantly outstretched hand. Even though she was far removed from the scene, Penelope could sense the powerful undercurrents flowing through the hall. Lady Shellingham smiled seductively up into his lordship's eyes while her husband glared angrily from her side. His hands clenched and unclenched as he viewed the play between his wife and the marquis. It

14

seemed as if Lord Shellingham was preparing to vent his anger when the viscount of Harrington rushed into the hall to exchange greetings with the arriving guests. Instantly the tableau dissolved and the tension eased. His arrival seemed casual, but Penelope had seen the truth. When the Shellinghams were announced, he had rudely pulled away from Lady Buxley and headed for the door. His timing was no mistake; he deliberately intended to insert himself between the Shellinghams and Ashford. But why?

When everyone had left the entry hall, Penelope puzzled over the question. When no answer came, she reluctantly retired to her bedchamber. Her brief glimpse of life in "polite" society made her restless. She lay on the hard bed, but sleep eluded her. All of the sermons her father had preached on the futility and emptiness of the moneyed existence echoed in her ears . . . yet the regret remained.

Would it be so awful to be a member of the ton, Penelope wondered. Their money could do so much good in the world, if only they cared. Surely their life could have substance. Her parents had scorned their heritage, but must she? Her eyes closed. Visions of being presented at court filled her mind. Then slowly the scene merged into an imaginary assembly at Almack's. Music was playing. A man was bending over her hand, begging leave to have the next dance. She could almost feel his warm grasp. Then . . .

With a start she jerked herself upright. Such nonsense must stop! She had thought Constance hen-witted; at least Constance was not wasting her time on empty dreams, dreams that would never possess reality, dreams that only brought sadness, not joy. Quickly, she got off the bed and reached for one of her father's books of edifying homilies. There was no comfort in the familiar words. She threw the book aside. What was the matter with her? She crossed the room and stared out the window; she was blind to the gardens below. Instead, the image of the marquis smiling down at Lady Shellingham returned to haunt her, and with it the vague feeling of remembrance.

With a shrug she pushed the image aside and reached for the discarded book. Before she could settle, the horns blew, calling the riders for the hunt. As if drawn by a force, she rushed to the windows of the upstairs parlor. Below on the gravel drive the riders, horses, and packs of hunting dogs were all milling about. The huntsmen blew their long brass horns again and the riders mounted. Without thought, Penelope looked for the marquis. She conceded he was a fine figure of a man; he needed no corseting or padding to aid nature. Indeed, he was almost too muscular; his bulging thigh muscles marred the smooth line of his breeches. With practiced ease he swung onto the back of his ebony black stallion. The horse pranced and threatened to rear. He pulled it down with a masterly hand. Penelope glanced over the rest of the guests and saw Constance edging her little mare closer to his side. Her effort was wasted. As she approached, the horns blew for the third time and the dogs were released. The hunt was begun.

Penelope pressed her face against the glass, her eyes upon his lordship's galloping back. There that feeling was again. Why did the marquis strike a chord in her memory? Her father had been vicar in the Ashford parish, but his lordship was seldom in residence. She was sure he had never graced their small church. Why was he so familiar? Now the riders were galloping across the fields, nearing the first jump. As she watched him soar over the hedgerow, the reason suddenly came. He was the imaginary beau of her dreams: the same chestnut hair, the strength, the powerful features; she could see it all.

She remembered. The marquis of Ashford was no

16

stranger to her. Several years ago she had seen him from afar. They were at the local fair day when he arrived with some of his fashionable friends. Everyone was agog at their presence, yet she saw nothing but him. The years rolled away as the event replayed in her mind. How conveniently she had forgotten! All this time she believed she had created her ideal, when if fact be known, she was but remembering the vague image of a schoolroom miss's infatuation with the unattainable. What an utter fool she had been! "I vow no more," she muttered as she slammed the door to her bedchamber. With a determined nod she grabbed the book of homilies and sank down on the bed. It was time to put away such childish nonsense. The handsome marquis could never have a place in her future, either in her dreams or reality.

CHAPTER TWO

The hunt was a smashing success. Penelope could hear the guests gaily chatting as they clattered back into the manor house. She wrinkled her nose in distaste. Riding was a favorite sport of hers, but not riding after a kill. Culling any herd of deer was necessary, she supposed, but this vestige of barbarism disturbed her. Why must they make sport in such a way? With a sigh she acknowledged, "That's but another reason why the tonnish life would not fit."

All through the house she could hear chamber doors slamming as the guests started to change for dinner and the ball to follow. At the thought of dinner she realized she was hungry. Before she could descend, there was a rap at her door and Rosie entered bearing a heavily loaded tray. "I made bold to bring your supper, Miss Stanwood, seein' as how you'll miss the sit-down."

"Rosie, you shouldn't have bothered. I could have come."

The cook fussed around Penelope as she settled her in the chair and laid out the meal. "'Tis good to be out of that kitchen. Besides you need to eat. If you get any thinner, the wind will blow you clear to Londontown."

Penelope smiled wanly. Rosie was correct as usual. Since her parent's death she had eaten little and knew she must resemble a scarecrow. Obediently she sampled one savory dish after another while the cook beamed with pride. There was thick chicken soup, oyster pie, pheasants stuffed with carp, roasted pigeons, vegetable fritters, and, for dessert, a small meringue basket filled with beautifully iced petits fours. When she had eaten her fill, the cook gathered up the dishes. "Sure wish you'd change your mind and go to that ball. A little dancin' do your heart a world o' good."

"I think I will read, instead," said Penelope with a laugh. "That will do my mind a world of good."

"Humph! 'Tis no fittin' way for a young lass to spend an evenin'. You listen now, no bluestocking lady ever did catch herself a beau. Still say you ought to be dancin', not readin'!" With that stern reproof she left.

The house quieted as the guests descended for the sumptuous dinner. Penelope used the opportunity to slip downstairs and enter the study by the back way. A footman had lit a fire in the room, so she felt cozy and warm as she curled up in the big leather chair in the alcove to read. Later she could hear the band tuning up and knew the dance would soon start. For a moment she wished she could be whirling around the room in a waltz or forming part of a set for a country dance. She pushed her thoughts away and returned to her book.

The strains of the music floated into the room as the ball commenced; with determination Penelope concentrated on the pages of her book. It worked. She became so lost in the story that she was startled when the door opened and someone entered. Who could that be, she wondered. The alcove wall blocked her view. She was about to rise and check when she heard a deeply masculine voice observe, "Not the most romantic place for a rendezvous milady, but it's apparently the best this dreary place has to offer."

"I don't care," a woman's voice answered seductively. "Even the butler's pantry would have done, just as long as we can have a few moments alone!"

Penelope silently laid the book down in her lap. Her

hands trembled. What should she do? She certainly would not dare interrupt such an interlude. She could only hope that the couple had slipped into the study for a brief flirtation . . . maybe one stolen kiss and then quickly back to the ball.

As if the woman had sensed her thoughts, she pleaded, "Oh, Alex, hold me! Kiss me!"

Penelope blushed when she heard the rustling sounds and murmured words of the embrace. She could not see and dared not leave; she had to endure the scene in silence. It seemed to go on for a vast age, until finally she heard the man softly tease, "Millicent, I've always thought you were a vixen or a siren or some such mythological being. Now I know it's true."

"Why, whatever do you mean?"

"I mean, I'll be dashed if I can figure out how you lured Chester away to the cardroom. I thought he never would leave your side. He's as possessive as a rooster with a flock of prize hens."

There was a throaty laugh. "I believe I shall leave you, Alex. I don't fancy being compared to a hen, even a prize one. But unfortunately you are right. My husband is getting to be a crushing bore! You should think he would be pleased the marquis of Ashford dances attendance to his wife. Any other husband in our set would be."

Penelope heard a chuckle. "If it weren't for this damned ball, I would do much more than merely dance attendance to you, milady." He paused, his voice deep with desire. "My *chérie amante,* I have missed you."

"Mmm, Alex, I love it when you call me that," she purred contentedly. "Say it again."

"*Chérie amante,* it is but a phrase. I would rather my actions beguiled you than my words. Shall we see which is the most enticing!"

There was another long, passionate pause. Penelope

yearned to be gone, but dared not try to tiptoe out. Her face burned with embarrassment. Lady Buxley's words about the marquis's reputation came to her mind. For once, Penelope thought, she did not exaggerate. Indeed his lordship was a rake! That woman in his arms was obviously married to another!

Millicent's silky voice broke the silence. "Alex, enough. You'll crush my gown."

"You've never objected before," he teased.

Penelope could hear the rustle of a taffeta skirt as the woman moved across the room. Millicent spoke again. This time her tone was different. A pleading note had entered her words. "No, Alex, I am serious. Please come no nearer. We must talk. There will be time later for . . . other things."

He sighed, but agreed. "I intend to hold you to that promise, fair lady. Now what is it you wish to discuss?"

"It's Chester. He is growing suspicious of us. Do you know he even had the nerve to enter my chamber this evening while I was dressing and hurl accusations at me? Thank goodness my dresser speaks only French!"

"Shellingham is a fool. I can't think why you married him."

"Alex, be serious! He is threatening to make his suspicions public. He even said he would go to the Queen. If he does, I could lose my place at court. You have to protect my good name! There must be no scandal!"

"Are you saying you wish to end our affair, Millicent?" A hardness had entered his tone.

"Oh, Alex, no!" she cried. "But we'd best be a little more discreet. If only there was a way to convince Chester that his beliefs are unfounded."

"I don't see how we can. Maybe you should try and find a ladybird to divert his attention."

"Alex! Such an idea. You put me to the blush."

Penelope heard Millicent cross the room and there was silence. When she spoke again, her voice was low with passion. "I can't let you go. I won't! You do feel the same! Tell me you do."

He answered with another kiss, and Penelope heard the woman in his arms sigh. Her words were softly pleading as she begged, "Alex, my love, there is a way to divert Chester's suspicions. Promise me you will listen."

"Must be deuced unpleasant if you have to plead with me to listen to it," said Alex ruefully. "Well, let's hear it. How can we convince Chester of your virtue and my honor? As you know, I cannot afford to have a public scandal attached to my name either just now."

She hesitated for a moment, then ventured her suggestion. "There would be no hint of our relationship if you were to marry."

"What!" he roared. "Have you suddenly turned into a ninnyhammer?"

"Alex, you promised to listen. And please lower your voice. We don't want Chester to come barging in on us."

"Sorry," he muttered, "but I tend to yell when confronted with absurdity."

"It is not absurdity! You must marry and set up your nursery soon anyway, unless you wish that mutton-headed cousin of yours to inherit. Do you wish that?"

"You know I don't. I will never allow Ashford to pass to Percy, but, on the other hand, neither am I ready to be shackled to some shrewish wife. One possessive spouse between us is enough."

"Darling, that is just it. If we plan this correctly, neither of us will be encumbered by a suspicious mate. Think how delightful that would be!" she murmured.

He started to protest, but Millicent stilled his lips. After a space she continued with her plea. "Please consider the idea. Truly, my dear, your marriage would make things so

23

much easier for us. Chester's such a dullard he will never think a bridegroom has . . . hmm . . . other interests."

"Chester may be a dullard, but from what I have observed, the young misses making their bows this season are not," Alex argued. "If I'm not properly attentive, my bride is liable to put up a screech and that would be unbearable! It might even create a worse scandal than Chester's blustering."

"Very true, but who says you must choose a bride versed in the ways of society. Would not some countrified miss, with no knowledge of the ton, be better? She would be content to reside at Ashford while you and I enjoy London. You would scarce know you were married."

When he made no reply, she urged, "Please consider well what I have suggested. It would answer for everything. If you were safely married, Chester would be satisfied; your duty to continue the Ashford line would be satisfied; your mother, who I know has been urging you to marry, would be satisfied; and," she whispered silkily, "I would be satisfied."

"Oh, devil take it!" he grumbled. "What a damnable coil!"

"Yes, I know it is, darling. But all can be well if you do as I suggest." A tinge of jealousy shadowed Millicent's words. "I shall hate the thought of your sharing a bed with another, but it must be. After all, it won't be as if your heart is engaged."

Penelope heard her taffeta skirt rustle as she moved toward the back of the room. "What we need is a convenient bride, good birth of course, but undemanding. One who will be satisfied with the few crumbs of attention you give on your rare visits to the country. You might even be generous and allow her a season in London." She laughed seductively. "Once in a great while. I shall look over the prospects outside and see if any of these country lasses will suit."

"I have not yet agreed."

"I know, my love, but it is the only way. We can't have Chester stirring up a ruckus. Neither of us wants to become the latest on-dits."

Penelope heard the door to the back hall open. "We ought not to be seen returning together. Wait a spell before you follow." Millicent blew a kiss and was gone.

Alex angrily paced across the room. "Hell and damnation!" he cursed as he crashed his fist down on the desk. He continued pacing. Why did this have to happen now, he asked himself? Why now when Sir Chinningsworth was on his puritanical crusade?

The words of Lord Sythe's warning returned to his mind. He had requested a meeting with the Tory leader to discover why his appointment to fill out his father's term in the House of Lords had not been received. The elderly statesman's answer was blunt. "Ashford, it's because of all the gossip concerning your reputation. Normally the appointment would have been given without question. However, the actions of the Prince Regent and his set, of which you are a prominent member, have angered Sir Chinningsworth and other Puritans. Because of this, they are challenging the nomination."

Alex vigorously defended himself. His appointment to the House of Lords was not mere whim. He was deeply concerned about the future direction of England and believed he could make a valuable contribution. Further, he asserted his personal life was his own and should not be used as a basis for judging his political potential.

Lord Sythe agreed, at least in theory. "Frankly, old boy," he said, "I don't give a fig for the way you choose to live your life. I've known you since you were in knee breeches and realize how much this appointment means to you. You'd be an asset to our party too, no doubt about that. But in this matter I have to answer to the other cabinet ministers. Take my advice, keep your affairs very quiet and discreet until I can ram through your nomination. Mind now, there must be no scandal, no cause for gossip. Any further whisper against your name and Sir Chinningsworth and his group will prevail. I shall be powerless to help you. Your father's seat in Parliament will go to another."

The marquis continued to pace through the study as he tried to find some solution to the dilemma. His affair with Millicent had been diverting, but it was not the grand passion of his life. Truly he would hate to see it end, but maybe it must. Wouldn't that still the gossiping tongues? He angrily rubbed his forehead. No. If he let Millicent go, there was still no guarantee that Lord Shellingham would not create a public scene. His behavior was too erratic. When he was in his cups, which lately had been more often than not, he was totally unpredictable. Even a drunken accusation by Chester might give Sir Chinningsworth enough ammunition to mount his crusade, and his hopes for a political future would be dashed.

"Damn, damn, damn!" Alex muttered savagely. He was determined not to let that seat in the House of Lords slip away, but what to do? Reluctantly he returned to Millicent's suggestion. The thought of marriage was distasteful. His heart had only been touched by one woman, and after that he had vowed never again to be so vulnerable. Nevertheless, he had always known that marriage was inevitable. As marquis of Ashford he had a duty to his heritage. The line must not be allowed to pass to his cousin. With a sigh he conceded that marriage might be the answer.

With a rueful smile he thought of his mother. At least she would be happy if he started setting up his nursery. Then the smile faded. There must be no scandal for her sake either. Since his father's death, her health had deteriorated. He feared for her if their proud name was dragged through the mire.

While he paced and muttered, Penelope sat silently in the chair, afraid to move. She heard his pacing cease, then doors to the cabinet in the corner open and slam shut. "You'd think Buxley would have at least one bottle of brandy in this cursed place!" his lordship growled. He opened another cabinet and slammed it shut.

Penelope's hand flew to her mouth as she heard his step turn toward the alcove. She silently scrambled to her feet, intending to slip behind the heavy brocade drapery. She had forgotten the discarded book laying on her lap. It fell to the floor with a thud.

In an instant he was at her side, glaring down at her with a thunderous scowl. "Who the deuce are you?" he demanded. "Why were you spying on us?"

Penelope's first instinct was to flee, but he was blocking her way. All of her emotions were jumbled. His towering presence was so disturbing! After the disgraceful interchange she had heard, her mind told her to give him a crushing set-down and leave with dignity. A rake deserved no more! Yet she did not move. The words did not come. For her heart was remembering the man of her dreams. She peeked timidly up at him. Her breath came quicker. Even when fury marred his face, he was still handsome. There was something so uncompromisingly masculine about him that he forced an unwilling response from her. Small wonder Millicent was desperate to hold on to his love.

When she remained silent, he repeated his question and added, "I do not intend to be cozened by some chit out of the schoolroom. You will answer me! Why were you eavesdropping on us? I suppose now you will demand payment for your silence. Well, how much do you want?"

27

Penelope was stung by his words. Without measuring her response she snapped, "The unpleasant results of the coil you have woven about yourself and your guilty conscience will be sufficient payment, milord."

Surprisingly he laughed. "What a little hellcat you are! I had expected you to put on missish airs. I much prefer this."

"Frankly, I don't care what you prefer. Please stand aside. I wish to leave."

She took a step to brush by, but his hand detained her. "Not yet." His words were hard once more. "You won't pass until you have answered my questions. Why were you hiding in this alcove?"

Penelope glanced down at the hand grasping her arm, then back up into his face. Reluctantly, he let his hand drop and took a step back away from her. She met his gaze calmly. Her heart was pounding, but there was no evidence of her turmoil as she replied coldly, "I was not hiding. I was here reading when you and your lady friend entered. And never fear, I would not sully my lips by repeating what I heard. The secret of your tryst is safe with me. Your discussion with Lady Shellingham shall go no farther."

"I vow I think I have encountered a prude," he teased. "At least you are a change from the usual young ladies I have met." He gallantly bowed and smiled down into her eyes. "Let us begin again. May I have the honor of your acquaintance?"

A smile tugged at the corners of Penelope's mouth. He really was irresistible! "Milord, I'm Miss Penelope Stanwood. My father was vicar of this parish."

His glance flickered over her. As a connoisseur of beauty he was not particularly impressed with what he saw. Her hazel eyes were appealing enough and the delicate bone structure betrayed her genteel breeding, but she was

28

far too thin to be attractive. But he did note that she wore the faded and patched dress with dignity. He was pleased that she made no apology for her poverty. Her head remained high. He nodded reflectively. "Oh, yes, you must be the poor daughter of the good vicar," he mimicked Lady Buxley's condescending tone exactly. "She bored me with a long recital of their generosity earlier this evening. If you are a guest here, why aren't you at the ball?"

Penelope lowered her eyes and murmured the excuse about still mourning her father's death. Suddenly she felt Alex's warm hand gently lifting her chin. Her eyes fluttered open; she was forced to meet his serious look.

"That's a hum if I have ever heard one, Miss Stanwood. You really ought not to tell a lie unless you can tell it convincingly." She started to argue, but he said, "Don't try to defend them. Lord and Lady Buxley and their incredibly boorish daughter thought you would put them to the blush so they shunted you off into this room. I am well acquainted with their type!"

Before she could explain that not attending the party had been her idea, the door opened and a man's voice called anxiously, "Alex, are you still here?"

The marquis stepped from behind the alcove wall. "Hullo, James, come and join us."

"Join you?" he croaked in a harried voice. "Didn't come to join you. Came to warn you! You've got to send Millicent away and now! Chester left the cardroom, couldn't find Lady Shellingham, and some old tabby told him she was in here with you. He's—"

His sentence was never finished. At that moment Lord Shellingham came crashing through the door. "Where's my wife?" he shouted in a drunken roar. "Know she's in here with you, Ashford. Saw you making sheep's eyes at her earlier."

Alex looked from Chester to the curious faces of the

other guests gathered outside the study. His mouth was grim. This was the type of public scene he had feared. He tried to remain calm as he answered, "Stop making a cake of yourself, milord. Lady Shellingham is not here."

"That's a lie!" Chester raged as he stumbled across the room. "Graham came to warn you so you could hide her. Know you two have been playing me false. Where is she? Where's my wife?"

Alex was quickly assessing the situation. Chester was too drunk to concede his error and apologize even when he found Millicent was gone, and word of his accusations were sure to reach the ear of Sir Chinningsworth. Hell and damnation, Miss Stanwood was right. He was going to pay dearly for the coil he had woven. Then an idea formed. Yes, it must be. "Lord Shellingham, you are foxed and therefore not responsible, so I will excuse the slur against my character. But I must insist you say no more. I repeat, your wife is not here. Search the room if you wish, but you will not find her. As for your other implication, the viscount of Harrington did not come here to warn me. He came to discuss my forthcoming wedding. He is to be the best man and—"

"Your wedding! Ha! Can't get married. My wife's already married to me!" he bellowed almost incoherently.

"Enough!" ordered his lordship. "I can not allow such nonsense to be uttered in front of my future wife."

"I may be a little foxed," scoffed Chester, "but not foxed enough to believe that Banbury tale. Do you really expect me to believe you are marrying an invisible wife?"

Alex heard suppressed snickers from the group gawking at the door. Without a word he walked to the alcove, put his arm around Penelope, and drew her forward. She tried to resist. It was futile. His arm was like an iron band. She was so stunned by his announcement that words failed her; she was silent as they emerged into the room. A rosy blush stained her thin face as she felt the warmth of his arm encircling her waist. "Lord Shellingham, may I present the future marchioness of Ashford, Miss Penelope Stanwood."

Chester blinked as Penelope appeared at Alex's side. A frown creased his brow as he noticed her scrawny looks and dowdy dress. She didn't look at all like the type of lady the marquis would be paying court to. His mind was befogged by the wine, but not befogged enough that he didn't suspect a trick. He was somewhat unsteady on his feet, but he managed a shaky bow. "Y'servant, Miss Stanwood." He turned and yelled to the people outside. "Did you hear that? Ashford's getting married. Come and wish them happy."

It's time for this nonsense to cease, thought Penelope. She started to protest, but before she had said two words, the marquis swept her into his arms and kissed her. She tried desperately to avert her face, but his embrace was too strong. Finally, he released her crushed lips, but his mouth hovered close as he whispered, "Be silent! We will settle this later." His arm remained around her as he confronted Lord Shellingham and the crowd at the door. "There, we have made a public declaration of our betrothal. I am sure you will understand if we delay receiving your congratulations for a time. As Miss Stanwood started to say, we had intended to keep our engagement a secret a while longer, but, hmm, circumstances forced an early announcement."

Lord Shellingham still had doubts. He demanded, "When is the wedding to be, Ashford? Are we all on your invitation list? By Jove, it will be one wedding worth attending."

Alex uttered a curse to himself. Chester was deliberately forcing his hand. The coil was tightening. "The wedding will take place very soon, but you will have to read the details in the *Gazette*. Miss Stanwood is still in mourning. The ceremony will be private."

Chester tried to focus his bleary eyes on the marquis. "I'll be watching with great interest for that announcement, milord." There was a veiled threat underlying his words, which Alex did not miss.

"So will I. Let us both wish you happy," a woman called from the doorway. Penelope recognized the voice instantly. For the first time she saw the woman Alex had held in his arms. How lovely she is with all that dark hair curling about her beautiful face, thought Penelope. Her own hair cast her into the dismals. It was dull gold in color, but with no life or sparkle, and being naturally straight, it would do nothing but hang limply about her thin face. Usually she kept it braided, for no amount of effort could force a single curl from its heavy mass. Penelope also envied Lady Shellingham's cool elegance as she strolled leisurely into the room. The red taffeta gown molded to every curve of her lush figure, and, by contrast, Penelope knew she must look like a positive dowd.

For her part Millicent was well pleased with the situation. One glance at Penelope reassured her. In truth Alex had found the perfect wife, one who could never compete with her for his attention. She almost purred with pleasure as she laid her hand on her husband's arm. "Chester dear, I have been searching everywhere for you. I stepped outside for a breath of fresh air, and when I returned, you had disappeared. Pray, let us go and leave these lovebirds alone. I have been saving a waltz for you." She guided her husband toward the door, but before she left, she glanced saucily over her shoulder and winked at the marquis.

James was about to follow, but Alex detained him. Once the door was shut, he immediately removed his arm from Penelope's waist and started pacing again. James watched with a perplexed frown, then finally ventured, "It won't work, old boy. Shellingham will yell the roof down when that announcement does not appear in the *Gazette*."

"It will appear. Wish me happy," he sneered sarcastically. "The famous marquis of Ashford is catched at last and to . . ."

Penelope was certain he was about to use some very uncomplimentary description, but he bit back the words. She raised her head proudly and stated, "Milord, this whole situation is a lot of stuff and nonsense! There will be no marriage. I have no intention of being your bride."

Alex stared at her. The harsh lines returned. "Leave us for a space, James. Miss Stanwood and I have something to discuss. I will meet you later, and we can settle the details of the wedding. Please see that we are not disturbed."

When they were alone, the marquis said, "As I mentioned before, I do not like missish airs, so stop all the blather about not wishing to marry me. You have no choice."

"I certainly do!" she challenged. "I will not be forced into a marriage I do not want."

"Stop playing the fool!" he snapped. "Think of what I am offering. As the marchioness of Ashford you would possess an honored place in society, be mistress of one of the great houses of England, never want for money, have servants by the score to instantly satisfy any whim and—"

"And I would also have a husband who longs for the arms of another woman. No thank you!"

"That's a typically feminine response, but one not worthy of someone with eyes as intelligent as yours. Actually your knowledge of my . . . mmm . . . other interests ought to work to our advantage. At least our marriage will commence with honesty and not the usual romantic rubbish. Yes, I fancy we can brush through very nicely."

"Well, I fancy we cannot," she argued. "You are offering a marriage to satisfy my material being, but not my heart. What if after we are wed, I fall in love with another?"

"You are in a pother over nothing!" he scoffed. "Love is for simpletons! It can only lead to disillusionment. Trust me, I know."

A thread of painful remembrance clouded his words. Penelope felt compassion for his hurt. Instinctively she knew some woman had wounded him deeply. For a second she wanted to hold out her arms to comfort him and convince him that not all women were untrue. But she didn't, and the cynical twist returned to his expression. "Yes, it's best to have a marriage where love is not involved. We can be friends and partners and leave love to the foolish poets. You heard the discussion between Lady Shellingham and myself, so you know what is required of my wife. Of that I need say no more." A small smile touched his mouth. "I grant the announcement will create a deuce of a stir. Ought to be interesting to hear the on-dits."

"Milord, you presume too much. I have not agreed."

Anger and determination flashed in his dark eyes. "Don't be mulish! You have no choice. Without conceit I know I'm a prime catch. Haven't an endless stream of scheming mamas and insipid misses put out their lures for me? How can you spurn my title?"

"Easily!"

"Then you're a ninnyhammer!" Alex walked across the room and stood towering in front of her. "I repeat, you have no choice. Are you goose-witted enough to believe life as a governess or companion would be better than being the marchioness of Ashford? Do you truly wish to grow old caring for others, never having a life to call your own?" The tone was harsh. "Or maybe you believe you will find another husband more to your liking." His eyes

34

raked over her figure. "Look at yourself. Who would marry you? You have no dowry or other, what shall I say, compensating appeals. I suppose some loutish farmer might condescend to wed one such as you, but your existence would be endless drudgery." He grasped her by the shoulders. "Look at me and tell me that would be better than being my wife."

Tears glittered in her eyes as she stared up at him. His words had resurrected all her fears about the future. Cruel though they were, they were true. She had no future. Why was she hesitating? Any other woman would hurl herself into his arms. Yet her heart yearned for words of love, not words of logic. She searched his face for some glimmer of understanding, but found only hardness. Could she endure the barren future of being his wife in name only. Could she endure an empty life if she refused?

When she remained silent, the pressure of his fingers increased. "Well," he demanded, "can you honestly avow that being a governess or paid companion would be better than being my wife? Answer me!" he ordered.

She trembled under the feel of his hands. "No." The words came out no louder than a whisper, but once uttered, her fate was linked now and forever with his.

Alex gazed at her poignant face a trice longer. His future was secure. The seat in the House of Lords was his. He relaxed his grip and stepped away. "Good. I knew you would see reason. You could scarce do otherwise." He paused a moment, then added, "I think we shall deal well together, Miss Stanwood." She wasn't at all sure, but withheld comment. He tucked her hand in the crook of his arm. "Are you ready to face all the old tabbies and gossipmongers outside? I don't scruple to admit it will be difficult, but we had best not delay."

Without a further glance at his bride to be he escorted her to the door, and they walked out into the crowded ballroom. Instantly there was silence. Even the dancers hesitated mid-step to take a peek at the betrothed couple. Squire and Lady Buxley were first to wish them happy. He seemed genuinely pleased, but Penelope detected a decided tinge of pique in Lady Buxley's congratulations. Everyone was agog to hear the details of their secret courtship. Alex said no more than that they had known each other for years and had been introduced by her father, who was the vicar of the Ashford parish. He also explained that the banns announcing their engagement had not been posted due to her recent bereavement.

As soon as was politely possible, Penelope escaped from the crush and fled to her bedchamber. She quickly changed into her old flannel nightgown and curled up in the chair. It was late, but sleep was far from her mind. Instead she sat and stared at the faded wallpaper. Why had she allowed herself to be trapped in this absurd situation? Was trapped the right word? Somberly she faced the truth. If she had wished, she could have stopped the charade at any time. She didn't. Why? She pulled a blanket off the bed and wrapped it around her. All of Alex's arguments returned to her mind. How could she deny he was right? Any fool would agree that being the marchioness of Ashford was preferable to the life of a drudge.

There was something more. Sadly the thought formed. Penelope, she told herself, you are a cheat, just as much as his lordship or Lady Shellingham. Best be honest and admit the truth. You did not consent to this marriage to guarantee yourself a secure future; you wanted the marquis for a husband!

Her heart knew the answer from the beginning. Alex was the beau of her romantic daydreams. That was why she agreed to his terms for a convenient marriage, not because she was trapped. The truth was painful, yet there was a note of hope. She knew she was mixing fantasy and reality, but in her soul she prayed they could learn to love. The image of that one moment when his mask of cynicism slipped to betray the hurt beneath floated into her mind. She remembered the bitter twist to his mouth when he mentioned love. He had lost faith, but she knew true and unending love could be found. Maybe, just maybe, they could find it together.

CHAPTER THREE

Penelope uncurled from the chair and crawled into bed. She needed rest. Tomorrow was sure to be a trying day. It was not going to be pleasant to face Constance and Lady Buxley after Alex's startling announcement. Even after the ball was over, and the manor house quieted for the night, sleep eluded her. She blew out the candle on the rickety nightstand. The darkness brought no comfort. Her mind spun in bewilderment. Her emotions were turbulent. Once she had made the admission of her own desires, doubts assailed her. It was like a fairy tale to be betrothed to the marquis. Never in her wildest longings did she believe such a splendid match was possible. Yet it had happened. She was to be the marchioness of Ashford. The tiny thrill in her heart at the thought couldn't be calmed. But in truth what did the name mean? She knew she would be his bride, not by choice, but by circumstance. He did not love her. He did not even desire her. His heart, if he possessed one, was pledged to another. The bed seemed less warm as she dwelled on these sobering thoughts. Had she thought the betrothal was like a fairy tale? Might it not end more like a nightmare?

Doubts tumbled on top of doubts. Penelope longed for her parents' comfort and words of advice. They had taught her the meaning of love, yet love might find no place in her future. How far her dreams had crumbled! Penelope had always believed she too would one day find the type of joy, happiness, and deep contentment that her parents had shared. Apparently this might not be. She tried to fluff up the hard pillow. It was no use. All that filled her mind was the remembrance of the lingering way Alex had gazed at Millicent, and the throb of passion in his voice as he called her name. Sadly she knew she was searching for the impossible. If only she could be like Constance, she mused, all would be well. Then she would be satisfied with the title, the position in society, and the wealth. Why must she hope for more? Why?

Dejectedly, she turned over on the lumpy bed. Her troubled thoughts allowed her no rest. Then the words of one of her father's sermons came back to her. Her troubled mind was soothed. On that Sunday he had spoken out against the blind acceptance of fate. His words now took on a personal meaning. She could make of her marriage whatever she wanted. It could be as miserable, or as wonderful as she desired. She knew it was up to her. Fate need not be accepted blindly. Fate could be challenged. She intended to challenge it! She would fight for what she wanted. Why had she wasted time on such dismal thoughts and endless doubts? She was enormously lucky! With a sigh of peace she settled back down under the covers.

Her future was secure. There would be no drab life as a companion, or the yearnings of a governess to raise her own, and not other people's children. A rosy blush swept over her face at the thought. She had not considered that! Children—she and Lord Ashford would have children. But to have children they must . . . The blush deepened. He had made no secret of his intention to have an heir, and that meant he expected his wife to . . . they would . . . Penelope put her hands up to her hot flushed cheeks. Her heart pounded. She sat up in bed and pulled the covers protectively around her. She felt like a very little girl. She was trembling.

Slowly, her reason gained control and a measure of

calm returned. That problem was far in the distance. Hadn't Alex said they could be friends and partners? Their feelings could develop slowly and then other things would come in time. She smiled sleepily and relaxed.

Resolutely, to still the lingering doubts, she dwelt on the imaginary details of their partnership. They would pay visits to their tenant farmers, to comfort the sick, or to admire a new baby. She could visualize sitting beside Alex on Sunday morning in the Ashford family pew listening to the new vicar. She rubbed her sleepy eyes. A small nagging voice told her these dreams were foolish, but they were pleasant; she ignored the warning and her thoughts drifted on. There was that huge gray granite house to explore. How fun actually to see the inside. Often she had ridden by on her old horse and stolen a moment to peer through the ornate gates at its splendor. Now she was to be mistress at Ashford. Other blissful thoughts floated through her drowsy mind. The image of Alex and his stallion clearing that first hedge returned and she smiled. They would ride together across his vast lands. Sleep finally neared, but one image remained. After their ride he would lift her down from her horse. She could almost feel his warm hands on her waist. He leaned nearer. His black eyes glittered. He smiled at her. Her last conscious sensation was to feel again the touch of his lips.

Once asleep no dreams disturbed Penelope's rest. She slept long and deep. The other members of Buxley Manor were not as lucky. As soon as the last guest had departed, Constance stormed up to her room and violently slammed the door. The noise reverberated through the still house and caused one of the maids to drop a plate. Lady Buxley glanced at her with vexation, but didn't stop to scold. Attending to Constance was far more urgent. She lifted her skirt and hurried up the steps after her daughter.

Constance's maid was trying to help her get ready for

bed. Every effort was met with abuse. "You idiot!" Constance shrieked. "Give me that brush. What are you trying to do, tear out my hair?" She yanked the brush out of the startled maid's hands and ordered, "Are you daft? Unbutton my dress. Do you expect me to sleep in my gown?"

"No, miss. I was only trying to—"

"Oh, do be quiet!" Constance snapped as she angrily tore the brush through her curls. "Hurry with those buttons!"

The nervous maid fumbled with the hooks. Constance was about to lash out again when the door opened and Lady Buxley entered. She took one glance at her daughter's furious face and said, "Thank you, Clara. You may retire. I will attend to my daughter. Please bring Miss Buxley's chocolate to her an hour later than usual in the morning. I know she will want to rest."

"Very good, m'lady." Clara muttered as she bobbed a curtsy and sped gratefully from the room.

Lady Buxley turned back to Constance. "That was quite a display you staged! Pray remember, you are a lady and not some sort of an ill-bred hooligan."

"But, Mama, that innocent little vicar's daughter you took in has made a fool of us all. She plotted and schemed and stole the marquis right out from under our noses. When I think of what she did, I could scream. She is nothing but a little hussy. I insist you toss her out!"

"Hush this instant! You are yelling loud enough to raise Lazarus! Do you want Penelope to hear?"

"I don't care if she does hear! She deliberately humiliated me and . . ."

"I realize you are overset, Constance, but that is no excuse for making a cake of yourself," her mother admonished.

"I vow you are already deferring to her when she . . ."

42

"When she is going to be the marchioness of Ashford," Lady Buxley finished the sentence firmly. "You had best get used to the thought. I admit I don't quite understand how it occurred. There hasn't been a snippet of gossip about them, but apparently it is all settled. There will be a wedding, and there is nothing you can do about it. We might as well accept the fact."

"What jabber! Do you expect me to accept the fact that that odious witch stole the most eligible bachelor in the ton from me," Constance squawked.

"Enough! She did not steal what you did not have. As I told you before, an alliance with Lord Ashford would be a splendid match, but one with some undesirable aspects. I vow if all the tales of his ladyloves are true, we may count ourselves lucky his attentions were caught by Penelope and not you. At least she will be married from this house. That ought to read very nicely in the *Gazette*. Let me help you out of that gown. The night has grown chill. You should be in your warm wrapper."

The pout remained on Constance's face as her mother fussed around her. She could not forget that a lowly vicar's daughter had bested her. She silently raged when she remembered how Penelope had let her chatter on about his lordship, when all the while they were secretly engaged. How she must have laughed at us! She will pay for that, Constance vowed.

Lady Buxley noticed the hard set to her daughter's mouth and quickly poured her a glass of ratafia. She knew that look well, and knew there was scant use trying to talk to her until some of the mulishness disappeared. Constance flopped down on the feather bed and her mother handed her the glass. As her daughter sipped the fruit cordial, Lady Buxley rather helplessly patted her shoulder. She waited for the tantrum to pass.

Finally, Constance sat up. There was a new glint in her

eye. The anger was gone. She seemed strangely excited. "Mother, we have almost made a muff of this whole ramshackle affair, but there's still time to salvage something from the wreckage."

"Whatever are you babbling on about?" A horrid thought occurred to Lady Buxley. "You aren't planning to challenge the wedding banns, are you? I know your father would never approve of that!"

"Mama dear, how you do go on! Rest easy. You are in a pother over nothing. I have no intention of stopping our little charity miss from wedding the illustrious marquis."

"I don't understand. What did we almost make a muff of?"

"The situation, the whole blessed situation!" Constance crowed.

Her mother stood up with a concerned look. She laid her hand on Constance's forehead. "You must be feverish. I declare you are not making a particle of sense!"

Constance grabbed her mother's hand and pulled her down beside her on the bed. "No, listen to me. We have not considered all the advantages to this situation. Think of it. Our own little charity miss, the one we took in and sheltered in her time of need, the one who is beholden to us, will soon be at the top of the ton. She will instantly be given vouchers to Almack's and," Constance paused to let her words penetrate, "she can easily procure them for her friends. Her sponsorship will assure the social success of anyone she favors. We must make sure she favors my debut!"

"Oh!" Lady Buxley whispered. "How stupid of me not to think of that." Her eyes sparkled. "Why your season in London is guaranteed. No door will dare be closed to the young friend of the marchioness of Ashford. You will have your pick of the most eligible bachelors." A small cloud darkened her pleasure. "Will Penelope do it? You have not exactly been a dear friend to her."

Constance frowned. Her mother's truthful words vexed her. Why should she have been a friend to that penniless nobody? She had no way of knowing her rudeness might rebound. "Well, from tomorrow on, I intend to be a very dear friend indeed. In fact, we all must be." With that settled she delicately patted a yawn, nestled down under the silk comforter, and motioned for her mother to blow out the candle. "See you in the morning, Mama. Rest well. We have much to do. We want Penelope to remember that we did everything possible to make her marriage a beautiful event."

Lady Buxley nodded earnestly and kissed her daughter good night. Yes, the future marchioness of Ashford must not be allowed to forget what she owed the Buxleys.

Penelope's changed status was instantly apparent in the morning. She was stirring awake when there was a tap on the door. Rosie entered with a heavily loaded tray. The news of her betrothal had obviously reached the servant's quarters, because Rosie treated her with a much more deferential air. Previously the cook had been kind, friendly, and a wee bit familiar. Now her behavior was much more correct and removed. Penelope was disturbed. Was she not the same person, she wondered. She strove to put the cook at ease. "Rosie, this was sweet of you, but it was not necessary. I could have come to the morning room."

"Now, miss, I knew you'd be tired after all the toing and froing last night." She fluffed up Penelope's pillow and set the tray down in front of her. Quickly she took the silver covers off the plates to expose the crisp toast, broiled ham, and her special cheese and chive omelette. While Penelope started buttering the toast, the cook poured her a cup of steaming hot chocolate, then stood back with her plump arms folded to admire the spread. When Penelope was finished with the omelette, she removed the plate and said, "Miss, I'd like to make bold and offer my best wishes for your forthcomin' weddin'. His lordship 'tis a fine figure of a man."

Penelope smiled at her and teased, "You see, a bluestocking lady can catch a beau."

"Oh, go on now!" Rosie laughed, and Penelope sensed her reserve had melted. She picked up the tray and leaned over to whisper. "Maybe it'd help Miss Buxley if she did more readin' and less dancin'!"

Penelope giggled and started to get out of bed. "No, you rest, miss. Lady Buxley wants you to stay in bed until Clara can come up and help you move."

"Move?" A fear gripped Penelope. Maybe her betrothal had so angered the Buxleys that they were going to ask her to leave. She knew Constance had hoped to have Alex's interest fixed on her. Maybe the squire also had anticipated an alliance with the Ashford lands. What was she going to do? There was no place else to go. Nervously she asked, "Where am I to go?"

"Why, to the dowager's suite of course. Lady Buxley gave the orders first thing this mornin'. And I'll tell you true, it sent everyone scurryin'. That suite hasn't been opened since the duchess of Northumberland visited here five years ago. You relax. The rooms won't be aired and cleaned for a while yet."

They certainly aren't angry, mused Penelope. The change of face was perplexing. Last night she had detected a decided note of pique hidden in the Buxleys' congratulations. Maybe they have simply decided to be gracious, she decided. Before she could reflect further on the matter, Clara arrived to help her dress and pack. Penelope was embarrassed at the maid's attentions. She had never before had anyone help her disrobe and was uncomfortable at her presence. How that one small word had changed her life.

46

Never again would she have to care for her own clothes, run errands, or do the bidding of others. It was a daunting situation. Was she truly prepared to be the marchioness of Ashford?

When her meager possessions were packed, she meekly followed Clara up to the dowager's suite. One look at the sitting room and she had to suppress a giggle. How typical of the Buxleys to overdo the decor. Everything was gilt and dark velvet. There were even silk tassels hanging from the settee. The whole effect was ostentatiously dreary. At least the bed proved to be a delight. It hadn't escaped the heavy touch. The hangings were of maroon velvet, and the spread was embroidered and re-embroidered with elaborate detail. Penelope took a closer look at the headboard and could hardly believe it. There were actually carved wooden cupids flying across the top carrying garlands of fruits and leaves. She sank down on the mattress. To her joy she discovered that it was filled with soft feathers. After the lumpy rock she had been sleeping on, this was sheer heaven. She was luxuriating in the feel when Constance and Lady Buxley entered.

"My dear," Lady Buxley cooed, "I hope you find these quarters acceptable. We do want your last few days with us to be pleasant. Naturally, we will see you in London, but it won't be the same as when you were our guest. Constance, please remind me to have flowers brought up." She beamed fondly. "I know how Penelope loves them."

"Yes, of course. We should have thought of that." Constance settled herself on the bed next to Penelope. "I want to tell you again how pleased I am about your betrothal. It's so exciting! Why, I vow I almost feel as if I were having a sister get married. I don't scruple to admit we were surprised, but delightfully surprised," she hastened to add.

Penelope stared from one to the other. How confusing!

An uncharitable thought crept into her mind. I wonder what they want? she asked herself. Immediately she felt guilty. They've been kind to her since Father died, why did she question their motives now? She smiled at them. "Thank you for your good wishes. I feared you might be upset."

"Upset? Whatever for? We couldn't be happier," gushed Lady Buxley. "But there is much to do. We must not waste time with idle chatter. When is the wedding to be, dear? I hope not too terribly soon. We have many plans to make. I want it to be a splendid affair. It will be our wedding present to you, one you will always remember when you are with your tonnish friends in London."

Before Penelope could answer, Constance bubbled, "What fun we can have when we're both in London for the season! There will be rout parties, musicales, and of course I'll see you at Almack's." She shot Penelope a quick glance. "That is, if someone is kind enough to help me procure vouchers."

She rambled on, but Penelope was not listening. A chill swept through her. What a slow-top she had been! There was no kindness in their attentions. They wanted her to help Constance gain entry to the ton. With a sigh she was forced to acknowledge once more how vastly different most people were from her parents. She wondered if she would ever find their type of unselfish loving and caring again. The prospects seemed dismal.

A rap on the door interrupted Constance's prattle. Clara entered and bobbed a curtsy. "There's a messenger below from Ashford, milady. His lordship wants to know if Miss Stanwood can receive him at four this afternoon."

Penelope started to speak, but Lady Buxley answered for her. "That will be fine, Clara. Have fresh flowers put in the red salon. She can receive him there. Has the seamstress from the village arrived yet?"

"Yes, milady."

"Good. Send her up. The fittings must not be delayed another moment."

Clara nodded her head and left. Penelope was about to ask a question when she heard Constance open the huge corner armoire, and start rummaging through her few dresses. "Simply everything must go, Mama. There's not a passable gown here."

Her disdain hurt Penelope. Every dress she owned had been lovingly stitched by her mother. They were links to her past, and were important. They might not be elegant or fashionable, but to her they were beautiful in spirit. Constance began dragging them off the pegs and tossing them on the bed. "Clara can come up later and dispose of these. Perhaps some of the servants can use them."

Penelope quickly ran to the bed and gathered the discarded garments into her arms. With dignity she faced Constance and Lady Buxley. "These are mine! I will not allow you to dispose of them. The servants are not to touch them!" Tears gathered in her eyes as she hugged her mother's handiwork. "Do you understand? I want them left alone."

Lady Buxley glanced at Constance, who shrugged her shoulders as if to say, if the hen-witted fool wants to keep the rags, let her. "Now, dear, don't set up such a screech," Lady Buxley soothed. "If these clothes have a sentimental value to you, naturally you may keep them. But you must realize they will never do for your trousseau. What would Lord Ashford think if we let his bride arrive in, er, these unsuitable garments? The village seamstress can not match the efforts of the Bond Street modistes. Still, you ought to have a few new things to wear until you can get to London to shop." She noticed Penelope's look of unease and commented, "Please don't fret. We know you are not plump in the pockets just now. These dresses will be a gift from us." Penelope tried to protest, but Lady Buxley would not be deterred. "If you are worried over accepting them as a gift, consider them a loan. I'm sure there will be a way for you to repay us, someday."

The seamstress entered, and before Penelope could object, the fittings began. She was swept along and there seemed to be no gracious way to reject the gift of the trousseau. Her conscience was finally salved by the basic truth of the situation. Why shouldn't she accept their bargain? They had given her lodgings after her father's death. She owed them something. Would it be wrong to help Constance during the season? With a sharp pang she remembered Millicent's plan for Alex's countrified wife to rusticate at Ashford, while they romped together in London. Surely convention would not allow him to abandon his new bride in the country. Yes, Penelope decided, he will have to take me with him. Maybe, her secret heart added, when he sees me in this new finery, he will be proud to have me on his arm.

The fittings seemed to go on interminably. Penelope was truly exhausted when Rosie finally arrived with the tea cart. "I thought you ladies might be needin' your tea 'bout now. I know 'tis a little early, but with that marquis fellow comin' at four, I thought it was time."

Lady Buxley thanked her and reminded her to have a tea tray prepared to serve when Lord Ashford arrived. Penelope's heart fluttered at the sound of his name. The touch of his kiss lingered in her mind and a blush stained her cheeks. Luckily Constance and Lady Buxley were too busy with the scones and crumpets to notice her flushed face. Calm returned as she sipped the scalding tea and nibbled at a sweet biscuit.

After Rosie removed the tea cart, it was time to get ready to receive her future husband. She was fortunate that the seamstress had a day dress of pale blue muslin in stock, which could be quickly altered to fit Penelope's thin figure. Constance and Lady Buxley exclaimed over how divine it looked on her. When she turned to gaze in the cheval glass, she was dissatisfied. The gown was attractive enough with its high waist and fluttering ribbons, but somehow it wasn't right. But then, none of her clothes seemed to be. She sensed something was amiss, as with Constance wearing that light pink riding habit, but her taste in fashion was so inexperienced she didn't know what needed to be changed. Besides, she had no choice. The blue muslin was the only dress ready to wear, and all of her feminine instincts rebelled against meeting Lord Ashford in one of her old faded dresses.

While Clara was braiding up her heavy hair, the chimes sounded. Alex had arrived. Constance and Lady Buxley rushed down to receive him and told Penelope to follow when she was ready. It took a few minutes to finish her hair, and a few more minutes to gather her nerve, but finally she descended the stairs and moved toward the red salon.

She approached silently across the heavy oriental rug. Her heart pounded as she caught a glimpse of Alex leaning against the mantel. She paused a moment to gather her wits. Was it really possible she was going to marry this man? How handsome he was! His appeal was like an invisible physical force that reached out and snared anyone near. Even Lady Buxley wasn't immune, as she coquetishly bantered with him. For his part he was obviously restless. Penelope knew that slight curve of his lip, which Constance and Lady Buxley thought was a smile, was really a measure of his boredom. His eyes flickered to the door. He caught sight of her. "Ah, the bride has arrived. Come in, Penelope, we have been waiting for you."

Penelope took one look at the devilish glint in his eye

and hesitated. She entered slowly, reluctantly. He noticed her faltering step. His merriment increased. In two strides he was at her side. Before she could utter a protest, he swept her into his arms and soundly kissed her. Penelope stiffened, then tried to wiggle free. His arms were unyielding. Finally, he released her bruised mouth and teased, in a voice only for her to hear, "Must keep up appearances, you know."

Penelope tried to withdraw, but he kept his arm firmly around her waist. Her emotions were a jumble. She was furious at his presumption; yet she couldn't deny that the touch of his lips sent a wave of weakness flowing through her body. But the remembrance of Millicent stood between them. She was determined he would never know of the power he had over her. She remained rigid in his arms.

He knew she was incensed and was silently amused by her reaction. Quite unexpected, he thought. Most females would swoon if he deigned to notice them. She wanted to slap his face. This marriage would no doubt prove interesting. The conquest was always sweeter if not too easily attained.

Lady Buxley chuckled indulgently at his indiscretion. "Obviously you are an impatient fiancé, Lord Ashford, but you will have to wait for your bride. News of the engagement must be published in the *Gazette;* we need time to prepare Penelope's trousseau; naturally we wish to give a prenuptial party in your honor; the seamstress hasn't even started on her wedding dress and—"

Alex had to raise his voice to halt her chatter. "Lady Buxley, the wedding will be this Saturday."

"What?" she gasped. "That's impossible!"

"It is not impossible. It will occur. Since the news of our betrothal has been made public, there is no reason to wait."

"But . . ." she sputtered.

"Your concern for Miss Stanwood is admirable," he observed with light sarcasm, "but unnecessary. If you will excuse us. Penelope and I would like to be alone. We must discuss our plans."

They were clearly displeased with his announcement and his mode of dismissal, but were too conscious of his rank to argue. When the door was closed, Alex dropped his arm from her waist and moved away. His eyes raked speculatively over Penelope's figure. She refused to lower her eyes. He was intrigued by her calm dignity. Yes, Miss Stanwood would do nicely for a wife. Of course, she could not compare with Millicent, but then he wasn't sure he would wish to be wed to Lady Shellingham. Millicent was like an exotic dish, thoroughly enjoyable to taste upon occasion, but undesirable as a steady diet. No words were spoken for several moments as they silently fenced with each other. Finally, Penelope observed, "I'm rather surprised at your visit, milord. I fully expected a note from you today canceling our agreement."

"I have no intention of crying off. As I told Lady Buxley, we will be married on Saturday."

A tiny thrill of excitement couldn't be stilled as she heard his words, but she had to demur. "That is quite impossible, milord. I cannot possibly have a trousseau gathered and a wedding dress finished by then. This may only be a marriage of convenience, but it is a marriage. I intend to be dressed as a bride. Further, propriety should be maintained. We need to give people no further cause for gossip."

"I had already considered that and have sent a messenger to London to pick up a wedding gown from Worth's. I included a letter with details of your size. There should be no problem."

Penelope's eyes flashed. "I am sure there won't be. No

doubt you have had vast experience ordering for your ladybirds."

"I see the kitten has claws," he observed blandly. "Beware that she uses them carefully. As I was saying, the dress will come from London along with some other things and, oh, damnit, I forgot a veil."

"Well," she countered coolly. "One could hardly expect you to remember all the details of female finery. You would hardly have been ordering wedding ensembles for your, mmm, other friends."

Alex's eyes flashed with anger. He took a step toward her. For an instant she felt afraid. There was a hardness about his look that would brook no opposition. She must remember that he was a man who could not be pushed too far; the passion lay close under his thin veneer of well-bred refinement. Penelope quelled under his gaze and retreated. She held up her hand, then dropped to the floor in a graceful curtsy. She peeked up at him and smiled hesitantly. "A truce, milord?"

A twitch of amusement appeared in the corner of Alex's mouth, then he threw back his head and roared with laughter. When his mirth had subsided, he reached down a hand to lift her up. "Miss Stanwood, you are an original!"

His warm grasp tried to draw her into his arms again. Penelope adroitly maneuvered away. His change from rage to ardor was so perplexing. She needed time to find her dignity. She asked demurely, "May I pour you tea, milord?"

"Tea? After dueling with you I need a large dollop of brandy, but I suppose Buxley locks it away. Yes, Miss Stanwood, a cup of tea would be nice."

Penelope seated herself carefully behind the tea cart and willed her hand not to tremble as she poured from the silver pot. "Won't you be seated, milord?" she suggested as she handed him the china cup.

"Miss Stanwood, don't you think all of this formality is somewhat passé. Let's not be skittish about convention. My name is Alex. May I call you Penelope? After all, I will hardly be able to call you Miss Stanwood after Saturday."

A delicate blush stained her cheeks. Saturday—it was so near. In a few days they would be married and Lord Ashford, no Alex, would be her husband. But a husband in name only. She must never forget for one instant that his arms yearned to hold another, that the kisses he gave were but for display. A shadow of sadness appeared in Penelope's eyes as she answered, "There is no need to be in a basket over appearances." She paused, then finished, "Alex. You have my permission to use my name."

He sensed her withdrawal. What do you suppose cast her into the dismals, he wondered. Oh, devil take it! Why should he care? With a careless shrug he asked, "I assume you are agreed on Saturday for our wedding. There will be no time to get a veil from London. Possibly the Buxleys will have one you can borrow."

"That won't be necessary, milord, I mean Alex. I will be married in my mother's wedding veil." Penelope proudly lifted her head. "It has been in my family since one of my ancestors accompanied King Henry VIII to France. A Saturday wedding, though, will not please Lady Buxley, I fear."

"Her opinion does not make a particle of difference to me, nor should it to you." When she started to defend the Buxleys, Alex argued with cutting logic. "Their treatment of you before the ball was shabby, but I fancy all that has changed. You are now a valuable prize they wish to exploit. It wouldn't surprise me if they moved you into that horrid relic they term the dowager's suite. The only reason they wish to host a prenuptial party is so their name will be linked with mine. It will not be."

"Alex, they did take me in after Father died. I do owe them that much."

"Yes, I agree, and that is why Squire Buxley will be allowed to give you away." His tone was autocratic. "They will have to be satisfied with that brief announcement in the *Gazette*. I can not afford to have this sham engagement drag on interminably." He stood up to take his leave.

Penelope walked with him to the door. "Vicar Wesley, the young man who took over your father's parish, has agreed to perform the ceremony in the Ashford chapel at three, Saturday. When the messenger returns, I will have him deliver the gown and the other items to you. I know you will be busy, I shall not intrude again."

There was no warmth or emotion in his voice. He could as well have been discussing the horses at Ascot as his marriage. Penelope yearned for even a tiny sign of his caring. There was none. He formally bowed over her hand and was gone.

CHAPTER FOUR

Penelope gasped as she pulled the white dress from the layers and layers of tissue. She had never seen anything more lovely. Worth had truly created a masterpiece. She held the wedding gown up in front of her and swirled so Constance and Lady Buxley could see. The dress was of white silk overlaid with finely wrought Brussels round-point lace. It was designed in the style Empress Josephine had made famous, with a high waist, slender skirt, and delicately puffed sleeves. But Worth had added his own personal touches, such as the deeply scalloped neckline and the magnificent aisle side train that fell from the shoulders. Her eyes sparkled as she turned back to thank the messenger for delivering the wedding gown and the other packages from London.

The liveried servant bowed low. "'Twas a pleasure, miss." He pulled another package out from under his coat. "His lordship sends his compliments."

With a puzzled frown Penelope took the flat box. It was covered in velvet and had a tiny gold key in its lock. She turned the key and slowly opened the lid. Her eyes widened. She was too stunned to speak. Constance stepped forward and peered over her shoulder. "Mama!" she shrilled. "It's the Ashford diamonds!"

"They are indeed," agreed Lady Buxley after she had taken a look. "I had forgotten how magnificent they are." She dismissed the messenger and hurried Penelope upstairs. "You must try this gown on at once. It may need altering."

It didn't. It slipped over Penelope's head and nestled against her figure like a glove. The marquis's instructions had been precise. As I surmised, Penelope admitted ruefully to herself, he's had a lot of experience in ordering female finery.

Lady Buxley was ecstatic. "My dear, you will be a lovely bride. I wish you weren't quite so thin, but it makes no sense being atwitter over something that can't be changed. Obviously you please Lord Ashford as you are."

Her words sank a shaft into Penelope's glow. She was thrilled over the beautiful gown and for an instant had forgotten the terms of their bargain. She suddenly felt cold. Still, she had agreed to play the blushing bride. She put on a brave smile as Constance observed, "Mama, there is no tiara in this set of diamonds. What is Penelope going to wear on top of her veil?"

"Oh, dear," her mother fussed, "that is a puzzlement!"

"I could fashion a wreath of white roses," Penelope ventured. "I often used to make them when I was younger." A note of sadness crept into her voice. "My mother had no jewels, but she loved beautiful things. When she and Father went out to a village dance, she would wear a wreath of flowers in her hair. I always thought they were prettier than the emeralds, diamonds, and pearls the other ladies were sporting."

"You believe flowers are prettier than these?" Constance snorted as she held up the Ashford diamonds.

Constance was about to make a further cutting remark, but Lady Buxley intervened. She threw a warning glance at her sharp-tongued daughter and soothed, "Yes, dear, that is a capital idea. I well remember how fresh and lovely your mama always looked at our village socials. Besides, we have no other choice. Let Clara help you off with that gown. You must try on these other things."

Package after package was opened to reveal such trea-

58

sures as Penelope had never seen before. There were several pastel morning dresses of softest muslin, a tan traveling coat deeply caped in beaver with a fur close bonnet to match, a wrapper in blue velvet, white silk embroidered inexpressibles, a walking dress with matching poke bonnet, a riding habit, and even a ball gown in pale yellow satin. It was impossible to hide her excitement as she tried on dress after dress. She had never had such lovely things before. Every instinct was thrilled as she pivoted and turned in front of the looking glass. The excitement brought a pink tinge to her cheeks and the haunting sadness, long her companion, began to fade from her eyes. In its place, an appealing soft feminine quality emerged. Nonetheless, Constance still privately grumbled that she found it difficult to imagine why the marquis had chosen this penniless girl over herself for his bride. Her mother shushed her. Their plan must not be jeopardized at this late date.

The last days of Penelope's old life sped by. Already many things had changed for her: the servants were more deferential; Lady Buxley no longer flung orders at her; even Constance swallowed back her acid comments and was the soul of friendship. Penelope might have been raised in the sheltered existence of the vicarage, but she wasn't totally an innocent. She always wanted to believe the best of people, but the Buxleys' motivations were too obvious to be ignored. Lady Buxley and Constance were so transparent. They are not doing this for her, Penelope sadly acknowledged, but because she would soon be the marchioness of Ashford.

The marchioness of Ashford—that thought always sent her heart racing. Penelope didn't covet the wealth or position of Alex's name. For her he was still the beau of her youthful fantasy. Even his disgraceful scene with Millicent could not tarnish the image she held in her heart. She desperately wanted to believe the dream. Reason was ignored.

The night before her marriage Penelope's sleep was filled with a kaleidoscope of images, each of which dissolved itself into a vision of Alex. It all seemed real. He so filled her every thought that she was startled when the soft light of the dawn, filtering through the maroon velvet hangings, awakened her, and she found that her wondrous dreams possessed no reality. This was her wedding day. The words echoed through her sleepy mind. She stirred. She had always dreamed romantic dreams of this day. Time and again she had imagined the joy of whispering "I do" to the man she loved. Now she was to be wed to the marquis of Ashford. Had those dreams just been dreams? Or was there a chance to turn them into fact?

That stubborn glimmer of hope brought a smile as Penelope jumped out of bed. There was much yet to do before three o'clock. She took off her flannel nightgown and was struggling with the buttons of one of her old morning dresses when Clara entered. "Miss, you shouldn't be adoin' that alone. Why didn't you ring for me? 'Tis my job, you know."

"I know, Clara, but it's so early. I didn't want to disturb you."

"Now, miss, don't you fret about that. Besides, I've been up this past hour or so. Couldn't sleep even if I'd a mind to, not with the whole house in a pelter over this wedding." She stood back and looked somewhat disapprovingly at Penelope's old dress. "Lady Buxley said I was to pack your portmanteau. You do want me to put in only the new things, don't you?"

Penelope glanced down at the faded dress her mother had made so long ago. It was like an old friend, and like a friend, not to be easily discarded. Somehow it brought her closer to her parents and gave her confidence. Yet she understood Clara's befuddlement. Why should she want to take her old patched dresses when she had all of this new finery? The fact remained, she did. "Please pack all of my things." She stressed the word all, then started for the door. She turned and said, "Please tell Rosie I will eat later."

Quickly, before the maid could protest, Penelope hurried from the room. Once outside the house her step slowed. She savored the freshness and beauty of the morning as she walked across the grounds. The dew dampened her kid slippers; it was of no importance. This was her wedding day. She stood for a moment and looked back at the manor house. How unsure and frightened she had been that first day when she arrived here after her father's funeral. Now her life had taken another twist, and she was unsure again. Penelope shook her head. No regrets—she would allow no regrets or doubts to mar this day.

With a purposeful step, she turned toward the rose garden, then remembered she had come out without a knife. The door to the gardener's shed was open. She knocked. With a sinking heart she saw the old crotchety caretaker emerge. Why did it have to be him? He was a dour Scotsman, who didn't take kindly to her cutting his carefully nurtured blooms. She smiled her prettiest smile. "Mr. MacDougar, I hate to be a bother, but could I borrow your garden snips?"

"What ye be needin' 'em for, lassie? My roses ain't recovered from the last bunch, ye took." His sharp eyes challenged her. "Ye don't need to be takin' no more."

"I'm afraid I must. But this time," she reassured him, "all I need are some white roses and a few slips of ivy."

"Be ye the one gettin' married, lassie?"

"Yes," she admitted. Penelope had an inspiration. She smiled again. "Yes, I wanted to wear your beautiful flowers in my hair today. I think they are lovelier than jewels or other frippery." She sighed sadly. "But if you can't spare any blooms, I suppose I understand."

Penelope peeked at him, and knew she had touched his weakness. It would never do to unbend too far, but his expression did soften a bit. "I daresay a weddin' 'tis special, lassie," he conceded gruffly as he grudgingly handed her the snips. "But don't be cuttin' more than ye need, hear!"

With a gay laugh she took the snips and slipped off to the rose garden. Quickly she cut an arm load of fragrant white roses and glossy green ivy, then started toward the house. Her pace halted. No, she didn't want to return yet. The day was too perfect; she didn't want it spoiled by Constance's ceaseless chatter about the London season, or Lady Buxley's subtle, but constant, reminders of the debt she owed them.

As before, when she wanted to be alone, she headed for the cool shade of the grape arbor. Grateful for the serene surroundings, Penelope sank to the ground and began to weave her wreath. Under her skilled fingers the flowers and foliage quickly became entwined into a beautiful headpiece. There were several roses that remained when the wreath was complete. She looked down at them, with a twinge of guilt for cutting too many. Then luckily remembered she must also have a nosegay to carry down the aisle, so she deftly created a round bouquet from the blossoms. The white ribbons could be added later. As she worked with the lovely blooms, her mind ranged back to her brief altercation with old Mr. MacDougar and she chuckled.

How familiar that scene had seemed. Many times she heard her parents have the same argument. Her mother wanted to fill the house with flowers; her father wanted them left in the garden for everyone to enjoy. Penelope laid the finished wreath and bouquet down in her lap and smoothed out the faded skirt. At the thought of her parents, a few tears gathered. She blinked them back. This was not the time for sorrow. Yet the tiny pang of regret that remained could not be ignored. How she wished for her parents on this day! Her eyes closed. She could almost see her father standing at the end of the aisle, ready to bestow the time-honored vows, and her mother watching from the front pew. Probably her mother would have shed a few tears as the ceremony progressed, but her dominant emotion would have been happiness. Penelope opened her eyes and felt warm at the reflection. Her parents seemed very near. Happiness was what they truly would have wished for her and today she was happy. They would have been content. A glow of confidence filled her heart as she stood up, brushed the scraps of leaves and stems from her skirt, and headed back toward the manor house.

Penelope handed the wreath and nosegay to a waiting maid and asked her to tell Rosie that she would be in the morning room. Lady Buxley was there sipping hot chocolate when Penelope entered. She put down the cup and exclaimed, "My dear, where have you been? We were beginning to fear you had decided to cry off, and that would never do."

"I was in the garden working with the flowers for the wedding."

"But of course, how hen-witted of me not to think of that. Are they done?"

"Almost, all I need to add are some white ribbons."

"Good, for I vow the time for the ceremony is almost upon us and there is still much to do." Lady Buxley picked up a small silver bell and rang it vigorously. "That cook has been in here every five minutes to see if you had arrived, and now when we finally need her, she seems to have disappeared. I declare, I hope you have better-trained servants at Ashford. They are an endless trial here, so lazy, disrespectful, and—"

Her tirade was interrupted when the door opened and Rosie entered with a large covered tray. Her eyes twinkled as she served the bride, and she beamed as Penelope ate up every morsel. When the dishes were empty, she gathered them up, but hesitated at the door. Lady Buxley stared at her with irritation. "You are dismissed."

"Very good, milady, but first the staff has asked me to give their best wishes to Miss Stanwood."

"Thank you, Rosie," Penelope smiled. "Please thank everyone for me. I will miss you all."

The cook dropped a curtsy and left. Penelope started to rise, but Lady Buxley restrained her with a warning hand. "My dear, that will never do!"

Penelope looked at her with a puzzled frown, "I'm afraid I don't take your meaning. What will never do?"

"Your familiarity with the servants," Lady Buxley admonished. "A lady must always remember they are but paid menials, and thus not worthy of regard." She saw the angry flash in Penelope's eyes and hurried to explain. "My dear, I am only telling you this so you won't make a grave blunder at Ashford. I realize that life at the vicarage was very simple. I'm sure it had many, hmm"—she struggled for a word—"mmm, admirable qualities, but you must admit it didn't prepare you to deal with a large staff of servants. Please listen and heed my advice. You simply must remember to keep them in their proper place; distance must be maintained, otherwise their behavior becomes very insolent. We can't tolerate that, can we?"

Penelope had to bite back her angry words. She may not have learned to manage a staff of servants at the vicarage, but she had learned something more important. She had learned to treat all people, no matter what their station in life, with courtesy and respect. It was useless to try to argue with Lady Buxley. Her mutton-headed attitude would never change.

Satisfied that her advice had been duly received, Lady Buxley stood up. "Come, Penelope. Clara has your bath drawn. I have given her some of my scented salts to put in the water. They came all the way from India, so they are rather special. I trust you will enjoy their fragrance."

It was sheer luxury to soak in a hot tub before the fireplace once more. It reminded Penelope of home. Since coming to the manor house, her baths had all been cold. Servants, no matter how menial, could not be wasted hauling hot water up for a penniless guest. She wiggled lower in the soothing water. This will be one of the nicest prerogatives of wealth, she decided. Never again would she have to shiver in a cold bath. The fragrance of the bath salts floated up around her. The essence of frangipani and jasmine filled the air. The scent was exotic, mysterious, alluring. Somehow it made her feel the same. There was a light feminine quality that was vastly different from the heavy musky perfumes so in fashion with the ton. She liked it.

The tension that had filled the days since her father's death seemed to seep out of her body and flow into the warm water. For the first time since that tragic day she completely relaxed. Too soon the world returned when Clara came bustling in to wash her hair and help her from the bath. The towels had been warming by the fire; they felt good and comforting as the maid wrapped them around her. More were used to dry her hair, and at last it was time to dress for her wedding.

She thrilled anew as the white gown was unwrapped from the tissue. Clara slipped it gently over her head and laced up the bodice. It could not fit more perfectly if she had stood for a dozen fittings. Carefully she smoothed out the silk skirt and sat at the dressing table. Clara braided up her hair and arranged it in a coronet about her head. She was tucking the last tendril in place when Constance and Lady Buxley entered. Penelope smiled at them. "Milady, I want to thank you for those bath salts. They were delightful!"

"Then you certainly ought to have them. Clara, pack the jar in Miss Stanwood's portmanteau."

"Lady Buxley, I truly must not accept anything more from you. You have already been generous to a shade."

She walked over and inspected Penelope's hair. One braid had slipped a fraction. She directed Clara to resecure it. When that was done, she patted the bride's shoulder. "You are talking stuff and nonsense, Penelope. We are only too glad to be supportive. It's what the dear vicar would have wanted." She met Penelope's eyes in the mirror. "I am positive we could count on your aid, if we were ever in need for anything." No further elaboration was necessary, but she did wish to elicit a promise. "Isn't that true, Penelope dear?"

Her meaning was clear. Penelope had only one choice. "Of course, milady. You need only to ask."

Lady Buxley exchanged satisfied smiles with Constance. Her daughter's season was assured. With a contented smirk she ordered, "Clara, please bring the train and veil. The squire will have the coach around in a trice. We mustn't dawdle."

The aisle-wide train of silk and lace was attached to the shoulders of Penelope's wedding gown with pearl rosettes. The scalloped hem trailed gracefully on the floor as she turned. The maid picked up the lace veil, which was laying across the bed, but before she could cross the room, Constance remembered, "Mama, we forgot the Ashford diamonds!"

"Heaven above!" her mother cried. "I shudder to think

66

what his lordship would have said if his bride had arrived without them. Clara, fetch them at once!"

The maid hurried from the room. Constance walked to the window and looked out. "Papa is coming around the drive with the carriage. We must hurry. It would never do to keep the marquis waiting at the chapel."

Lady Buxley paced across the room and stared into the sitting parlor. "Where is that doltish maid?" she complained. "Penelope, you see, it's as I told you. The servant problem is insufferable! They're lazy and never about when you really need them. It quite puts one off! I . . . oh, there you are," she fussed as Clara came rushing in the door carrying the jewel case. "It took you long enough! Here give it to me. Your fumbling hands will only delay us."

She grabbed the velvet case from the maid and unlocked it. Carefully Lady Buxley lifted the diamond necklace out and let it glitter for a moment in the sunlight. Constance's eyes narrowed as she saw its splendor. Her resentment returned. The Ashford diamonds should be hers, not little Miss Nobody's! She wasn't foolish enough to show her bitterness, though. After all, there was the season in London to be considered. But she vowed that someday she would pay Penelope back for her treachery.

The animosity flowing through the room didn't touch Penelope. She was staring at the necklace. It was the visible symbol of her new life. It felt cold when it was placed around her neck. But there was scant time to dwell on omens. A footman rapped on the outer door and announced that Squire Buxley was ready to attend the ladies. Constance hurried to the mirror to fuss with her curls one last time as Lady Buxley struggled to screw on the matching diamond earbobs. Penelope had never worn any jewelry before, and she longed to look at herself in the mirror, but Lady Buxley forbid it. Instead she sent Clara for the veil.

The maid had carefully washed and blocked the delicate French lace. Lady Buxley had not seen it before and exclaimed over its unique beauty. The lace was so sheer and finely wrought that it seemed almost weightless as the maid placed it on Penelope's hair, yet each detail of the elaborate design was clearly etched. It was like a soft cloud as it billowed around her and fell to the floor. Clara secured the white rose wreath on top, lowered the front edge over Penelope's face, handed her the bouquet, then stepped back. Finally Penelope was allowed to turn and see herself in the looking glass.

It was as if a stranger returned her gaze. Was it possible this lovely vision was the same girl who had cried in the grape arbor and feared for her future? There was no fear now. She was to wed the man who had drifted through all her dreams. With a smile she turned and started from the room.

CHAPTER FIVE

The old traveling coach of the Buxleys' swayed and rumbled over the post road toward Ashford. Constance maintained an unceasing stream of chatter, but Penelope was not attending. She was in a world of her own thoughts. The bridal veil that was drawn over her face helped shield her and hide all of the fluctuations in her spirits. The doubts about marrying the marquis were gone. The commitment had been made. It would be honored.

The thought of standing by his side at the altar created a shiver of excitement deep within her. Penelope had played the scene over in her mind so many times, when she dreamed of her imaginary beau. Now the dream was real. The joy made her breathless; yet a question remained. Did she have the ability to be Alex's wife? Would she shame him by committing some social blunder? Could she handle the servants and manage the vast house? Would she have the strength to stand at his side and smile, when she knew his thoughts and desires were with Millicent?

"Fate can be challenged!" Her father's words reassured her; her tension eased. She was not without resources. She had common sense and, more importantly, determination. Somehow it would work out. Fate could be challenged and the future molded to suit her wishes. Her marriage might not be as perfect as her parents'; nonetheless, it was better than the grim future she faced before Alex's offer. As always and forever his name sent a tremor of pleasure through her body. The glow of warmth followed her as the coach jolted to a stop in front of the Ashford chapel and Squire Buxley handed her out.

The chapel was built of the same granite as the great house. It would have been a bit forbidding if its stern walls weren't softened by masses of ivy climbing and entwining up its sides. The large double doors were standing open. Penelope could see glimpses of the dim interior as she neared. Patterns of color played across the floor as the sunlight filtered through the stained glass windows. The gaily flickering light seemed to draw her forward. She smiled quietly as they mounted the three steps to the portico of the small chapel.

Lady Buxley fussed around her adjusting the wreath of white roses and straightening the train. She lifted the long veil that fell from the back of the wreath and tried to fix it, but it twisted and would not fall gracefully. "Constance, help me," she urged, "this veil won't fall correctly." Constance was straining forward to peer into the chapel and pouted when she had to return to the bride, but she came. The two ladies picked up the edges of the lace veil, held it high, and let it flutter to the ground. It floated softly around Penelope and reinforced the quality of ethereal purity that seemed to surround her. Finally, Lady Buxley smoothed the white ribbons falling from Penelope's nosegay and stepped back. "My dear, you do us proud. I know we cannot take the place of your beloved parents, but remember that our best wishes will always go with you. Come, Constance, we mustn't keep his lordship from his bride."

When the two ladies had entered and were seated in the front pew, Squire Buxley held out his arm to escort Penelope into the chapel. Lightly she laid her fingers upon his arm. They moved to the center of the doorway. It was time.

No music played as Penelope moved slowly down the

aisle. Dimly she was aware that Vicar Wesley's wife was in the left pew and the viscount of Harrington was at Alex's side, but, in truth, she saw little other than her future husband. Her breath came quickly. How elegant he was. How easily he dominated the small chapel. His broad shoulders seemed to strain the seams of his delft-blue velvet coat. He wore the coat over a plain white waistcoat. No fob, watch chain, or other foppery detracted from his strength. The only jewelry he sported was a sapphire stick-pin nestled in the folds of his lace-edged neckcloth and a heavy gold signet ring on his finger. His black eyes flashed for a moment in appreciation, as she neared. Alex reached out his hand. His grasp was warm against her chilled fingers. He smiled slightly as he held her hand.

Vicar Wesley waited until Squire Buxley was seated before he began the cherished words of the wedding ceremony. Penelope felt as if she were in a play. The age-old words that united them as husband and wife seemed remote and detached. Even Alex sliding the heavy gold ring of entwined lover's knots onto her fourth finger had no meaning. She was in a daze. She feared she would wake to find it was all just another dream. It wasn't until Alex gently lifted her veil that the realization hit; she was married—for better or worse—to this man. Alex bent toward her. His fleeting kiss brushed her lips. The ceremony was complete. Penelope's fate was joined forever with his.

The Buxleys crowded around to congratulate them. Constance had already sighted a new quarry and was making sheep's eyes at James. If a marquis wasn't available, maybe a viscount would do. James squirmed under her attentions and threw pleading glances toward Alex. But his friend could be of no help, because Lady Buxley was busy recounting to him the tale of their ceaseless generosity to his bride. The shadow of boredom quickly descended over Alex's chiseled features. His answers became more curt. Penelope wanted to intercede, but Vicar Wesley drew her aside. He offered his best wishes, then commented sadly, "I was honored that his lordship asked me to officiate at your wedding, but I realize I was a poor substitute for your father."

Penelope smiled wanly. "I know he's here in spirit watching over us. I think he is pleased."

"I'm sure he is," the vicar reassured her. "You made a splendid match. His lordship is a fine man. We only wish he resided at Ashford more often. As you know, there is so much to do in the parish. We could certainly use his help."

"Yes, Father always said he scarce knew which problem to confront first."

The vicar's young wife joined them. He smiled at her. "I'm afraid it's still the same. Your father did admirable work, I should know since he helped raise the money for my seminary schooling, but there is still much left to do. That's why Harriet and I are glad his lordship married a local girl and not some belle of the ton. I know you care for our parish and will set a good example for the people."

"I will certainly try. You must let me know how I can help."

"Best watch what you offer," Harriet teased. "Albert will put you on all of his committees and charity drives, and that would scarce be the ideal way to spend one's first few weeks of marriage." She noted Penelope's delicate blush at her words and was pleased. The new mistress of Ashford was not putting on airs. She felt an immediate kinship and hoped she had found a friend. "Please come and have tea with us when your time permits. I know you will enjoy seeing the vicarage again. Your mother's rose garden is particularly beautiful this year."

Penelope was anxious to hear news of the parish, but

Lady Buxley pulled her away. "My dear, we need you to settle an argument. You simply must convince his lordship that the announcement of your marriage in the *Gazette* deserves more than a mere few lines, conveying but the bare bones of the matter. After all, you were married from Buxley Manor. That should be mentioned. And I know you would wish Constance's name to be included. It will seem a sadly ramshackle affair, if we aren't listed as attending you."

Alex's eyes were hard. "I'm sure we will brush through handsomely without all that folderol. I have already informed you that Squire Buxley's name will be listed."

"But," Lady Buxley sputtered, "the marchioness of Ashford deserves better than that. All the ton will be eager to read the details of the ceremony. Your marriage will be the topic of much curiosity."

"I am not in the habit of pandering to vulgar curiosity." Alex's tone was autocratic. "The brief announcement will be sufficient."

Lady Buxley turned entreatingly toward Penelope. "Milady, as the new marchioness of Ashford, you ought to be concerned with appearances. Do you wish your marriage to be considered a hole-in-the-wall affair?"

The use of her new title startled Penelope. Members of the nobility had always seemed so distant, so removed from her existence; now she too was called "milady." Her questioning eyes sought Alex's, but he made no response. She glanced back at Lady Buxley's determined face. What a puzzlement! Someone was going to be furious. But, in truth, there was but one choice. "I fear I must agree with his lordship. It is true my period of mourning is almost complete, but still I do not wish the details of my wedding to be bandied about on a passel of tongues. I much prefer a small dignified announcement."

Anger flashed across Lady Buxley's face; she was

tempted to make a sharp comment about ingratitude, but did not. Constance's season in London must not be jeopardized. Penelope's debt would have to be called sometime in the future. Instead she put on a simpering smile. "Then it should be as you wish, my dear." A change in tactics was in order. She turned back toward Alex. "I vow it has been a vast age since I have seen the inside of Ashford. It will be a pleasure to see the lovely rooms again."

Alex raised a brow at her presumption. His response was cool. "Yes, I am sure it will be. We have not had a ball at Ashford since my father's death. No doubt we shall wish to entertain our neighbors as soon as we are settled."

"Milord, stop twitting me," Lady Buxley gushed. "I was referring to the traditional wedding feast this evening."

"My wife and I are dining alone." When she began to protest, he stilled her with a curt rejoinder. "Surely you would not wish to intrude on our first evening of marital bliss."

There was a strong current of irony that underlaid his words. Penelope perceived it, but, as usual, Lady Buxley was impervious to any subtlety. She blanched and replied stiffly, "We would not think of it!" Abruptly she turned away and snapped, "Constance, get your father. We must leave."

"But, Mama, you said—"

Lady Buxley raised her voice until it was almost shrill. "Don't argue with me! Please, have your father summon the carriage. We're leaving!"

They departed with an unmistakable air of injured dignity, the Wesleys followed, and Penelope was alone with her husband and James. "That is the first time I have ever seen Lady Buxley bested, milord. I thank you. I was not relishing another evening in their company."

"Nor was I. They are incredibly boring people. I sup-

74

pose we will have to recognize them once we are in London, but I refuse to do anything more to further their social aspirations. They shall not hang on my sleeve!"

Penelope's heart skipped a beat when she heard his words. He was planning to take her to London for the season. Her eyes sparkled; she smiled radiantly up at him. James did not miss her reaction. He wasn't happy. He knew his friend well, but his friendship didn't blind him to Alex's faults. Heartbreak would surely be ahead for Penelope, if she allowed herself to fall in love with her husband. He longed to tell her, to warn her she had best not forget the circumstances and terms of their unusual marriage. A woman like Millicent was capable of handling Alex. She knew the rules of his game and would emerge unscathed, but there was a softness, a vulnerability about Penelope that was dangerous. He shook his head. If she wants more than Alex's name and his wealth, he mused, she is doomed to disappointment. That would be a shame, for he liked the dignity and honesty he found in her nature. What a damnable coil! Best be out of it. He bowed over Penelope's hand. "Lady Ashford, I must be off as well. It was an honor to attend your wedding. I bid my farewell."

Before Penelope could reply to his gracious speech, Alex chuckled, "Did you think my set-down of Lady Buxley included you, James? Believe me, I never find your company boring."

"But . . ."

"Don't get in a fidget. You will of course join us for dinner and spend the night at Ashford. I want your opinion of a sweet-goer of a hunter I picked up at the local horse fair. I think you will agree it was quite a find. Besides, it's late, and the only inn near is that bedbug-ridden, Peacock and Plume."

Alex glanced at Penelope to see if she supported his

75

offer. She refused to meet his look. She was feeling a bit shy. The Buxleys were an irritant to be sure, but at least they provided a buffer between her and her new husband. Alex's moods were so unpredictable that it made her feel unsure. She couldn't imagine sharing an intimate dinner with him. What would they talk about? She possessed no gift of sparkling wit to keep him entertained. No doubt he would consider her a rustic bore! To cover her bashful uncertainties, she urged, "Yes, Lord Harrington, please join us." She smiled at him. "Slapping at bedbugs sounds like a poor way to spend an evening."

He threw up his hands. "I concede, but I have two conditions. First," he joked, "you must never tell anyone I dined with you on your wedding night. If that tale ever got about, Alex's reputation would be ruined forever."

"Ah, yes"—Penelope laughed and twinkled up at her husband—"rumors of his vaulted reputation had even leaked into the vicarage. We must do all we can to preserve his image. I agree with your first condition. What is your second?"

Her spirited reply forced James to revise his view of her personality. She might lead Alex a merry chase yet. Should be interesting to follow their battle. "Secondly, you must call me James. Everytime someone says 'Lord Harrington' I look around for my father."

"Agreed." She smiled again. "Shall we go, James?"

Alex was pleased at the interchange. Granted this marriage had been foisted on him, but now that the deed was complete, Penelope was his wife. He was delighted at her social grace and easy repartee with his friend. Yes, she will do admirably. Even Sir Chinningsworth, that old fussbudget of a Puritan, could not question his life-style as long as she stood beside him. No one could doubt her purity or innocence. She would be an ideal shield. His life could continue as planned. The seat in the House of Lords was secure, and so were his other diversions.

They left the chapel. On the portico Penelope turned for one last glimpse. Only then did she notice that there were no flowers on the altar. It appeared stark and bare, almost unfriendly. She wished he had cared enough to notice. A little tinge of disappointment tried to mar her day. She pushed it away. A man can't be expected to think of floral decorations, even if they are for his own wedding, Penelope decided. She put it from her mind, and as Alex helped her into the carriage, her thoughts turned toward Ashford. She fervently hoped that the decor was less oppressive than the dowager's suite at Buxley Manor. Another night spent in such surroundings would surely give her a fit of the vapors.

The well-sprung carriage was a delight to ride in. The interior was luxurious. The seats were of tufted velvet with the Ashford coat of arms emblazoned on the back in gold thread. Penelope was content to rest and listen to the two men discuss the latest humorous foibles of their friend, the Prince of Wales. The chapel was at the far edge of the Ashford estate; it took a while to arrive at the main house. As they were about to turn around the last curve in the road, Alex commented, "I fear there will be quite a welcoming committee to greet us. My valet informed me this morning that the entire staff, both inside and outside, plans to be present when I formally introduce you. Don't try to remember all of the names. The only ones you need be concerned with are Jenkins, the butler, Mrs. Grayson, the housekeeper, and Earnest, the bailiff."

Penelope gulped as the huge gray house came into view. Its enormous facade was daunting, but worse still was the mass of servants lining both sides of the drive. As Alex had warned, everyone was present, from the liveried footmen to the rough-clothed stable hands. How would she ever manage? They were all agog to see their new mistress, but were too well trained to break rank. Her knees quivered as she descended from the carriage. She was grateful for Alex's supporting arm. He guided her to the center of the drive, then announced in a loud, clear voice, "I present to you, my wife, the marchioness of Ashford. I'm sure you will make her welcome."

Applause rang out and shouts of good wishes. Penelope smiled and relaxed a bit when she saw a few familiar faces in the crowd. These were her parish neighbors, the ones who had attended services in her father's church and danced at the village socials. She found it easy to be gracious as each group approached to be presented. Finally, everyone departed and only three servants remained.

Alex beckoned for them to approach and pay their respects. The butler, Jenkins, was an old man who bent stiffly from the waist. His manner was correct and proper, but Penelope detected a gleam in his eyes which she liked. He seemed approachable. Earnest, the bailiff, was a large man with a ruddy complexion. He doffed his cap respectfully when they were introduced. He had little to say. Mrs. Grayson was another matter entirely. Her black skirt rustled stiffly as she neared, and the keys hanging at her waist jangled menacingly. No smile accompanied her curtsy. Penelope reserved judgment.

The housekeeper's words were clipped as she turned back toward the house. "Milady, if you'll follow me, I'll show you to the bridal chamber. I'm sure you are fatigued." When they reached the huge double doors that gave entry to the house she paused and bobbed a curtsy to Alex. "Milord, dinner will be served at eight."

Her back was ramrod stiff as she marched across the entry hall toward the curving staircase. The hall was impressive in its rugged splendor. Massive suits of armor, from an earlier age, guarded the hall. Their long pikes pointed to the hunting trophies hung high above. The engraving on the armor was intricately beautiful, and Penelope wished she had time to study the detail, but the housekeeper's pace would not slow. With a sigh, Penelope gathered up her skirt and followed her up the stairs. It seemed that they walked through miles of corridors. Penelope was thoroughly lost when Mrs. Grayson finally stopped in front of a set of white doors. She turned the golden doorknobs, which were formed in the shape of swans, and threw open the doors.

Penelope couldn't help but gasp. She had never seen a more beautiful room. There was no ornate vulgarity of the type that marred the dowager's suite at Buxley Manor. The furniture was of deep rich mahogany wood with ormolu trim. The lines were simple and the hangings were all of white silk trimmed with a gold braid edging. A white and gold plush rug muffled her step. Even the fireplace was of white marble with flecks of soft gold.

Mrs. Grayson stood stiffly until Penelope completed her tour. Then she walked to the wall by the bed and yanked the bell pull. "I have assigned Kate to be your personal maid. Please inform me immediately if her services are wanting." Without waiting to be dismissed, she left, closing the doors firmly behind her.

What a female dragon, thought Penelope. She prayed Kate wouldn't be as intimidating. She wasn't. Penelope took one look at the cheerful girl, who came bouncing into the room, and smiled. She sized her up at one glance. Kate was a simple apple-cheeked country girl eager only to please. Under Kate's soothing hands, Penelope began to relax. The maid helped unpin the wreath and lifted off the bridal veil. Then she undid the pearl rosettes and removed the train. Penelope hadn't realized how heavy it had been, or how tired she was, until the weight was gone. She stretched and patted a yawn. "Will you change for dinner, milady?" Kate asked. "Your portmanteau arrived and I made bold to unpack it." When she saw the tiny frown of uncertainty on Penelope's face, she ventured, "The yellow gown might be nice for tonight."

"Yes, that will be fine."

"Very good, milady. Let me help you off with your wedding dress." Kate laid the gown carefully across the great white bridal bed, turned back toward Penelope, and helped her snuggle into the warm velvet wrapper. When her mistress was comfortable, she observed, "'Tis a pleasing scent you use, milady. 'Tis not like that heavy musk or sweet ambergris the other ladies be favoring. It suits you. You lay back on that day chaise there and let me brush out your hair. 'Tis the remedy my sainted mother always used when I was all in."

Kate's soothing strokes calmed Penelope's jittery nerves. Surprisingly she dozed. As she slept, Kate moved quietly about the bedchamber. The wedding gown was repacked in tissue and stored in the armoire. As she started to close the doors to the cabinet, she caught sight again of the old dresses that she had found folded in the bottom of Penelope's trunk. At first, she thought they had been packed in error and was tempted to dispose of them, but her common sense saved her. The ways of the aristocracy were strange, she realized. One never knew what new fashion they might follow next. Maybe dressing in faded, patched garments was the latest masquerade in the ton. She had heard tell of balls where everyone dressed as shepherds and shepherdesses, why not a ball where everyone dressed as beggars? With a shrug she had hung up the tattered dresses, but she still wondered.

Kate's gentle touch on her shoulder awakened Penelope. She sat up and rubbed her eyes. It was time to dress for dinner. The pale yellow gown of moiré silk was beautifully designed and fitted perfectly. The softly gathered neckline was cut low enough to display her slender shoulders to advantage and set off the Ashford diamonds, yet something spoiled the effect. The light color seemed to fade the natural color from Penelope's skin and made her appear a bit wan. She shook her head sadly as she stared in the looking glass. She supposed she was searching for a miraculous transformation. She expected the finery to turn her into another Millicent, but that could never be. Why must she persist in chasing these rainbows?

Penelope glanced at the clock ticking softly on the mantel and pushed further reflection away. Dinner would be served in a very few minutes and her hair was still unbound. She must not delay. Nothing made a man more peevish than to sit and wait while his dinner turned cold! Kate wanted to try a new hairstyle, but there wasn't time. Quickly she explained to the maid how to braid up her hair in a coronet, then walked down the stairs toward her future.

CHAPTER SIX

Penelope paused for a moment and stared in awe as Jenkins formally opened the door to the dining room for her. A huge walnut table by Sheraton dominated the room. Lavishly upholstered chairs to seat twenty-four were arranged down each side, a mirrored vermeil centerpiece graced the middle, huge silver candelabra, placed at intervals along the long table, provided glittering light, and bowls of fragrant flowers scented the room. She felt more than a little lost as she slowly walked toward Alex and James, who were lounging on a sofa at the far end of the enormous room. They stood as she approached, and Alex observed with a sweep of his hand, "It's a frightful morgue of a place, isn't it? Never fear, we shan't have to dine here often. Usually dinner is served in the green salon, but Mrs. Grayson wished to impress you. I fear we are at a stand."

He held out his arm and escorted her to the table. Three places were laid at one end of the long table. He seated her to his right and smiled, "I know as hostess you should properly be seated at the far end, but I think shouting across this expanse would make conversation rather tedious. Don't you agree?"

"Certainly, milord, but then we could always hire an extra footman to run messages back and forth. There is solution to any problem if you but apply yourself."

Alex threw back his head and laughed, "Footmen running messages, indeed. Penelope, as I said, you are an original!"

His laughter set the mood for the festive dinner. Penelope enjoyed herself. At first, when she saw the bewildering array of silver on either side of her plate, and the numerous styles of wineglasses setting above, she panicked. She had not ever seen some of the types of silverware before and had no idea how they were used. But she took her lead from Alex and did not blunder as course after elaborate course was sat before them. First they were served a mixture of oysters, lobster, and shrimp in a sharply spiced sauce, then oxtail soup with crisp croissants, followed by entrees of duckling in orange glaze and a roasted baron of beef. There were a variety of fresh garden vegetables, and dessert was fresh raspberries in a rich custard cream. A different wine was poured with each course. Penelope tried to demur. She had never had a drop of liquor before, and would have preferred lemonade or a cordial, but Alex was insistent. "I'll be dashed if you can toast your wedding night with a glass of lemonade! Let Jenkins pour you a little of this champagne. I am sure you will find it more to your taste than that usual insipid ratafia most of you ladies favor."

For a moment Penelope was startled. His mention of their wedding night put her nerves aflutter. Hesitantly she peeked at her husband through lowered lashes. He had been drinking heavily all through the meal; she feared what effect the wine might have on him, but he appeared in complete control. There was no devilish gleam in his eyes. She let out her breath. Tentatively she sipped the chilled champagne. After all the thundering her father had done from the pulpit about the evils of drink, she was certain it would be vastly unpleasant, but it wasn't. In fact, she rather liked it. Carefully she took another sip, then another. A warm glow enveloped her and her nervousness and sense of inadequacy eased. Alex noticed the change and smiled to himself.

After the luscious raspberries were finished, Penelope

expected the men to retire for cigarillos and brandy, but they merely pushed back their chairs, loosened their neck-cloths, and continued their discussion. Jenkins placed a decanter of brandy at Alex's elbow and motioned for the other servants to withdraw. Penelope sipped her chilled champagne and listened in polite silence until the subject of land enclosure was raised. After the defeat of Napoleon the wool trade with Flanders had resumed, and the price of raw wool was rising each year. Both of the men were large landholders and were considering the economic advantages of enclosing their fields and converting the farmland into pasture to raise sheep.

Penelope could hold her peace no longer. Her eyes flashed. "And what of the farmers you drive off the land, milords? Where will they go? How will they feed their families? They know no other trade but working the land. They are your responsibility!" She looked from one to the other. "You say the wool trade will help England prosper, but how can it when every acre turned into pasture throws a farmer and his family into the ranks of the beggars, or worse, turns them into thieves? Are the few gold coins you would add to your already bulging purses worth this?"

James laughed. "Ah," he observed good-naturedly, "the lady not only has beauty, she has fire. Have you considered, though, that the wool industry is providing as many jobs as it destroys and . . ."

The animated debate continued. Penelope refused to concede the point. Alex leaned back and drank his brandy as the two sparred with each other. He was satisfied. He admired spirit in a woman. The insipid, clinging misses who had cast their lures for him always left him quickly bored. He filled his glass again. He was indeed pleased that Millicent's plan was evolving so admirably. A few weeks of the tonnish whirl in London should satisfy his countrified wife, and her presence would still the wagging tongues of society. Then she could return to the obscurity of Ashford, and he could take his proper seat in Parliament. Even his discreet liaison with Lady Shellingham could continue. He raised his glass of brandy, gave a silent toast to the promising future, and drank deeply. His eyes roved lingeringly over his wife's figure. Yes, the plan was working—and it might have some pleasurable aspects Millicent had not considered. He smiled as he refilled his glass and drank again.

The bantering argument between James and Penelope continued for a spell. She might not be versed in the ways of polite society, but her natural wit and sharp intelligence made her an interesting companion. James was favorably impressed with the new Lady Ashford. He knew well the unusual conditions of their marriage, but he would lay down his blunt that Alex had not married the type of undemanding, acquiescent, nonentity that he wanted for a wife. The future should prove to be entertaining! The candles burned lower. Finally, during a lull in the conversation, Penelope glanced at the clock on the sideboard and saw that it had grown quite late. Gracefully she rose. "Milords, I have kept you from your cigarillos far too long. Please excuse me." The men were also on their feet. James bowed. Alex took her hand and drew it to his lips. His touch sent a wave of fire flashing through her body, and her hand trembled. Quickly she dropped a curtsy and sped from the room.

Kate was waiting outside the door to escort her mistress back to the bridal chamber. The rosy glow that had flowed through Penelope at her husband's touch lingered. Penelope was content. The maid swiftly unlaced the satin gown and helped her step out of it. As the cool air hit her bare skin, a whiff of the exotic fragrance swirled up about her once more. It seemed to be part of the magic of the evening. Penelope glanced toward the bed expecting to see

86

her flannel nightgown laid out for the night; instead, there was an exquisite lace and silk chiffon negligee with a flowing wrapper to match. Kate noticed her look and explained, "Lord Ashford had it delivered from London. Are you pleased, milady?"

There were no words to describe the delicious sensation of the silk gown against her skin. It fit closely, revealing every curve of her slender body. Penelope didn't know whether to be thrilled or slightly embarrassed. Kate held out the diaphanous wrapper. She felt a bit more secure as the silk cord was knotted firmly about her waist. A blush stained her cheeks, but her voice was calm when she replied, "Yes, I am pleased. It was most kind of his lordship to think of such a lovely gift."

When the maid had been dismissed for the night, the suppressed excitement of the day bubbled to the surface. Penelope twirled in front of the looking glass and watched the chiffon swirl out around her. Everything was so perfect! Even the room seemed more beautiful in the twinkling candlelight. There was an unreal, magical quality about everything.

Penelope felt so happy she spun and danced through the room. Then with a smile she crawled into the warm bed and snuggled under the down-filled comforter. She blew out the candle on the bed stand. The crackling fire in the fireplace softly lighted the room. The shadows thrown out by the blaze formed patterns on the wall. Penelope let her fantasy take hold, and her mind created all sorts of images from the flickering light. There was a knight jousting with a dragon, two men boxing, a lady waltzing at a ball, and then without conscious volition she saw a different vision reflected from the leaping flames. The image of her husband emerged from the pattern of shadows. She and Alex were alone. There was a smile in his eyes as he gazed at her. Her heart pounded as she envisioned him crossing the room to her side. His arms went out. Gently he drew her to him. Penelope could see it so clearly. He tilted her blushing face up until their eyes met. A fire smoldered deep within him. A strong hand caressed her trembling lips, her neck, her face. She felt herself on fire. He drew her nearer. Slowly his lips came down to meet hers and . . . Crash! A log fell down off the grate. The beautiful illusion was destroyed. Penelope buried her burning face in the pillow and wept.

When her tears were spent, she left the bed and knelt by the fire, seeking its familiar warmth. Her long hair fell around her. Visions of Millicent being passionately held in Alex's arms tortured her mind. Over and over she scolded herself for playing the fool. Somehow she must find the strength to defend herself. Alex must never know of the desire his slightest touch produced within her. Penelope knew she was nothing to him, less even than his prize horses. At least those he chose himself, while she had been forced upon him. He has Millicent. It's her lips he wants, her arms, her body, her love, she reminded herself time upon time.

The misery was so intense that she didn't hear the door to the connecting chamber open. Alex's voice came from across the room. "Come here, Penelope. You will catch your death of cold huddling like that on the floor. Besides" —he smiled crookedly—"my arms are warmer than any fire."

Penelope leaped to her feet. "What do you want here?" she demanded in a shaky voice.

"Why, you of course, my dear." His eyes roamed slowly, lingeringly over her body. She had no idea how the flickering firelight revealed her delicate form. It was an enticing sight! He moved nearer. His arms went out. "I want you!"

"How dare you!" Penelope's voice trembled as she moved away from him. "Get out of my bedchamber!"

His step was somewhat unsteady as he relentlessly moved closer. "It is our bedchamber, Penelope, our bridal chamber." His voice stressed the word our. "I don't intend to spend this night alone."

"Then seek the arms of Lady Shellingham, or some other idiot that would welcome your embrace," she raged. "You will not touch me! This was not part of our bargain!"

He seemed amused by her defiance. Usually women were only too willing to throw themselves into his arms and climb into his bed. Resistance was a novelty. It would make the conquest sweeter. A sardonic smile curved his lip. "Could it be you're jealous of Lady Shellingham? You needn't be. You are my wife. She is but"—he casually waved his hand—"a passing fancy. She'll never bear the Ashford heirs you will."

"Never!" she swore.

Panic seized Penelope. She quickly backed away from his approach. It couldn't be like this! It must not be like this! She turned to flee. The day chaise barred her way. Alex's throaty laugh rang mockingly in her ears as he gathered her into his arms. She fought wildly as the brandy fumes assailed her. His hold didn't slacken. His kisses rained down on her face and neck, and finally he claimed her mouth. Her mind willed her to struggle and fight to be free, but his touch couldn't be denied. She couldn't force him away. Alex sensed her weakness. His brutal kisses became softer and more deeply passionate. Slowly, skillfully, he forced Penelope to respond. Her resistance ebbed as the kiss went on and on. At last, with a soft moan, her arms crept up around his neck and she urged him closer.

When he finally released her, her head fell back against his shoulder. A smile touched his lips as he saw the look that love's first passion had lit in her eyes. With a satisfied growl he pulled her back to him. Again her mouth quivered under his touch. Flames of desire swept through her as his hands roamed over her body. A soft yank released the silken cord of her wrapper. It fell to the ground. His lips nuzzled her neck as he swept her into his arms and stumbled toward the bed.

Penelope's eyes closed. Alex pulled back the covers and gently laid her down on the bed. He stretched out beside her and stared down at her for a moment. Penelope's eyes fluttered open and she saw him smile. Slowly he lowered his head. The touch of his lips was at first light and soft; then when he felt her response, his mouth became more passionate, more demanding. Resistance was gone. She pulled him nearer ever nearer, as he whispered words of endearment into her ear. With a deep rumble of desire, he murmured, "Ah, *chérie amante*, I . . ."

Alex's words, the same words of desire he had murmured to Millicent, shattered the spell of her passion. He used the same words, Penelope's heart cried, the same words! It is Millicent he is thinking of! It is Millicent he wants to make love to! She struggled from his grasp. Tears poured down her face. She was nothing to him, she silently raged. She was just a convenient substitute for the one who isn't here. How could she have submitted to his caresses? Shame flooded through her. How? How could she have forgotten for one moment whom he truly desired?

Frantically she fought against him. His eyes, which a moment ago had been dark with desire, glared down at her in fury. Roughly he pushed her back on the bed. With one deliberate motion he reached down and ripped the sheer silk from her body. In terror Penelope lashed out with her tiny fist. She caught the edge of his mouth. Her wedding ring slashed his lip. Drops of blood fell on her skin. Alex wiped his hand across his mouth and looked at the red staining his hand. He shoved her away, muttered an oath, and stood up.

His eyes flickered over the trembling figure before him. A cynical twist contorted his smile. "Fools never learn," he taunted. "I actually thought you might be different, but all women are alike! From countesses to strumpets, you're all deceitful! You tempt, promise, beckon, then play the tease! Well, Lady Ashford, I won't play!" His voice was incredibly bitter, almost hurt. "I hope you enjoy your wedding night . . . alone."

The door slammed. Penelope was alone—alone on her wedding night. How dreadful everything was! Tears choked her throat. She trembled again when she tried to draw the tattered remnants of her nightgown around her. Another slam reverberated through the room. Was Alex coming back?

Fearfully she crept out of bed and ran to their connecting door. There was no bolt, no lock, no protection. What if Alex returned? Would she be able to resist him again? Quickly she shoved the desk in front of the door. As she moved, the tattered gown fell to the floor.

A sense of shame raged through Penelope's body as she remembered his caresses and her fiery response. She shivered. The trembling was not entirely due to fear. She could still feel the touch of his hands against her skin, his hard embrace, his kiss that demanded her surrender. Angrily she rubbed her hand across her bruised mouth. How dare he come here—How dare he think she would—How dare she almost—

With a swoop Penelope gathered up the torn gown and threw it into the fire. The flames eagerly licked across the silk. Soon nothing was left, nothing but ashes. She struggled into the warm wrapper and curled up by the fire, deliberately turning her back on the bridal bed. Her arms protectively encircled her knees, and she rubbed her cheek against the soft velvet of the robe. Back and forth she rocked as she stared at the flames. Why—why had it happened?

"Alex was foxed, no question of that," Penelope muttered aloud. "Maybe he had an excuse; there was no excuse for what I did." Her voice broke. "I behaved like a—like a . . ." The words faded. She didn't even know the name for that type of woman. "Why?" she raged at herself. "Where was my pride? I should have rejected him, but no, I welcomed his embrace until . . ."

The remembrance of the words that drove them apart was painful, so was the truth. What had happened was not entirely Alex's fault. It was their wedding night. He was her husband. She had willingly returned his caresses. Often Penelope had dreamed of being in his arms. When it actually happened, she couldn't resist playing out the fantasy. No more dreams! Not ever again! There must be no more fantasies! They were dangerous, so dangerous she almost found desire without love.

Abruptly Penelope stood up. The anger was gone. Her husband was a rake, not the ideal beau she had created in her mind. Yet she couldn't deny his powerful attraction. Even now the thought of his towering presence sent a tremor of desire through her body. Yes, he was a rake, but he was an engaging rake. She turned toward the bed. A hot blush spread across her face as she remembered what had almost happened there. This time she did not turn away from it. She and Alex were married. That fact had not been destroyed tonight. There would be a way out of this tangle, there always was. Tomorrow they could talk and try to make sense of their marriage.

Penelope went to the armoire and found her old flannel gown. The knot of the wrapper was stubborn. It finally came loose and she hung up the robe. The familiar warmth of her old nightgown was comforting, but still her hands trembled slightly as she smoothed out the crumpled linen sheets. A few tears tried to fall. She squeezed her eyes shut, blinked them back, and quickly climbed into the lonely bed. A whiff of Alex's cigarillo floated up from the pillow. She held it tightly in her arms as she fell asleep.

Kate brought Penelope a breakfast tray the next morning. A perplexed frown flashed across her cheerful face when she noticed her mistress's old nightgown, but she said nothing. "'Tis a beautiful morning, milady. Do you wish the drapes to be opened?"

Penelope nodded and sipped her hot chocolate. Everything had seemed simple last night. She would talk with Alex and they would come to some new understanding. This morning she was not sure. She longed to see him, yet what was there to say? She dawdled over her chocolate and nibbled slowly on the warm crusty rolls. They were sweet and rich with butter. She tasted little.

Kate bustled about the chamber, straightening up things and relaying the fire. Once in a while she cast a concerned glance at Penelope and shook her head. Went to bed in silk, woke up in flannel, 'twas not a good sign.

Her mistress did not have the look of a happy bride. Kate went to pick up the breakfast tray. "What dress do you favor this morning, milady? There was a chill in the air when I arose, but it's right warm now."

The maid's question forced a decision. Her confrontation with Alex could be delayed no longer. Penelope swung her feet to the floor. "The blue muslin will do." The choice of the dress was deliberate. She had worn it during a happier meeting, maybe he would remember. Nervously she fiddled with the ribbons as Kate plaited her hair. What would Alex's reaction be to her this morning? He had been bitter and angry last night. Would he talk calmly or give her one of his thundering set-downs? When Kate finished pinning the braids into place, Penelope smoothed out the rumpled ribbons and left the bedchamber. She hesitated at the top of the stairs, then slowly started down.

The house was silent. No one was about. She found her way to the dining room where they had eaten the evening before; it was empty. What had Alex said? Oh, yes, the green salon, that was where he took most of his meals. He must be there. Penelope's hand trembled as she reached to touch the knob. She swallowed once, stiffened her back, then boldly opened the door. Alex wasn't there. No breakfast was laid. The room was coldly still.

Penelope tried another door and found the library. The sight of all the books tantalized her. She ran her fingers lovingly over the leather covers and felt the titles tooled in gold. The books looked well read, not like the ones at Buxley Manor. Countless authors she had always wanted to read were here. Her hand started out to lift Spenser's *The Faerie Queen* from the shelf. She pulled back her hand. No delays. She must see Alex. Regretfully she closed the door.

Maybe he was still asleep. He might not be feeling the thing this morning after all that brandy. Mrs. Grayson would surely know. Penelope wrinkled her nose at the thought of the housekeeper. I daresay she will unbend in time, she thought as she re-entered the green salon and yanked the tapestry bell pull. In a few moments Mrs. Grayson entered and stood stiffly by the door. "You rang, milady."

Penelope clasped her hands together to keep them from trembling. She prayed her voice would not break as she asked, "Has Lord Ashford partaken of breakfast yet? I wish to speak with him."

Mrs. Grayson gave her a disapproving stare. "His lordship and the viscount of Harrington returned to London this morning. Is there anything else?"

Penelope's heart pounded. Gone—Alex was gone! No

word, no letter, no good-bye. He had left her. What was she to do? With a nod she dismissed the housekeeper and sank down on the settee. Tears trickled through her fingers and splashed against the muslin of her gown. They fell on the bodice ribbons and formed watery blotches on the silky surface. It didn't matter. Alex was gone. She had driven him away. She was alone again.

CHAPTER SEVEN

In the days that followed Penelope descended into her own personal hell. She could hear the servants whisper behind her back, but she held her head high and would not show her heartbreak. Only at night, in the bed where she had held Alex in her arms for those brief moments, did the tears come.

One night, as the moonlight flooded her bedchamber, Penelope clutched the pillow closely and wondered again how it would be if she had not spurned Alex's passion. Would he be beside her? A hot blush stained her cheeks as she remembered the feel of his hard lips. She yearned to feel them again. Even the fury she felt at his whispered words had not burned out her love. She threw the pillow away from her and got out of bed. The breeze from the open window cooled her face and calmed her overtaut nerves. She leaned against the jamb, staring at the garden below. Penelope shook her head. The dismals had gone on long enough. She had best accept the situation and stop acting the goose-witted fool. The countryside was full of springtime beauty to explore, the Ashford tenants needed visiting, and she had duty calls to pay on the local gentry. Alex had seen fit to leave, but that did not mean she had to rusticate here alone. Somehow she had to fill the empty hours of the day. Maybe a spot of tea at the vicarage would cheer her. Tomorrow, yes, she would do that tomorrow.

In the morning Kate noticed a new spirit about her mistress. The deep sadness still haunted Penelope's eyes, but at least she ate more than a few nibbles of breakfast. 'Twas a good sign.

Penelope dressed in her riding habit and walked down to the great entry hall. Mrs. Grayson was there directing a footman to polish the bronze sconces. She turned when Penelope reached the last step. She did not curtsy. Penelope refused to be daunted by her forbidding manner. Her voice was polite, but contained a note of authority. "Mrs. Grayson, please have a groom bring round a mare. I wish to ride this morning."

The housekeeper's mouth formed a thin, hard line. "That isn't possible, milady. Lord Ashford left no instructions concerning which of his horses you might ride."

"My husband," Penelope stressed the word, "is not here, therefore he cannot be consulted." She paused, then added firmly, "I do not expect to have to issue my request again."

The footman snickered. Mrs. Grayson glared at him. She would not yield. "I can't take the responsibility. Lord Ashford is most particular about who rides his horses."

"It is not your responsibility," Penelope countered. "It is mine. If you will not summon a groom, I shall go and select my own mount from our stables."

Mrs. Grayson sputtered a reply. Penelope ignored her, turned, and walked out the front door. It felt good to have some of her spirit return.

A groom was mucking out one of the stalls when Penelope entered. She jumped back as the odoriferous pile came sailing through the air. The groom's face blanched when he saw what he had done. He took off his battered cap and twisted it nervously in his hands as he waited for her furious scold. Penelope merely smiled at him. "What is your name?"

"Jem-groom, milady," he stammered.

"Jem, will you please help me select a horse. I feel like a gallop this morning."

His mouth was agape. No person of quality had ever spoken so kindly to him before. Jem unbent even further when he discovered her love of his precious stock. As they moved along the row of stalls, Penelope paused time and again to stroke a soft muzzle or whisper gently to one of the horses. When they responded with playful nudges, she laughed. Horses be wiser than people for judgin' a person, Jem thought. They knew she'd be a kind mistress. At the end of the row of stalls Penelope's smile faded. Alex's great black stallion stomped and whinnied at her approach. The sight brought back some of her unhappiness. She turned away. "Which horse do you suggest, Jem? The little sorrel looked pleasing."

The groom scratched his head. "That mare be a sweet-goer, 'tis true, but she be skittish as well. If I might make bold to suggest the bay. She be—"

"No, the sorrel will do nicely." When Penelope saw his concern, she added, "Don't fret, I am not a cow-handed rider."

Jem shook his head, but saddled the little mare for her. He also saddled an old plug for his mount. Penelope sighed. She had ridden alone for years, but those days were past. The marchioness of Ashford could not ride without an escort. Before they cantered out of the stable, she instructed Jem to have one of the other grooms ride to the vicarage and tell Harriet she wished to pay a call in the afternoon.

The morning was beautiful. She let the little mare have her head. They took off at a gallop. The wind ruffled her hair and whipped against her face. It was wonderful to be outside and riding again. Too long she had moped in the dismals. She vowed no more.

On a small rise she reined in her horse and dismounted.

The field around was filled with fragrant wild flowers. She picked an armful before remounting. Ashford stood majestically in the distance. It was a magnificent house, no question of that, but without Alex there it seemed cold and unfriendly. Penelope stroked the gleaming coat of the little mare and laid her cheek against the horse's neck. The horse nuzzled her hand, then tried to nibble on the flowers she had picked. "You had best not do that," she scolded gently as she pulled them away. "Are you ready for your oats?" The horse neighed as if it understood. Penelope laughed. "All right, we will return."

On the ride back Penelope passed the bailiff, who was busily directing a crew of men in the repair of a stone fence. His rudely shouted orders displeased her. She slowed the mare to a walk. Immediately his tone changed. He respectfully doffed his cap. His manner was servile as he bowed in her direction. She did not like his attitude, nor did she like Mrs. Grayson's when she returned to the great house. The housekeeper looked disapprovingly at the bunch of wild flowers Penelope handed her and sniffed with displeasure when she was told to put them in water. Penelope frowned. That woman was a trial!

After lunch Penelope read and then rang for Kate to help her dress for the visit to the vicarage. Harriet and Vicar Wesley were delighted to see her and warmly welcomed her. Her old home glowed with their happiness. She was truly pleased they were there. They walked through her mother's treasured rose garden. Her eyes grew misty as she remembered the loving hours her mother had spent among these flowers. She picked one yellow rose and carried it back to the house with her.

Harriet poured tea for them in the parlor. The warmth of their friendship soothed Penelope's spirit. She enjoyed talking with Vicar Wesley about the parish news and laughed over the latest foibles of Miss Bessie Crump, the village gossip. Harriet knitted quietly and missed none of the conversation. She was not cozened by Penelope's cheerful chatter; something was definitely wrong at Ashford. She bit off the yarn and spread out the tiny blue wool blanket. Penelope saw her fold it and questioned, "Should I start shopping for a nursery gift? Mama always said the pink bedchamber would be ideal for a wee one."

"Harriet," Vicar Wesley asked with a grin, "are you hiding secrets from me?"

"Oh, no—I mean"—Harriet colored rosily—"the blanket is for that young Mrs. Thomas. She had a baby boy last week," she explained quickly. "Dick Thomas is one of your tenant farmers at Ashford."

Penelope brightened. "Do you think we could pay them a call this afternoon? I have been wanting to meet some of our farmers."

Harriet was delighted with her interest. Lady Ashford has a kind heart, she noted with pleasure; far different from her husband who is a . . . well, enough of that! It is best to hold only charitable thoughts. Vicar Wesley hitched a horse to their old carriage and the two ladies set off. The Thomas cottage was small, with a steeply pitched thatched roof. Petunias grew in the flower boxes and there was a small vegetable garden on the side. Mrs. Thomas answered their knock. She was astonished to find the marchioness of Ashford at her doorstep. The floor of the cottage was of packed earth, there was only one room, but everything was neat as a pin. Mrs. Thomas felt shy as she stood back and let the two ladies enter.

As Harriet and Penelope cooed over her new son, Mrs. Thomas gained confidence, and they were all soon chatting like old friends. The baby woke up and fussed a bit. Harriet and Penelope tried to rock his cradle, but he continued to kick and squall. He was not the least impressed by his noted visitors. "'Tis his nursin' time," his mother

101

explained as she picked him up. She settled in the creaky rocker and nestled the baby against her breast. Instantly the cries ceased.

Penelope looked at them, mother and child, and her throat filled with tears. She imagined a child with Alex's curly chestnut hair, and her arms ached with emptiness. As the feeding was ending, Dick Thomas came into the cottage. He was a big strapping man with a ready smile. Dirt clung to his heavy clogs and his hands were rough and calloused. Proudly he stood by his wife and new son and greeted them. Penelope talked with him about the farming conditions at Ashford. His answers were honest and direct until she mentioned the bailiff. He stammered, stopped, then muttered something about milking the cow and quickly left. She wondered what was amiss. Harriet was on her feet ready to leave; she had no time to find out. When they left, the little baby was sleeping contentedly under his new fluffy blue blanket.

Day followed lonely day. No word came from Alex. There was some news though. The London papers were posted to the estate, and Penelope read that Alex's appointment to the House of Lords had been confirmed. He had what he wanted; he could forget she existed. She rubbed her forehead. What else did she expect? The newspaper also discussed the stir his maiden speech in Parliament had created. Alex had spoken forceably against the unhealthy conditions in the new factories and the long hours worked by the child laborers. Many industrialists were angered by his stance and challenged his assertions. The paper noted the marquis of Ashford had not withdrawn his accusations. Penelope was pleased by that article, but her hurt returned when she read in the *Gazette* of a rout party hosted by Lord and Lady Sefton. Lady Shellingham and Alex were prominently listed among the guests. Lord Shellingham was not. A few more tears fell that night.

Working in the rose garden helped relieve the tedium of the days. Penelope would rise early, don one of her old dresses, and walk outside. The warm sun felt good as she weeded, pruned, and slowly let the hours slip by. One morning she had returned from the garden and was in the great entry hall, when she heard a carriage clatter to a stop on the drive. Alex—maybe it was Alex. She glanced down at her faded gown. Why did she have to look like this when he returned? She whirled to run upstairs; there was no time. The bell rang imperiously once, then again. Jenkins slowly creaked open the door and bowed low.

A tall, slender woman with pure white hair advanced slowly into the hall. She was dressed all in black and leaned heavily on a cane. Her back was straight, her eyes glittered. "Milady," Jenkins bowed again, "we did not expect you. May I say it's a pleasure to have you at Ashford again."

The woman regally nodded her head. She spared a glance toward Penelope as she answered, but thought she was a new maid. "Yes, it is good to be back. I wish I could have returned under more pleasant circumstances, though. However, I would as lief not delay the matter." Her voice was bitter as she demanded, "Pray inform that —that creature who shackled Alex that the dowager marchioness of Ashford is here and wishes to see her." She advanced slowly across the marble floor, placing each foot carefully before she took a step. "I will receive her in the morning room."

Alex's mother! The color drained from Penelope's face. She heard the hatred in her voice when she asked for Alex's wife. She wanted to turn and flee, but there was no place to go. Jenkins coughed uncomfortably. He glanced from one woman to the other, then cleared his throat. His old voice croaked a bit as he announced, "Milady, may I present the marchioness of Ashford."

The dowager's eyes swept the room. She looked at Penelope, who had dropped into a deep curtsy. "Stuff and nonsense!" she snapped. "Jenkins, are you daft? This chit cannot be Alex's wife. I am in no mood to be roasted. Call Lady Ashford at once!"

Penelope rose from the curtsy and folded her hands before her. In a quiet voice she responded, "I am Penelope Ashford, milady."

The dowager studied Penelope carefully. She took in every detail of her unassuming appearance. When Alex had written to tell her of his marriage, she suspected he had been trapped by some scheming hussy. Why else would Alex not bring his bride to meet her? Everything she had believed was obviously wrong! This child before her was no bit of muslin or other disreputable woman. There was a mystery here and she intended to find the answer. She smiled at Penelope. "Child, please forgive my outburst. Come, let us have a cup of tea together. I am afraid the trip fatigued me more than I expected."

Alex's mother leaned on Penelope's arm as they made their way to the green salon. Mrs. Grayson brought hot tea and sweet biscuits, then they were alone. "All right," she insisted, "what is the truth about this marriage? Where did Alex find you? Who are you?"

Penelope swallowed nervously. "My father was Vicar Stanwood. Ashford was his parish until his death."

"Yes, I knew your parents well. They were good people. Now finish the tale. How did this marriage come about? Why did Alex hesitate to tell me of your attachment?"

Penelope stared down at her tightly folded hands. "Maybe he felt the difference in our rank would distress you."

"That is pure twaddle!" the dowager insisted. "Alex

may seem remote, but he is a loving son. If you two had fallen in love, he knows no difference in rank would have mattered to me. Stop the hum! I want the truth!" Penelope remained silent. She could not betray Alex's secret. Finally his mother asked, "Does all this have anything to do with Lady Shellingham and his appointment to the House of Lords?"

Penelope's eyes flew up. Spots of pink appeared high on each cheekbone. "It's as I suspected," his mother nodded wisely. "Alex got himself all in a basket over his involvement with that woman."

She started to deny it. The dowager raised her hand to stop her. "There is no need to fly up in the boughs. I may have been in deep mourning, but that does not mean I have not followed Alex's raffish career. I heard about the lovely Millicent from several sources. I suppose that drunken lout she is married to threatened to create a stir." She patted the seat beside her. "Best come over here and tell me everything. I fancy we can clear up this muddle."

Slowly, painfully, the whole story came out. Penelope told her everything, everything except about the scene on their wedding night. All the time that Penelope was speaking, the dowager was judging her. She was pleased. The girl had spirit as well as innocence—an irresistible combination. She would do very nicely for Alex. Plan, she must make plans to draw them together, but she was too weary to think more today. Penelope helped her upstairs and sat with her while they ate a bite of dinner. By the time Penelope tucked her gently into bed, Alex's mother was sure that her daughter-in-law was worthy of the Ashford name.

That same night in London others were also thinking of the new Lady Ashford. The Prince of Wales was hosting a magnificent ball at Carlton House. Between dances a group of his friends clustered around to hear about a

Rubens painting he had acquired. Alex walked by on his way to the card room. "Lord Ashford, come and join us," the prince shouted. "I have not seen you for a vast age. You must have been rusticating with your new bride. I always said honeymoons were smashing fun!" He chuckled as he poked a neighbor in the ribs. "Bring Lady Ashford over and present her."

The crowd parted. Alex reluctantly walked over to join the prince. "Damn!" he muttered under his breath. "Prinny would have to be in one of his jovial moods tonight!" His cravat felt unusually stiff about his neck. "Sir, Lady Ashford could not attend your ball this evening. She is still in the country."

"I want to meet her," the prince insisted again. "Everyone's agog to see the lady who captured you." He laughed knowingly. "When can we expect her?"

Alex could hear snickers behind his back. Penelope's absence was causing a passel of gossip. Until now he had been safe. His aloof manner had stopped anyone from questioning him, but Prinny would not be put off. "Sir, Lady Ashford is still in mourning for her father. She will come for the remainder of the season when that time is over."

"Not good ton to desert your bride, old boy!" Prinny teased. "Could make a deuce of a stir."

"Damn, damn, damn," Alex cursed to himself. Casually he snapped open his snuffbox to gain a moment to think. He took a pinch. "Sir, I had to come to London to claim my seat in Parliament. I could scarce do otherwise."

"What is the charmer like? A local miss I hear. By Jove! I guess we should all go out and see what the country has to offer," he bellowed. "Ah, Ashford!"

James quietly stepped to Alex's side. When Prinny pressed for more details, he answered, "I was honored to be at Ashford's wedding, sir. I assure you Lady Ashford is indeed charming, quite out of the ordinary."

"Good, good, can't wait to meet her."

The music began and Alex and James made their escape. "Damnit, James, this is a nasty coil! Why did you tell Prinny that? He will be expecting a belle of the ton, and when Penelope is presented, he will think I have bats in my cockloft!"

"Hardly think so," James disagreed. "Penelope is uncommon, far from ill favored, you know. Ought to be able to brush through."

Alex looked at him with a frown. Why was James so complimentary of Penelope? It was a puzzlement. He should be glad his friend liked her, yet a bit of resentment lingered. There was a light hint of sarcasm as he replied, "I am glad you find such favor with my wife."

Before James could answer, Millicent glided up. A tiny pout marred her lips. "Lord Ashford, you are down for this waltz."

Alex bowed gracefully, begged her forgiveness, and they danced off. As they whirled around the ballroom, Millicent laughed gaily. "Our plan is working splendidly. Chester does not suspect a thing. He even apologized for that drunken scene at Buxley Manor."

Millicent felt Alex's arm tighten around her as they spun across the floor. He leaned nearer, his voice was deep and sensually warm. "That is delightful news."

"Yes, and I have other delightful news, milord. Chester will be leaving soon to hunt grouse in Scotland. My court duties will not permit me to accompany him. How very sad!" she added with a wink.

"You must let me know when Chester departs." He smiled down at her, then commented with special meaning, "I can tell him where the hunting is best."

Millicent's throaty laughter floated across the ballroom.

Her heart beat faster as Alex continued, "Ah, *chérie am* —" His words suddenly died. The image of Penelope's tear-stained face thrust its way between them. His eyes left Millicent. A vague frown clouded his handsome features. He stumbled over a turn.

The woman in his arms felt his abrupt withdrawal. To regain his attention, Millicent forced a sparkling smile. "Alex darling, why did you stop? I adore it when you call me *chérie amante.* Say it again," she pleaded.

The waltz was ending, but she would not let him go. "Please, Alex, say it."

He removed his arm from her waist. "No!" His voice was curt. "It is trite nonsense!"

Millicent was startled. Desperately she wanted to find some assurance of his continuing devotion. "Meet me at the Diana fountain after we dine."

Only after he had nodded his head in agreement did she let another partner claim her hand for the next dance.

Alex was surly company during the supper. James looked at him and wondered. When the music began again, he slipped outside and strode to the fountain. Even Millicent's assurance that her husband would not stir up a ruckus did not mellow his mood. He paced impatiently. Finally, with a soft rustle, Millicent was at his side. Without a word he swept her into his arms. She returned his embrace with passionate intensity; her lips melted under his, her arms pulled him closer. When he released her, Millicent stared up into his face. Their kiss had been satisfying, and yet something was missing. She kept her arms around him and did not let him see her concern. "Alex," she murmured, "it has been a vast age since you held me like that." Her voice was low and seductive. "I have thought of you every day, and especially every night."

Alex smiled down at her. Millicent was an incredibly

beautiful woman, a sensual woman. An unwelcome thought intruded. How many others had held her like this? How many times had she said those same words before? To blot out the question, he drew her back into his arms. Only the sound of the fountain disturbed the night.

Long moments later Millicent sighed, "I do believe you missed me. No doubt that born antidote you married left you eager for my arms."

He pulled away from her grasp. "Alex, pray what is wrong?"

In truth, he wasn't sure. Her possessiveness and acid tongue had never angered him before. Why did it now? "Millicent, you are not to refer to my wife in that way." His tone was harsh. "She is Lady Ashford, don't forget that!"

Tears glittered on the ends of Millicent's long lashes. His set-down jolted her. She pressed close against his body. For the first time she was unsure of holding a man. What had changed him? Why did he suddenly seem remote? His kisses were ardent enough, but something had changed.

CHAPTER EIGHT

With each passing day Penelope grew fonder of Alex's mother. The feeling was shared. The dowager asked Penelope to call her Amelia. She was delighted with the warmth and understanding of her new daughter-in-law. Amelia was not yet fully recovered from her husband's death. She was growing stronger, but still needed to rest each morning. Penelope used this time to explore the countryside around Ashford. She even paid a duty call to Buxley Manor, but found the Buxleys were in London for the season. In the afternoons Penelope would walk with her mother-in-law through the gardens or read to her in the library. They asked Harriet and Vicar Wesley to visit, had other members of the local gentry over for tea, and the dowager tried to teach Penelope to tat. Lace making was definitely not her craft. The spindles flew everywhere and the delicate threads ended up in a jumbled heap. Alex's mother took the mess from her hands, laughed, and handed Penelope back her embroidery frame. They enjoyed each other. It was fun to laugh again.

The peaceful days came abruptly to an end. Penelope was out riding early one morning and decided to visit Mrs. Thomas. The baby had had a slight cold the day before and she was concerned. She fixed a poultice and rode off. The small cottage was past a bend in the road. She heard the angry shouts before she could see the trouble. She urged the little sorrel into a gallop. Earnest, the bailiff, was standing in the road shouting at the young farmer. Dick Thomas blocked their doorway. He had a pitchfork in his

111

hands. He aimed the sharp prongs at the bailiff and yelled, "Not one step closer. Ye back up!"

Penelope gulped when she saw the bailiff draw a pistol. Without thinking, she hurled the horse between them and sprang to the ground.

"Put that away!" she ordered the bailiff. "Dick, you set that pitchfork down."

When the men were slow to move, she stormed over and grabbed the pistol from Earnest. He was so surprised he let her take it without a scuffle. "Dick!" she ordered again. Slowly he put his rustic weapon aside, but he did not move away from the doorway. Penelope looked from one to the other. "All right, who is going to tell me what this set-to is about?" Neither spoke, neither moved. Penelope took a step toward the door. "Come, we will go inside and discuss this problem calmly."

Dick refused to move. He pointed. "That man's an out-and-outer. He ain't settin' one foot in my house!"

"It ain't your house no more," the bailiff yelled back. "I told you to get out."

"That is enough!" Penelope intervened sharply. "What is the trouble?"

Both men started arguing again, finally the story came out. Dick was a quarter behind on his rent, and the bailiff was determined to evict him. Penelope asked the farmer, "Have you ever fallen behind on the rent before?"

"No, never. I wouldn't have this time neither except there's been nary a drop of rain. The corn's shriveled up and the oats won't head out. Can't sell what won't grow. 'Tis a bad spell we've been havin'."

"Rain or no rain, he's behind," the bailiff argued. "I've a duty to turn him out. Lord Ashford would be angry if I let him stay. Ain't my fault he's a poor farmer."

"That's a lie!" Dick shouted. "My father tilled this land

before me. He was a good farmer and he made me into a good farmer I—"

"Gammon!" the bailiff roared. "Lady Ashford, don't listen to him. I know . . ."

Their yelling match continued at full volume. Fists were clenched. Eyes glared. They were beyond reason. Penelope feared a mill was inevitable unless she acted. She lifted the pistol toward the sky, closed her eyes, and pulled the trigger. A shattering report split the air. The men were startled into silence. Inside the cottage the baby wailed.

"I fancy you are now prepared to listen to reason." She looked sternly at the bailiff. "Dick Thomas and his family are to stay in this cottage until I can investigate your charges. They are not to be turned out. Is that understood?"

"Yes, milady," he snarled unhappily, "but you'll have to answer to Lord Ashford's anger when he finds out what you've done."

The matter settled, Penelope remounted her horse and turned toward the great house. She supposed Alex would be furious with her interference. Yet she knew she had done the right thing.

Amelia agreed with her when Penelope told her of the incident over lunch. "My child," she reassured Penelope, "the Thomas family have been farmers here as long as I can remember. They are good tenants and honest people. We are not going to turn them out without a hearing. I do wish we could be sure of the truth though, before we take this matter any further."

"If anyone knows the true state of affairs, it will be Vicar Wesley," observed Penelope. "Papa knew everything and everyone in his parish."

"Capital idea, child. Ring that bell. Let us send a message inviting the vicar and his sweet wife to tea this afternoon. No reason to dawdle."

The dowager sparkled in anticipation and visited the kitchen to supervise the baking of some ginger cakes. Penelope noticed her new energy and decided part of her decline was due to boredom, not ill health. She must find some way to keep Amelia interested in life.

The vicar and Harriet arrived on time and they had a nice visit. The tea was hot, the cakes sweet; things were pleasant indeed, until Penelope described the ugly scene she had interrupted on her morning ride. Vicar Wesley was deeply concerned. He wanted to know all the details. When she had finished her tale, he shook his head. "I vow trouble of this kind has been festering for a long spell. I am sorry it had to involve that young Dick Thomas."

Both Penelope and Amelia wanted more information. The vicar told them the bailiff's charges were probably true. Many farmers were behind on their rent because of the dry weather. But this had happened before, and the tenants had not been shoved off the land. They demanded to know why this time was different.

The vicar hedged; they insisted. At last he said, "I hesitate to speak ill of anyone, but there is a rumor about which claims your bailiff is involved in some, shall we say, less-than-honest dealings. I do not know the details, but several farmers have come to me for help. It seems they have been hounded off their land, the land is then enclosed to raise sheep, and the thankful wool merchants are generous in their payments to your bailiff. Mind you, I have no facts. However, I have heard this same story from several honest sources."

Penelope nodded her head. Her mouth was grim. She had heard tell of a similar thing occurring in the Worchester parish. The rising price of wool made men greedy. Did Alex know? Was he a part of the scheme? Did he also receive payments from the wool merchants?"

At supper that night Amelia was unusually quiet. Penelope was concerned until she saw the glint in her eyes. It reminded her of Alex, when he was up to some mischief. After the meal they strolled in the rose garden. Alex's mother still walked with a cane, but her step was surer now. They sat in the gazebo as dusk gathered and sipped their tea. "Penelope, I have decided you must lay this matter before Alex, and without delay."

"That is impossible! He would not welcome my interference."

"He would not welcome having his bailiff act dishonestly," his mother countered. "It reflects on our name."

"But . . ."

"Child, listen to me. Alex may indulge in the foolish amusements of the ton, but underneath he truly cares for his people. Neither you nor I have the power to stop the bailiff if he is determined to evict this family. They are behind on their rent. He can turn them out if he wishes. You must go to London and talk with Alex. He must know what is happening here." And, she added silently to herself, "It is high time you and my son were together again."

"I should not leave you," Penelope protested. "You are not well. What if—"

"Stuff and nonsense! I am no better, nor no worse than any other woman my age. The death of my beloved Robert was a sad blow, but he would not wish me to mourn him forever. I willed myself into this decline, I have decided it is time to stop!"

That response drew a wan smile from her daughter-in-law. She was uncertain. She wanted to see Alex again, but feared what his reaction would be. All that filled her mind was the look of bitterness and anger that clouded his face the night he left her. The dowager tapped her hand. "Penelope, pray attend me. You seem far away."

115

"Forgive me." She pulled her attention back. "I am sorry. What were you saying?"

"I was saying that this trip will also give you a chance to shop for some more acceptable clothes. The few things you have from Worth's are all right, of course, but they are hardly enough of a wardrobe for the marchioness of Ashford. You do have an image to maintain, you know."

"I doubt if Alex will allow me to stay in London, even if he grants me a hearing on the Thomas matter." Penelope hesitated, then chose her words carefully. "He can be stubborn at times."

"Where is your spirit, child? Stand up to him. You are his wife. You are an Ashford now. Alex is like his father. You must meet fire with fire." The dowager looked away. "Robert used to call me his little hellcat. He teased me about it, but"—she chuckled merrily—"he could never abide the clinging, insipid miss type. Trust me, neither can Alex."

Penelope smiled. "Hellcat," that was the very word Alex had used at their first meeting. The smile faded. The thought of facing him made her tremble. She stood up. "It is growing dark. I think we should go in before you catch a chill."

Amelia noticed her uncertainty. A wee extra push was needed. Maybe it was time Penelope learned the truth about her son. "Come up to my bedchamber with me please."

Penelope helped her change for the night. She draped an ivory lace bed jacket around Amelia's frail shoulders and folded back the covers for her. When she was settled against the mound of pillows, the dowager patted the bed beside her. Penelope sat down. "Alex was our only child. Robert and I wanted more but . . ." She shrugged the memory away. "I suppose we spoiled him terribly. I know we were too protective. Maybe that is why he was not

116

ready to handle the games played by the ton." A look of remembered sadness wrinkled her brow. "He went to London for his first season and fell desperately in love. She was a beautiful girl, a girl of good birth; we were happy for him. Suddenly she left him. She cried off without a word, or explanation, or a good-bye."

"But why?" Penelope whispered. "If they were in love . . ."

"I said Alex believed himself to be in love, the girl never was. When a duke began to pay her court, the lowly marquis was quickly forgotten. It did not matter that the duke had already buried three wives and had children older than she. His rank, his wealth, the place at court were too attractive to be ignored."

"Alex has never forgotten his loss, has he?"

"Loss?" His mother laughed. "She became his mistress shortly after she became a duchess. The affair was diverting enough for a while, but Alex soon found other interests. Don't look so shocked. I am not blind to my son's faults, for you see, I know the true reason he wanders from, shall we say, flower to flower. He is searching for something he has never found. Child, look at me." She put her hand over Penelope's and squeezed gently. "You love my son." It was not a question. "I see it in your eyes when his name is mentioned."

"I . . ." Penelope stammered. "I am not sure."

"Go to London, go and find out. This Thomas business is the ideal excuse." She leaned back and wearily closed her eyes. Penelope started to tiptoe from the bedchamber. The dowager stopped her. "Promise me that you will not delay." She chuckled and settled down under the comforter. "I would like to rock my grandchild before I die."

Alex's child! The thought echoed through Penelope's mind as she tried to sleep. She wanted that, she wanted his child, but only if love came with his desire. Was it possible he might learn to care? She would never discover the answer if she stayed in the country. "Fate can be challenged." The remembrance of her father's words decided the issue. Tomorrow she would start for London and Alex.

Penelope ate breakfast in the morning room with Amelia. The dowager's brisk orders sent servants scurrying in every direction. In a short time the traveling coach was loaded and Penelope's trunk was packed. It was time to leave. Penelope helped her mother-in-law down the curving staircase. Mrs. Grayson and Jenkins were there to watch their mistress take her leave. Penelope kissed her mother-in-law on her wrinkled cheek. Tears glistened in her eyes. "Take care of yourself," she whispered. "If you are not feeling the thing, I will return at once."

"Do not overset yourself about me, or that Thomas family. No one is going to turn them out until you have talked with Alex. Remember," she teased, "I shall do you mischief if you do not keep me posted on developments."

Penelope kissed her again and drew the tan traveling coat around her. The beaver collar and close bonnet felt warm and snug as she settled in the coach. She leaned back against the Ashford coat of arms. The coachman snapped his whip. The coach lurched forward. The last words she heard were, "Remember the tale of Robert's hellcat, Penelope."

Penelope chuckled to herself as the coach swayed around a curve. She did not feel much like a hellcat. Maybe she could pretend. Life in the ton was artificial; she could play a role. As a child she had acted in scenes from Shakespeare. Her father had said she made a smashing Ophelia, why not a hellcat? She laughed at the absurdity of it all. It helped calm her nervousness as the carriage rumbled on toward London.

The Ashford mansion on Grosvenor Square was even

more daunting than the country estate. It was located right on the walk, with no garden to soften the austere lines. The coachman helped Penelope alight from the carriage. She stepped out and stared at the towering facade. It rose five stories above her. There was a large brass lion-headed knocker on the massive front door. The coachman raised the clapper and let it fall. She could hear the noise echoing eerily inside.

A liveried butler, who looked for all the world like a younger version of Jenkins, opened the door. He blocked the entrance. "Stand aside, man," the coachman snapped, "and let Lady Ashford enter."

Penelope fancied she saw a glimmer of surprise flash across the butler's normally impassive countenance. "Milady, we were not informed of your pending arrival. I fear your suite will be quite chill. It has not been aired since the dowager marchioness left."

She walked up the five stone steps and entered the cavernous hall. Her heels clicked as she stepped onto the muted green and white marble of the parquet floor. She glanced around at the elegant entry. Family portraits dating back to the time of the Plantagenets lined the oak-paneled walls, and an enormous cloud-filled mural of Aurora graced the vaulted ceiling. It was far different from the cozy vicarage.

"Milady, if I may make bold to suggest, why don't you retire to the study, whilst I have your chamber readied."

"Thank you, hmm . . ."

"Hemnings, milady." The butler bowed.

"Thank you, Hemnings. Some hot tea would be nice."

"Certainly."

Hemnings opened a door off the entry hall and Penelope entered. He turned to leave. "Hemnings please see to the comfort of the servants who accompanied me from Ashford. Inform the coachman they need not return until tomorrow."

He nodded his head. "Do you wish me to call a maid to assist you, milady?"

"No, that is not necessary. I will wait until the chamber is aired."

He closed the door behind him. Penelope took off her traveling coat and laid it across the back of a chair. The bonnet followed. There was a mirror over the mantel. She stood and stared at her reflection for a space. Could she attract Alex? Would he ever see her as more than a convenient means to continue the Ashford line? She rubbed a weary hand across her forehead. The tea arrived and the scalding brew helped revive her spirits.

After her second cup of tea she wandered about the room. Alex's presence hovered everywhere. Books of essays by Burke, Rousseau, and Thomas Paine cluttered the tables, and on the desk was one of his half-written speeches. Penelope settled in his leather chair and picked up the sheets of paper. Alex's bold scrawl flowed across the pages. No secretary had composed this speech. She smiled as she read his hard-hitting words. Statistics on the death rate of child laborers glared up from one page; on another he attacked the use of young boys to sweep chimneys and—

The sound of the knocker boomed through the still room. Penelope neatly restacked the sheets of paper and stood up. She heard Hemnings's low words convey a message, then she heard Alex roar, "Hell and damnation! What does—Where is she?"

Penelope braced herself. She stood in the center of the room. Her heart was beating so rapidly it hurt. The door crashed open. Alex stomped into the study. A frown furrowed his brow. The line of his mouth was hard, uncompromising. Without taking his eyes off his wife, he ordered, "Hemnings, bring a decanter of claret, then leave us. We do not wish to be disturbed!"

Silence. Neither spoke. Penelope felt weak. His towering presence sent waves of—waves of—she could not identify the feeling. She knew for certain it was not fear. Alex's eyes never left her face as they waited for the butler to return.

Hemnings entered with a silver tray, the decanter of wine, and two glasses. He bowed, backed out of the room, and firmly closed the door.

Alex finally looked away and walked over to pour himself a glass of the Burgundy. He did not offer Penelope one. He leaned against the mantel with apparent unconcern, studied her a moment longer, then demanded, "Well, what the devil do you want?" He paused. His eyes glittered strangely, then he added, "Lady Ashford."

Penelope trembled slightly. She refused to look away. "There is trouble at the country estate, milord. Your mother felt you should be informed immediately and—"

"My mother! What the deuce is my mother doing at Ashford?"

A vague smile hovered around her lips. "She came to save her only son from the bit of muslin who had entrapped him. Actually, we get on quite well. She is a lovely woman."

"Such cant phrases as 'a bit of muslin' are unbecoming on the lips of a lady.

"I thought you detested simpering misses. I must remember to be more demure."

"Demure! You? You have always been more the hellcat type." Unconsciously he rubbed his hand across his mouth where her wedding ring had struck him.

Penelope chuckled at his phrase. "What the deuce is so funny?" he demanded irritably.

"Nothing really." She stifled the smile. "You reminded me of something your mother said."

"What?"

She ignored his question. "Seriously, Alex, we must talk. Your banter, as always, is most diverting, but I did not come all the way to London merely to bandy words with you."

Quickly she described the argument between the bailiff and Dick Thomas. He laughed when she explained how she had stopped their fight by firing the pistol. There was no smile though, when she told him of Vicar Wesley's suspicions.

Alex paced across the room. His glance flickered to her, then away. He said nothing for a long time. Then he walked over and yanked the bell pull. Hemnings opened the door. "Send Mr. Carling to me at once."

When his secretary entered, Alex introduced him to Penelope. She detected the same note of surprise that had flashed across Hemnings's face. "Charles, you are going to have to ride out to Ashford. There is a problem between the bailiff and our farmers." He described the situation. "You are to investigate this matter thoroughly, and if Earnest has been lining his pockets, give him the boot. Under no circumstances are the tenants to be moved off the land! Have Hemnings help you pack. Plan to leave in the morning." Alex glanced at Penelope. "You can accompany my wife back to Ashford."

Penelope smiled serenely and sat down on the settee while Alex and Charles finalized the arrangements. When Charles had gone, Alex instructed, "Please assure my mother that no one will—"

"I think not!" she calmly interrupted.

"You think not what?"

"I think I shall not be discussing this matter with your

mother. Mr. Carling can give her your message. I have no intention of returning to Ashford tomorrow."

"Frankly, I do not care a jot what you intend. You will go back!"

Penelope stood up and pretended to pat a yawn. Inside, she was all aflutter. There was no way she could respond calmly to this man when just being in the same room with him sent tremors through her body. But she would not let Alex see the power he held over her. Instead, she coolly commented, "Please lower your voice. You are yelling like a fishmonger. Do you wish our domestic quarrels to be bantered about the servants' quarters?"

"Damnit, Penelope, you cannot stay here!"

"I can and I will." She strolled across the room and let her hand casually trail across the top of the desk. "I do believe that it was part of your arrangement with Lady Shellingham to allow your countrified wife a season in London." She spread her hands and smiled. "Well, your countrified wife is here. It is the season. I intend to stay." Penelope noticed the angry flash in Alex's eyes, but she bravely continued, "You must tell me which modiste on Bond Street to favor with my patronage. I shall need many items for the ton parties."

With two strides Alex was at her side. He grabbed her shoulders and gave her a shake. A thunderous scowl marred his chiseled features. His eyes were black with anger. "You will not exert your caprices on me!" he raged. "You will do as I say!"

Penelope stared up at him. She tried to wiggle from his hard grasp. His hands were hurting her. As she struggled, a faint whiff of her perfume reached him. Memories—it brought back the memories of their wedding night. Alex remembered her fiery response to his touch, the feel of her lips that willingly parted under his, the softness of her body . . . her rejection. Abruptly he dropped his hold and

123

turned away. His hand was not steady as he poured himself another glass of wine.

Penelope rubbed her sore shoulders. The currents of emotion still ran through the room. She tried to make her voice light and unconcerned, "Is that any way to greet your wife, milord?"

Alex put down his wineglass. His eyes were flashing again, but not with anger. Penelope's breath came quicker. He took two steps toward her. His eyes slowly raked over her figure; his voice throbbed warmly as he observed, "I could think of a much more personal way, milady, but you would scarce enjoy it."

How little he knows, thought Penelope sadly. Not one night had passed that she did not yearn for his arms, his caresses, his love. Alex took another step. No! This was dangerous. It must not go on. She was not sure she could resist his kiss again. She was not sure she wanted to. Quickly she put on a bland smile and inquired politely, "How is Lady Shellingham, milord? I trust she did not lose her place at court."

Alex cursed under his breath. He came no closer. With a muttered oath he turned and started pacing through the room once more. He was at a stand. Penelope was here. If he tried to force her back to Ashford, she could put everything into a nasty spin. Maybe her arrival was not such a bad event. Prinny was most insistent on meeting her. She could attend a few musicales, card parties, and drums, make her curtsy to the Prince of Wales, and then he could pack her off to the country again. He smiled. Yes, that should stop the wagging tongues and satisfy his wife.

He stopped pacing and looked at her. There was no emotion in his voice as he agreed. "All right, you may stay for a spell. I am expecting guests for supper this evening. You will dine in your chamber." Without another word he slammed out of the study.

CHAPTER NINE

The suite of rooms Hemnings escorted Penelope to was even larger and more ornate than the one at Ashford. There was a sitting room with a Sheraton writing-table inlaid with brass, glassed-in bookshelves, a settee, and several armchairs. It had a gracefully bowed window that overlooked the formally laid-out back gardens. She paused a moment to admire the flowers in bloom, then followed the butler into the dressing room. It was comfortably outfitted with a lion-footed chaise, a beautifully hand-painted lacquer screen to conceal the bath, and a whole wall lined with massive armoires.

Penelope entered the bedchamber and stopped. She felt as if she had stepped into a bedroom in the court of China. It was the most elegant room she had ever seen. Oriental rugs in palest blue and apricot muffled her step, Ming vases graced the mantel, and an elaborate tester of rose-wood and swagged silk canopied the bed. The blues and apricots of the rugs were repeated in the window hangings and the silk upholstery covering the furniture. The chamber was lush and expensive; yet there was an air of tranquillity about it that pleased her.

Hemnings apologized once again for the delay in readying her rooms. He explained that the housekeeper was on holiday at Bath and would not return for a fortnight. Things were in a bit of a dither without her supervision, he admitted. Penelope assured him it did not signify and requested tea. He bowed and was gone.

She walked about the chamber, touching first one thing,

then another. Her step took her to a closed door—the door leading to Alex's suite. Gently Penelope laid her hand against the dark wood and caressed it. So close, he was so close. Without thought, her hand fell to the brass doorknob. Was he there? What would he say if she entered? What would he do?

She turned away. She knew the answer. Alex had made it clear that her presence in London was being tolerated, no more. There was no welcome, no pleasure that she had come. Secretly she had hoped for some reaction, but she believed Alex was totally indifferent to her.

Penelope was wrong. Alex was far from indifferent. He cared, he cared very much that she had come. In fact, he was very disturbed that she had come. He stomped across his bedchamber and glared at the door separating them. "Hell and damnation!" he muttered again. His valet took one look at his black mood and quickly backed out of the room. Why did she have to come and disrupt his well-ordered life? He knew he had to introduce his wife to society sometime, but why did it have to be now? Damnit, it was just too soon. If she had stayed tucked away at Ashford a little longer, he might have been able to forget, forget their farce of a marriage, forget their wedding night. He flung himself down in a chair and threw his leg over the arm. His fingers drummed impatiently on his thigh. Why did she have to come and stir up the memories again? He did not want to remember!

For the first time in his life he was ashamed of something he had done. He had been foxed, still it should not have happened. Alex rubbed his hand across his forehead. Why did Penelope's face, that tear-stained face, have to haunt his thoughts? Why wouldn't it go away? He remembered that night as if it were yesterday. Penelope had looked like such a child with that golden hair falling around her face, but her response to his kisses was that of

126

a woman. He closed his eyes. He could not forget the touch of her soft lips or how gentle her caresses had been; nor could he forget those tantalizing glimpses of her body through the tattered nightgown, and that perfume! "Damn, damn, damn!" he cursed as he got up and savagely yanked the bell pull. "Why did she have to come?"

Nothing his valet did that night could please him. No coat looked right, no cravat would tie properly, and the polish on his boots was not bright enough. The valet was most relieved when Alex's supper guests arrived and he was dismissed.

His guests found him just as surly. Alex had invited James and George "Beau" Brummell to dine with him. Then they were to adjourn to White's for a night of gambling. Even Beau's witty stories could not force a smile from Alex. James glanced at his friend and wondered. Must have had a tiff with Millicent, he concluded. Finally, as course after course of savory food was enjoyed, Alex's mood began to mellow. The men were enjoying cigarillos and brandy in the study when Hemnings knocked on the door and entered. He had a pale blue note on a silver tray. He extended the salver and bowed. "This came, milord. I thought you might wish to see it immediately."

Alex ripped open the seal and scanned the brief note. A smile lifted one corner of his mouth. He glanced up at Hemnings and ordered, "Have the phaeton brought round at once. I will drive myself."

When Hemnings had left, Alex tossed the note into the fire and commented to his friends, "Gentlemen, you will have to excuse me from White's tonight. Something has come up that I must attend to."

Beau smiled knowingly, but said nothing as Alex took his leave. "Well, James, it appears we have been left to our own devices this evening." He pinched his nose and disdainfully observed, "I really must speak to Lady Shellingham about that perfume. She even drenches her billets-doux with it. The odor quite puts one off." He took a sip of his brandy. "I suppose we could be angry with our host for deserting us, but no doubt our company is not as, mmm, stimulating as the lovely Millicent's." He swirled the brandy in his glass and smiled. "I wonder how Lord Shellingham is finding the grouse hunting in Scotland? Maybe he should have stayed. Obviously the hunting is quite good in London!"

James choked over his drink and quickly changed the subject. "Heard Prinny and Mrs. Fitz had another spat. Never did know what he saw in that woman. She is—"

"I am not the least interested in Prinny's domestic troubles. I want to know about Lady Ashford. You were at their wedding. What is she like? Why isn't she in London for the season? What is the mystery?"

James nervously cleared his throat. Beau was a good friend, but he was also a notorious gossip. Alex's private life was his own. He did not intend to reveal all the details to Mr. Brummell. The two men fenced with words.

Upstairs Penelope heard the shouted orders for the phaeton and later heard the front door slam. Alex was gone. She had half hoped he might leave a message for her or even drop in to say good night. Stop dreaming, she fussed at herself. You have his name and nothing more. The dinner the maid brought was excellent, but she had little appetite. She pushed the tray away and aimlessly walked through the bedchamber. The minutes dragged. London was no better than Ashford. Maybe that book of essays by Burke would help the hours pass.

Penelope walked down the staircase and entered the study. She was startled when two men jumped to their feet. She thought Alex's dinner guests had left with him. A blush reddened her cheeks, and she started to back out of the room. Then she recognized James and smiled. "I did not mean to intrude. I thought everyone had gone."

James bowed to her. "Lady Ashford, please do not leave. I would like you to meet a friend of ours." He turned to Beau and introduced, "Lady Ashford, please be acquainted with Mr. George Br—"

"George Brown," Beau quickly finished. He gallantly took her hand and raised it to his lips. "Y'r servant, Lady Ashford. Please join us."

James gave him a sharp look. What game was Beau up to with this Brown business? He did not like it.

Penelope glanced down at the plain gown she had on. The village seamstress had done her best, but she certainly was not properly dressed to receive guests. She felt the positive dowd, especially in front of this elegantly dressed Mr. Brown. His evening attire was subdued, but perfect to the last detail. He wore the dark blue coat, the white waistcoat, and the black pantaloons with the complete assurance of someone who knew himself well turned out. Her simple chintz dress was inappropriate. She wanted to snatch her book of essays and escape. Beau would not let her. He insisted she join them. After her first nervousness passed, she enjoyed their company. James was always a delightful companion, and she liked Mr. Brown. She fleetingly wondered why Alex had left without his friends, but soon George told another amusing story and her laughter made her forget the question.

The hour grew late and Penelope finally excused herself. Brummell sat there and stared at the fire, chuckled, then chuckled again. James wrinkled his forehead. "All right, Beau, what was the hum about introducing yourself as George Brown."

Beau smiled mischievously. A delightful scheme was forming in his mind. "I wished to become acquainted with Alex's rather mysterious wife without her knowing who I really was." He shrugged. "Women tend to put on airs if they know they are talking with the famous, or if you will, infamous, Beau Brummell. I wanted to discover if she really was as kind and unassuming as she appeared at first glance."

"And?"

"And obviously she is." Beau rubbed his hands together and chuckled again.

"George," James demanded, "what is so funny?"

"You know, James, this season has been a crushing bore! There has been no excitement—yet. I do believe I have a mind to play Pygmalion to Lady Ashford's Galatea. That should make an interesting stir."

"Are you daft? Who are Pygmalion and that Galatea person? Sound like foreigners."

"They are, James, they are. In fact, they are Greek."

"What do a bunch of Greeks have to do with you and Lady Ashford? Never did like Greeks, too short."

"No, Harrington, you have missed the point, but it does not signify. What I meant was, I intend to make Lady Ashford into a belle of the ton. You are going to help me."

"Have you got bats in your cockloft!" James sputtered. "Alex would call me out. Don't fancy getting run through with a saber. Besides, it won't work. Lady Ashford is uncommon, but far from an incomparable. Best leave it alone."

"My young friend, you have no vision. Lady Ashford is badly dressed and her hair looks like a German Hausfrau, but her bearing is good. I liked her dignity. Yes, there is a uniquely attractive quality under that dowdy appearance. We are going to make her into the first stare of fashion. Tomorrow, we start," Beau said bracingly.

James was silent for a long time. He knew Beau's vanity was tickled by the challenge of turning Penelope into a belle and stirring up the staid ton. Penelope meant nothing to the famous Brummell, neither did Alex. He was bored, nothing more. On the other hand, they both meant a lot to him. Alex had been his best friend since Eton. James had suffered through his first season with him and watched him drift from one affair to another. Millicent was just number—he did not know what. Now his friend was married, married unhappily. He never asked Alex what had happened on their wedding night, but he had sensed the anger and hurt as they drove hell-for-leather toward London that next morning. He had liked Penelope at first meeting. He knew the terms of their unusual marriage. Still, the fact remained, she was Alex's wife. She could well be what his friend had been searching for. Alex would never know as long as Millicent stood between them. Maybe Beau's plan would work. If nothing else, Penelope deserved a fling in London before she was exiled to the country.

"All right, Brummell, I will help. If Alex calls me out, you will have to stand as my second."

Beau laughed. "Here is the plan. You pick Lady Ashford up tomorrow afternoon and escort her to Lady Jersey's so we can begin work."

"Sally!" James choked. "How did she get involved?"

"She is going to help us also." Beau looked smug. "Sally is always ready for a lark. Lady Ashford can make her debut at their ball." He stood up. "We had best be off. There is much to do." He whistled merrily as they strolled to White's. The forthcoming scene should be amusing.

Beau's note, requesting a word with her, came up with Lady Jersey's morning hot chocolate. She yawned and took off her lace nightcap. She wondered what caprice Brummell was up to now, that he would appear on her doorstep before noon? She yawned again and rang for her dresser. Lady Jersey did not rush, but on the other hand, she did not dawdle through her morning toilet. Her curiosity was engaged. Lord Jersey and Beau were sharing a breakfast of kippers and toast when Sally entered the morning room. Her husband kissed her attentively on the cheek and held out her chair. Lady Jersey rang the little silver bell, ordered a fresh pot of coffee, hot crumpets, and a dish of strawberries in cream, then glanced at Beau. "You are up early this morning, George. Your business must be most urgent. How can we help you?"

"I have come to beg a favor. There is someone I wish you to add to the invitation list for your ball."

Lord Jersey stood up. "Sounds like a problem you can handle, my dear. I hate to leave you alone with this devilishly handsome man, but I have an appointment at Weston's." He kissed her again. They exchanged smiles. "I will see you tonight."

"An unusually solicitous husband," Beau observed blandly.

"Yes, he is. Actually, we are quite fond of each other." Lady Jersey sipped her coffee and took a bite of the strawberries. "The invitation list has already been sent to the *Gazette*. I fear it is too late to add a name."

"Perfect!" Brummell smiled. "I do not wish this name to appear in the *Gazette* before the ball."

"How intriguing! Who is this mysterious guest?"

"No one you know, Sally. She is completely unknown to the ton."

Lady Jersey's interest faded. "Beau, I am not of a mind to put up with one of your quirks, nor do I wish to sponsor a little Miss Nobody into society, even if she is one of your friends. Pray, let us hear no more of the matter. If you wish her to make a bow, have Prinny invite her to one of his boring dress parties at Carlton House. We have invited quite enough guests to our ball. We do not need anymore."

"She is not a friend of mine. In fact, I only met her last night."

"George, stop roasting me!" Sally insisted. "Who is this person?"

He smiled smugly, took a drink of his coffee, and casually answered, "Lady Ashford."

"What! Alex's wife!" Lady Ashford's eyes sparkled. "Tell me all. What is she like?"

"She is quite a fetching little thing, but totally unversed in the ways of the ton. Her father was a country vicar, I believe." Brummell went on to describe his meeting with Penelope, his impersonation as Mr. Brown, and his plan to present her at the Jerseys' ball. He saw Lady Jersey get a thoughtful look. His plan was working perfectly. Sally had despised Millicent ever since Lady Shellingham had cast her undoubtedly attractive lures toward Lord Jersey. Fortunately, he was an unusually devoted husband and had not been tempted by the bait. Sally had never forgiven her. "I thought," Beau continued, "that you might wish to help."

Lady Jersey smiled, chuckled, then broke out in laughter. "It would make Millicent furious! I do not scruple to admit I would enjoy that." Sally cocked her head and looked at him. "George, why are you doing this? It is scarce your style."

"To tell you true, Sally, I am bored with London, bored with the season, and bored with the present crop of insipid misses who simper and fawn about the ballroom. This girl has spirit, dignity, and—"

"Beau, cut the pother," interrupted Sally. "Confess you simply wish to put the season into a spin."

He laughed. "How well you know me, milady. Yes, I admit it should be amusing. Will you help?"

"Certainly. I would enjoy thrusting a spoke in Millicent's wheels. Is Alex to know his wife will attend?"

"I think not. He might object. He has made no push to introduce her to society. I believe it is up to us," he commented innocently. "Here is my idea. Harrington will bring Lady Ashford here at three, then we can all adjourn to Worth's to select her wardrobe. You should see her dresses. Even your upstairs maid dresses better."

"Worth will most assuredly not do, Beau. You know he has a gibbering tongue. Thirty minutes after we leave the whole ton will know of our plan. I suggest we try Mademoiselle Geneviève. She escaped from France when that monster Napoleon came to power, and went to Vienna. She has only recently crossed the Channel to England. Her designs are quite unique. Moreover, she is discreet."

Beau Brummell raised his coffee cup in a toast to the success of their plan.

The viscount of Harrington called for Penelope at half past two. As he handed her into his curricle, he commented, "Hope you don't mind, milady, I have made arrangements for us to have tea with George Br—hmm—Brown and Lady Jersey." James looked a little uncomfortable. "Thought you might like some advice on female finery and such."

"Lady Jersey!" she squeaked. "The Lady Jersey of Almack's."

"There is only one."

As they took tea with Lady Jersey and Mr. Brown, Penelope found out how her hostess had earned the nickname "Silence." Lady Jersey's ceaseless chatter dominated the conversation, but while she carried on her witty monologue, she was carefully evaluating the new Lady Ashford. Brummell's perceptions were flawless as usual. Penelope might not be an incomparable, but she was definitely not an antidote. There were possibilities—a gown of the first stare, a different hairstyle, yes, it ought to work.

After tea Lady Jersey sent the men out to bring around the carriage. When they were alone, she asked, "Lady Ashford, are you up to a lark?"

Penelope was startled. She was still a bit in awe of her famous hostess and now this. What would the ton consider a lark to be? She answered carefully, "If it would not hurt anyone, milady."

Lady Jersey's sparkling laughter filled the room. Originally her only interest was to overset Millicent; now she also wanted to help Penelope. She patted her hand. "This lark will not hurt anyone, I assure you. Lord Jersey and I are hosting a ball three days hence and would like you to attend."

"Oh." Penelope blushed. "I do not think my husband would—"

"Your presence will be a surprise to everyone. That is the lark!"

Penelope started to object, but Sally rushed on, "When everyone is in the ballroom, we will have you announced. Think of the fun! The whole ton is agog to meet Ashford's wife. It will make our party the hit of the season." She saw Penelope waver. "The Prince of Wales will be there. I know he wishes an introduction. Please say you will do it."

Penelope considered the idea. Alex's mother had suggested she show spirit, well, why not? This lark would certainly be spirited. What would Alex say? He could not be any angrier than he already was. If nothing else, it would force him to notice her. Phoo! The ball gown had been left at Ashford. She would have to decline. "Your invitation is most generous, but I fear I have nothing to wear, milady. I have not yet found time to visit Bond Street."

"An appropriate gown is no problem. We will attend to that this afternoon."

Before Penelope could object any further, Lady Jersey swept her outside and handed her into the carriage where James and Mr. Brown were waiting. Penelope wondered if this had all been planned. She hated to question people's motives, but it was curious.

Mademoiselle Geneviève's small shop was not on Bond Street, but the elegant interior bespoke her tonnish clients. Penelope hardly had time to catch her breath before the vivacious little French woman was draping first one exquisite fabric over her figure, then another, while her three new friends sat in front judging the effect. Geneviève tried a soft pink satin, a delicately made white raw silk, an ice-blue tulle, a pale yellow taffeta. Lady Jersey shook her head. "Something is amiss here. I fear none of these will do." She sighed. "At least we know Lady Ashford has the Ashford jewels. They make any gown seem lovelier."

"Sally, you are a sorceress! You have hit on just the thing."

"Thank you, George, but pray, what did I conjure?"

"The answer!" Brummel chuckled. "We will have Mademoiselle Geneviève design gowns to accent the Ashford jewels. Mademoiselle, do you have any emerald silk?"

"*Oui, monsieur,* but the pastels are much more popular."

"Lady Ashford shall set a new style." When she hesitated to do his bidding, he ordered, "Mademoiselle, please fetch the silk. We must see if I am right."

The little French woman scurried off. Soon she returned with a bolt of shimmering emerald-green jacquard-weave silk. She draped it across one of Penelope's shoulders and stood back. "*Mon Dieu—la différence!* The color, the color was all wrong!"

James agreed enthusiastically, "By Jove, that color is smashing!"

Beau was pleased. He knew his taste could not fail. "Lady Ashford, look in the mirror. You ought always to wear pure strong colors. The pastels wash the color from your skin and make your hair seem drab."

Penelope turned and stared in the looking glass. The difference was amazing! Her skin seemed to glow, her eyes had extra sparkle, even her hair looked less dull. She had known the soft colors were somehow wrong. Now she knew why. She turned back. "Mr. Brown, you have excellent taste, sir. Where did you learn so much about fashion?"

Lady Jersey and James doubled over in laughter. Penelope was quite puzzled by the mirth. There was some joke here she was not sharing.

Beau smiled at the success of his ruse. He accepted her compliment. "Thank you, Lady Ashford. It is pleasant to know at least one person considers me to be an authority on style and proper dress."

While they were talking, the little French woman was pulling the pins from Penelope's hair and unbraiding it. She brushed it vigorously. It fell to Penelope's shoulders and tumbled down her back. Where her dull hair touched the emerald of the fabric, sparks seemed to shoot forth. Geneviève pulled the heavy tresses to one side. "We will curl it so, then—"

"No!" Brummell snapped. "Lady Ashford is not the type for bobbing curls. Besides, I am bored with those crimped hairstyles you ladies favor. You look like so many woolly lambs. I like the simplicity of her hair the way it is. It must be trimmed, then we will let it fall naturally."

"George," Lady Jersey interrupted, "I have the perfect thing!" She grabbed a piece of emerald ribbon and laid it across the front edge of Penelope's hair. "We will pin the Ashford emeralds here, like a headband, instead of hanging them around her neck."

"Mmm," Beau Brummel sighed, "perfect! Everyone"— he winked with special meaning to Lady Jersey—"will be envious of your originality." He turned to Mademoiselle Geneviève. "The style of the ball gown ought to be very severe and simple. This emerald fabric will do for the Jersey ball. Also find the richest silk you can in ruby, sapphire, and amethyst. We might as well finish with the other Ashford jewels while we are ordering."

Lady Jersey added, "This order must be in the strictest confidence. If no word escapes, you can count on my patronage as well as that of my friends."

The little French woman was delighted with her good fortune, and so was Penelope. To have these thoughtful people befriend her and take time to advise her was unexpected. She had always heard tell that the members of the ton were too involved with their social whirl to be kind to a stranger. Evidently that was not true. She was dazed as Mr. Brown and Lady Jersey continued to plan garment after garment for her wardrobe. Walking dresses, morning dresses, tea gowns, cloaks, spencers, and pelisses were ordered, all with bonnets and slippers to match. They were having a grand time spending Alex's money.

Suddenly James, who had been sitting quietly amid all the hubbub, spoke, "Riding habit! Lady Ashford, you have to have a habit for riding in the Row, or do you plan to promenade in a barouche?"

"If you are not cow-handed, I would suggest you ride," Lady Jersey suggested. "It is most difficult to be seen in a carriage."

"Lady Ashford," Beau asked, "can you handle a horse adequately? Best be honest. There is nothing more absurd than someone who bounces all over the horse's back instead of staying in the saddle."

"I do not hunt," Penelope confessed, "but I can be a bruising rider if need be."

"By Jove! Do believe I have come up with a splendid idea," James said excitedly. "Alex always rides one of his great black beasts in the Row. We will find Lady Ashford a pure white stallion, and Mademoiselle Geneviève can make her a white habit. The contrast between the two Ashfords should be smashing!" He stood up and paced through the small room as he warmed to the idea. "I have three black horses in my stables. We can all accompany her to the Row, the day after the Jerseys' ball. Ought to create a stir!"

Lady Jersey laughed at his enthusiasm. "Quite right, James. However, I shall ride as usual in my barouche. Lady Ashford will be more striking as the only woman between you two gallants."

"Your idea is good, Harrington, but we will need a spot of color. Mademoiselle, please include a scarlet cravat with the riding habit and make up some sort of matching hat. Also find some scarlet gloves and boots, if you can," ordered Brummel.

"Please have all of these purchases delivered to my house," instructed Lady Jersey. She smiled at Penelope. "A flood of packages arriving at your address before the ball might make someone suspicious. We would not wish that, would we?"

Penelope was a little numb by the time they started back toward Grosvenor Square. In the space of a few hours her whole life had been replanned. She had taunted Alex about enjoying London in the season. He believed it to be an empty threat, since she knew no one of quality. Now she was to attend the Jersey's ball and meet the Prince of Wales. Life could be befuddling.

CHAPTER TEN

While Penelope and Lady Jersey were gaily planning her wardrobe for the ball, Alex was pounding out his frustrations at Jackson's boxing establishment. Everything was in a damnable coil! His wife was underfoot and his discreet rendezvous with Lady Shellingham had not passed off well. When he had arrived, Millicent was reclining on a chaise and looked enticing as ever in her sheer silk wrapper. As she rose to greet him, the wrapper parted to reveal glimpses of her bare legs, her breasts, her lush shoulders. Her arms were warm, her kisses demanding, until he told her his wife had arrived in London. Immediately she set up a well-bred, but nonetheless irritating, screech. Her jealousy grated on his nerves. There was a scene. He slammed out.

A pleading letter, well drenched with that musky perfume she favored, arrived early the next day. Millicent begged him to call. He threw the note into the fire. He was in no mood for any more of her ill-tempered freaks. He sent an under-footman with a curt note saying he would see her at the Jerseys' ball and left for Jackson's. The fisticuffs did not help his black temper, neither did a night of gambling at White's. His mood was foul.

The next day Alex was emerging from a fitting at Weston's, when he bumped into James. The sight of his friend cheered him. He fell into step beside him. "Where are you off to?"

"Hmm." James hesitated. "I've a mind to look at some blood stock."

"Good. I'll go with you. I am always interested in adding to my stables. I might even buy Lady Ashford a little riding mare. By the by, she is in town. You might wish to call."

James mumbled noncommittally. Lud! This is a deuce of a mess! Why did he ever let Brummell talk him into this charade?

The men spent several pleasant hours looking at the horses. Alex picked out a small gray mare for Penelope, then asked, "Anything particular you are hunting for? That black there looks like a good jumper."

He swallowed nervously. "Had in mind a white stallion, but I can look for it another day. Why don't we head for Waiter's? I fancy a glass of port."

"Nonsense! We are here, let us find your stallion."

They walked through the vast stable again. Alex stopped and pointed to a pure white horse that was snorting and rearing against his lead rope.

As they neared, the stallion pawed and whipped his head around to glare at them. Alex smiled. He liked a horse that needed a master's hand. "There you are, James. He is a magnificent animal!"

"Won't do, Alex. Looks like one of those wacking great beasts you ride. Don't fancy getting tossed. Best find something with less spirit."

They finally settled on another stallion. James was relieved. This horse was well proportioned, impressive in size, and had a gentle cast to his eyes. Lady Ashford should be able to handle him.

Alex returned to Grosvenor Square, pleased with the day's work. His good mood was restored. Millicent was still in a miff, but a present would handle that, and contrary to his expectations, Penelope's presence in London was not causing any trouble. He scarce knew she was in the house. They had run into each other once in the hallway. After exchanging a civil greeting, he politely inquired where she was off to; she replied a fitting, and they parted. That was all. There was no trouble, no screeches, no fits of the dismals. It was not a trial having her here. Penelope was not hanging on his sleeve or pitching jealous scenes like Millicent. He could almost forget he was married.

Alex whistled cheerfully as he dressed for the ball. When he nestled the emerald stickpin in his snowy neckcloth, he suffered a slight tinge of guilt that Penelope could not attend the night's entertainment. The feeling quickly passed. In a few days he would arrange for her to attend a musicale or the like. That should be sufficient.

Alex had been invited to the dinner party before the ball. Lady Jersey greeted him warmly. There was an extra sparkle in her eyes as she received his bow. Tonight should be fun! After dinner everyone made their way to the glittering ballroom. It was ablaze with candles. Those who had not been invited to dine were being announced by the butler's stately tones. Once their names were called, the guests walked down the great staircase toward the swirling dancers below. Alex made a turn about the room, nodding to acquaintances, and stopped for a moment to chat with Brummel. "You are here early tonight, George. Has some young belle caught your fancy?"

"Hardly! It is an unusually dull crop this season."

Alex laughed and moved off. He spoke a moment with James, saw the Prince of Wales arrive, and then lounged against the wall watching the dancers. Beau was right, it was an unusually insipid group of misses. Not like Penelope! She had spirit and—He pulled himself up sharply. A frown creased his brow. Why did she always have to intrude upon his thoughts?

Millicent noticed the glower as she made her way to his side. She laid a possessively caressing hand on his arm. He glanced down at her. His frown lifted as she commented, "Chester's witch of a mother is watching us. We had best dance."

Alex took her in his arms and they waltzed off. Millicent used every wile she possessed to entice her way back into his good graces. No man had ever walked out on her before. She did not intend for it to happen again. At each opportunity she pressed her body warmly against his. Gradually, she felt his arm tighten around her waist. Yes, it was going to be all right, if that country bumpkin he had married did not interfere. She really had nothing to fret about, Millicent reassured herself, that dowdy creature could never hold Alex's attention.

While Alex and Millicent were waltzing, Lady Jersey's dresser was helping Penelope with her final touches. After Alex left, Penelope ordered a carriage and made her way to the Jersey mansion. She stole through the servant's entrance and up the back stairs to Lady Jersey's suite. Sally was entertaining her dinner guests, but her maid was there to receive Penelope.

Quickly Penelope stepped out of her drab dress and slipped into the emerald gown. An unexpected pleasure greeted her gaze when she looked into the mirror. She actually had curves for the silk to cling to. The change had been so gradual; she really had not noticed that she had regained the weight lost after her father's death. No longer did she look like a skinny scarecrow.

The dresser was brushing out Penelope's hair when Lady Jersey came sweeping into the chamber. "Our other guests will be arriving in a moment. I cannot stay." She rapidly puffed a bit of powder on her nose and pinched her cheeks. "I wished to see how your gown turned out."

Penelope stood up and pirouetted. Lady Jersey clapped her hands gleefully. "Lady Ashford, you are lovely! I would have scarce believed a change of color could make such a difference."

"I wish you would call me Penelope."

"All right, Penelope." She laughed. "If you will call me Sally." Her smile faded. She sent her maid out of the room on an errand and looked at her young guest. "Penelope, I have grown fond of you. I am likewise fond of your husband." Her tone was serious. "Arranged marriages are most difficult, but I know they can work if you are willing to fight for what you desire."

Before Penelope could reply, Lady Jersey kissed her on the cheek. "The butler will call for you when it is time for your entrance." Hurriedly she rushed out of the chamber.

Sally's advice ran through Penelope's mind as the maid secured the Ashford emeralds into her hair. She had been nervous about this evening, doubting she should come, but no more. Fight! If she wanted Alex, she would have to fight to win him. She intended to do just that.

The butler knocked. Penelope could hear the strains of a waltz floating up from the ballroom. She paused at the top of the staircase, her hand poised on the carved railing.

The music came to an end. As the last notes died, Millicent whispered to Alex, "Promise you will save another waltz for me. If I cannot have your arms around me through the night, at least I can feel them here."

A waiter passed by with a tray of champagne. Alex took two glasses, handed one to her, and toasted, "To the nights that will be."

Millicent smiled silkily and sipped her wine.

There was a short break in the music, conversation stilled, the butler's voice boomed, "Lady Ashford."

Alex choked over his champagne. His eyes swept to the top of the staircase. He could scarce believe it. His wife, the wife he thought was home quietly reading a book, was slowly descending the stairs. One elegant hand trailed along the banister. The green gown clung provocatively to curves he had not noticed she possessed. Her neckline was cut in a deep square. It plunged to reveal the gentle swell of her breasts. The Ashford emeralds glittered against her hair, her hair that tumbled loose and free as on the night of their wedding. Alex could feel his blood warm. A man behind him let out a low whistle. Alex glared and took a step toward his wife.

Millicent's clinging hand detained him. "Alex, what is your wife doing here?" Her voice was icy.

"How the deuce do I know! Good God, she is talking to George. Hell and damnation! Brummell is escorting her out onto the dance floor."

Penelope was glad for Mr. Brown's support. Her knees felt weak as she glanced across the floor and saw Millicent's hand on her husband's arm. With determination she turned her attention back to the intricate steps of the cotillion and gaily laughed at a witty comment her partner made. She smiled and flirted with him as the patterned steps of the dance brought them together.

Millicent was furious! The countrified wife she had sneered at so disdainfully had disappeared. This woman was a threat! She glanced at Alex. His attention was riveted on his wife. She did not like it, nor did she like the famous Brummell paying court to Lady Ashford. She tugged on Alex's arm. "Did you put Beau up to this?"

"No!" he replied curtly.

Alex pulled his arm free and started to push his way through the crowd. His luck was out. The Prince of Wales stopped him. "Smashing wife, Ashford, smashing!" Prinny chuckled. "No wonder you have kept her hidden. Go and fetch her," he requested, "I want to meet her. Oh, good, Brummell is bringing her over to be presented."

Alex clenched his hands. There was nothing he could do but play out the farce. Penelope glided up to him and

146

smiled demurely. He took her hand and raised it to his lips. He squeezed it a bit hard as he blandly observed, "You look lovely tonight, my dear. May I present His Royal Highness, the Prince of Wales."

Penelope sank into a deep curtsy. She was glad for the chance to drop her head. The Prince of Wales was such a ridiculous figure, with his ornately brocaded coat bulging over his ample middle, that she felt inclined to giggle. Luckily, by the time he raised her to her feet, the fit had passed, and she could smile admiringly up at him as he complimented her on the originality of her gown. Beau stood at her side and was delighted with his prank. For once he did not find the party a dull bore.

"Champagne!" The prince bellowed. "Tell that dullard to bring some of that champagne over here."

The waiter brought over his tray of glasses. The prince offered Penelope one. "Thank you, sir, for the offer, but I must decline. The last time I tasted champagne I admit it was a pleasurable experience"—she glanced at her husband and smiled—"however, something happened and the glow did not last. I would prefer a glass of lemonade."

Alex stared at Penelope. What game was she playing? This was not the innocent miss he had left crying in their bridal chamber. He was puzzled by her behavior. Lord and Lady Jersey joined the crowd around the prince. While Prinny recounted the latest news on the building at Brighton, Lady Jersey took Alex aside. "You have a lovely wife, Alex. Her gown is most unique."

He raised an eyebrow. "It is surprisingly unique, considering she just came up from the country a few days ago. One would almost suspect she had some help with the design. Do you not agree, Lady Jersey?"

Sally tapped him on the arm with her fan. "It is bad ton for one to be too curious."

The orchestra began to play a waltz. The Prince of

147

Wales bowed over Penelope's hand. "Lady Ashford, would you do me the honor of partnering me for this dance?"

Penelope dropped another curtsy. "Sir, I beg that you will excuse me. My husband has requested that I save all my waltzes for him. I fear it is one of the prerogatives of a new bridegroom."

Alex was half amused and half angry when he heard her. She is a clever puss, he acknowledged, as he held out his hand to lead her onto the floor. Penelope danced beautifully as they whirled around the ballroom. The slightest pressure of his arm directed her step. Never did she miss a step even when he drew her close into his arms. "Penelope, you should not have told His Highness that hum. It was quite an honor that he asked you to dance."

"Oh, I enjoyed the honor of being asked very much," she replied pertly. "I would not have enjoyed being crushed in his pudgy arms, though, or being maneuvered into the conservatory for a stolen kiss."

Alex roared with laughter. When he recovered, he observed, "Nonetheless, you should not have committed me for all the waltzes. I do have other social obligations."

"Yes, milord, I quite understand." Penelope tossed her head in Lady Shellingham's direction. "I see one of your obligations over there tapping her foot. She appears a bit miffed. Never fear, I will not hold you to that commitment. I am sure some gallant will take pity on me and waltz with your countrified wife."

His arm tightened about her. "Did some gallant send you those flowers?" he asked as he indicated her gold filigree *bouquetier* filled with violets.

Penelope had selected the flowers herself to accent the color of her gown. She had no intention of telling him that. She put on a secretive smile and said, "Perhaps."

She felt his step falter. She was pleased. The waltz ended. He raised her hand to his lips. "You may tell your gallant, whoever he may be, that all of your waltzes are bespoken. You will dance, as you told the Prince of Wales, with your husband."

James claimed her hand for the next country set. When the dance was finished, he left her by the open windows and went off in search of a glass of lemonade for her. Penelope felt a tap on her arm, and someone gushed, "What was it like to dance with him? What did he say?"

Penelope turned and found Constance Buxley at her side. Lady Buxley was hovering right behind. The Bond Street modistes had tried; even they had not been able to prevail over Constance's stubborn will. The fabric of her gown was an exquisitely woven satin, and the neckline and hem were trimmed with brilliants and sequins. The color, however, was that same pale pink she had insisted on for her riding habit. It would have been a beautiful gown on anyone else; on Constance, it was dreadful! Maybe Mademoiselle Geneviève could help.

"Well," Constance demanded again, "what was he like to dance with? How did you meet him?"

"I am sorry," Penelope confessed. "I was not attending. It is nice to see you again, Constance, and you too Lady Buxley. I tired to call at the manor. You had already left for London. Please plan to come to tea. We are—"

"Lady Ashford"—Constance uttered the title with the slightest hint of distaste—"will you introduce me? I simply must meet him!"

"Yes, Penelope," Lady Buxley added, "it would be a gracious gesture. You were married from Buxley Manor. There is a connection. A dance with him or even a bow would assure Constance's season." Her voice was softly insistent. "I vow it is not too great a favor to ask after all we have done for you."

Penelope shook her head and looked puzzled. What

were they gibbering on about? "You already know Lord Ashford and the viscount of Harrington. I can hardly introduce you to the Prince of Wales. We spoke for only a short spell."

"Stop playing the hen-witted fool!" Constance commanded sharply. A note of awed reverence then crept into her words. "I am talking about the famous Mr. George Brummell, Beau Brummell, the most powerful arbiter of taste in the ton."

"I do not know . . ." Penelope's voice faded. A suspicion grew. She remembered James stumbling over George Brown's last name and Lady Jersey's mirth when she complimented him on his taste. George Brown—George Brummell. Her eyes narrowed for a moment in anger, then she had to laugh. It was indeed a capital joke! No doubt he had planned it all to put everyone into a spin. He succeeded. It didn't matter, though. She was here at a tonnish ball, and he had helped her create a style uniquely and attractively her own. Better still, Millicent was furious, Alex had agreed to waltz every waltz with her, and she had curtsied to the Prince of Wales. She chuckled again.

"I hardly think my request is amusing!" Constance snapped. "I thought you might wish to help me, considering all we—"

"Considering all you have done for me," Penelope finished the sentence. "I am ever mindful of your generosity. I will do what I can to secure an introduction to the famous Brummel for Constance. He has requested I save the quadrille for him. I shall speak to him then." She included Lady Buxley in her smile. "Do you suppose we might go shopping one day? I have discovered an excellent dressmaker. I am sure you would like her. Her name is Mademoiselle Gene—"

"No!" Constance answered abruptly. "I have had a

most trying time finding a modiste who will make the type of gowns I need. Worth was impossible! He actually said I should not wear pink. Naturally, he did not receive our patronage! How he received his reputation, I shall never know. Anyway, I have finally discovered a modiste who will do exactly as I tell her. I do not intend to change."

"Maybe you should meet Penelope's designer," Lady Buxley suggested. "Her gown is most striking."

Constance glanced quickly at Penelope's outfit. "I prefer pastels. I am told they are much more fashionable." A slight tinge of sarcasm coated her words. "I do not have Lady Ashford's exalted rank. I dare not be cast as an original!"

Her mother sighed. The season had not mellowed her daughter. She saw a hand signaling from across the floor. "Oh, Constance, look, Lady Cowper wishes us to join her. Remember dear, she is a patroness of Almack's. Do not make a muff of this introduction."

James appeared at Penelope's side with the iced lemonade. She smiled mischievously. "James, you just missed the Buxleys. Shall I call them back?"

He looked frantically around for a way to escape, then saw the glint of amusement in her eye. "Stop roasting me, Penelope. Can't stand the Buxleys, never could. Wasn't so bad before you married Alex. Miss Buxley was always casting her lures toward him, now it's me she's after." He shuddered. "Quite puts one off the whole idea of marriage!"

The lemonade tasted cold and good. Penelope was about to tease James a bit more, when Brummell joined them. He bowed to her. "I believe our quadrille is next, Lady Ashford."

"I am honored you remembered, Mr. Brown, or may I call you Beau?"

He chuckled. "Ah, I see my ruse has been discovered.

I trust you are not too angry with me for the little deception."

"I ought to be," Penelope replied archly, then softened it with a smile. "However, it was very handsome of you to take the time to advise me on my wardrobe. I shall forgive you."

Brummell gave an exaggerated sigh of relief. "I feared you might set up a dreadful screech and I do detest scenes. I am glad my caprice shall go unpunished."

"Did I say that?" Penelope asked innocently. "I fear, sir, you must pay for the stir you created or I shall set up that screech," she said sweetly.

Beau was amused by the interchange. It wasn't often someone had enough spirit to challenge the famous Brummell. It was diverting. "What is my penalty, fair lady." He made a dramatic gesture. "Pray that you will not wound this heart too deeply."

Penelope giggled. He really was not to be beat on any suit. She liked him. "I have a favor to ask, that is all."

"Ask for anything, except a loan," he said aside to James, "and I shall try to grant it."

"Good. I want you to go and dance with Constance Buxley."

"That female mushroom! Lady Ashford, surely you could not be that cruel to me?" he protested as he wrinkled his nose in fastidious distaste.

"Seriously, Mr. Brummell, I would appreciate it. The Buxleys were kind to me at a time I needed someone. A bow from you would help repay that debt."

"All right, it offends my sensibilities, but I shall do it for you." He looked across the room to where Constance was standing by her mother and Lady Cowper. "Are you sure I must do this? That pink gown is frightful! Lady Ashford, you simply must tell her not to wear that particular shade again. She looks like a sick petunia. Also tell her to put some cucumber juice on those freckles. They are dreadful!" He bowed over her hand. "Your appearance tonight has the ton intrigued. Your unique riding habit and white stallion we planned for your ride in the Row tomorrow will definitely establish you as an original. Remember, never follow, make polite society follow you."

"I will remember. Thank you for granting my favor."

"I vow if she dances as awkwardly as she looks, I will do you mischief!" Brummell muttered as he bowed again and started off toward Constance and Lady Buxley. He turned back toward her. "Since you have refused me this dance, I demand the right to be your partner for the midnight supper."

James quickly answered, "Don't try to cut me out, Beau. I am planning to escort Lady Ashford in to dine."

Brummell laughed. "She now has two escorts." He started across the ballroom, whispered a word to Lord Castlereagh, and continued on to beg a dance with Constance.

Penelope frowned as she saw the way Constance simpered up at him. She shrugged. She had done her best. Lord Castlereagh approached. "Brummell informed me you are free for this quadrille. May I have the honor, Lady Ashford?"

Penelope nodded her head and they joined the sets forming on the floor. Partner after partner followed, and she danced until the double doors were opened to the dining room and the supper was announced.

Alex had been standing at the side of the ballroom watching the whirling dancers when the butler announced the supper. He noticed that Penelope was alone and started toward her. His step halted when he saw that both James and Brummell had appeared at her side. A deep crease marred his forehead when he saw his wife gaily link arms with the two men and enter the dining room. Out of the corner of his eye he caught a glimpse of Millicent walking toward him. He quickly turned on his heel and marched into the card room. He was in scant mood for any more of her theatrics.

Lady Shellingham was forced to go into the dining room alone. Her pout became more pronounced when she saw the attentions being showered on Alex's wife by the two men at her side. Why did Brummell, of all people, have to be dancing attendance? His sponsorship guaranteed Lady Ashford's success. Millicent tapped her fingers on the lace tablecloth. She was not pleased with the way her plan was turning out. The convenient bride was not supposed to turn into a belle of the ton. She must think of some way to send Alex's wife back to the country.

Penelope's dining companions were delightful. She was in cheerful spirits when the music began again. The evening was an enjoyable rout until Lord Jersey claimed her hand for a dance. He was leading her out onto the floor when she caught sight of Alex and Millicent standing close together. Between steps of the dance she kept an eye on their conversation. At first Millicent was flirtatious. Her eyes were warm and sultry as she gazed up at him. Her lips parted in a smile as he responded to her. The pattern of the dance pulled Penelope away. She could not see what was happening. Lord Jersey made a humorous remark. She forced a smile. Was Alex still beside Millicent, she wondered. Slowly, the pattern changed and she could see them again. Penelope was gladdened. Evidently a tiff was brewing. Lady Shellingham's eyes were snapping in anger; she stomped her foot and flounced off. Penelope was happy for a moment, then she saw Alex start after his mistress. He took three steps and stopped. He turned, their eyes met across the room. Alex knew his wife had seen it all. With a shrug he headed for the trays of champagne.

James was there sampling some of the vintage wine. Alex was glad for his company. He had had enough of troublesome women for a while. He took a glass of the champagne. "All right, James, let me have the story."

"What story?" his friend asked innocently.

"Stop the hum! How did Brummell meet my wife?"

"Beau met her that night you left for your tryst with Lady Shellingham."

Alex was taking a drink of the champagne and sputtered. "How the devil did you know that's where I was going?" he demanded when his voice returned.

"No secret, old boy, her letter fairly reeked with that ghastly perfume she uses."

"I assume Beau also knew."

"Of course. Anyway, as I was saying, after you left Penelope came into the study looking for a book by some Murke fellow."

"Do you mean Burke?"

"Could be," James conceded. "Never was bookish, you know. Beau asked her to join us and—"

"And," Alex finished, "he thought up this bit of mischief to overset Millicent. No doubt Lady Jersey was more than willing to help. Lady Shellingham is not her favorite member of polite society. Am I correct?"

James nodded his head. He was surprised at Alex's reaction. He had expected him to be angry; his friend was more amused. Best not upset things by telling Alex of his involvement in the whole deal.

Alex chuckled. "Tell Brummell his plan worked splendidly. Millicent is definitely miffed. I may have to find a pretty bauble to restore her good spirits."

How could he still care for Lady Shellingham when he had Penelope for a wife? James looked at him. "Alex, you are a fool!" he observed harshly and walked away.

The last dance of the evening was a waltz. Alex tried to

draw Penelope close into his arms. She remained stiff and unbending. "You were a much more willing partner last time we waltzed, Penelope. What has cast you into the dismals?"

The scene she had witnessed between her husband and Millicent still haunted Penelope's thoughts. Why did he have to follow her, if only for a few steps? Her voice was chilly and remote. "I was only thinking of you, milord. I would not want 'anyone' to fly up in the boughs over the attention you are paying your countrified wife."

In a flash of anger Alex roughly yanked her into his arms. "You have a tart tongue, milady," he murmured as his hold around her waist became tighter. His embrace was warm and possessive as they whirled around the ball-room. She resisted for a moment, then yielded. His arms became even tighter when he felt her body relax. The feel of his touch sent her blood scalding through her veins. A twirl threw them closer. Penelope melted against his hard chest. All too soon the music died and he put her from him.

Her heart was pounding. She prayed he too had felt the desire rise. His eyes were dark as he pointed to her bouquetiere. "You had best tell your gallant I intend to escort you home."

His eyes searched her face. Was he showing a wee bit of jealousy? How marvelous! Penelope looked around the ballroom as if searching for someone. "Apparently my gallant has deserted me. You scarce need to bother, however, I have our carriage." She peeked up at him and noticed the grim set to his mouth. "The coachman was requested to stay. I thought you might have, hmm, other plans for later this evening."

"I do," he answered curtly. "I shall escort you home first." He took her arm. His grip was none too gentle.

Neither spoke on the brief ride back to Grosvenor

Square. Alex instructed the coachman to remain as he handed Penelope out of the carriage. Hemnings answered his knock. They walked into the entry hall. Alex dismissed the butler.

Silence. He stared down at her. A fire burned behind his gaze. Suddenly he reached down, yanked the violets out of her bouquetiere, and crushed the flowers in his hand. "There will be no gallants in the country, Lady Ashford. Be prepared to leave within the week."

Alex instructs the mechanic to remove as he
block of the water surface, all except. He swings around a
moment. They all then turn the car to hell. Alex stumbled
the bottle.

Shows Henry who gives her a few minutes behind the
car a short drive on. Henry slows, signed the noble car
It had not started, and stalled the new car in the back.
There will be no pulling up the country as fully awaited.
Be prepared no more when the world.

CHAPTER ELEVEN

A maid unlaced Penelope's gown and helped her step out of it. Her attentions were adequate, but Penelope missed Kate's cheerful smile. Oh, well, soon she would be back at Ashford and Kate would be brushing out her hair again. The Jerseys' rout would be only a memory. She put on her velvet wrapper, dismissed the maid, and curled up on the bed.

Alex's behavior had been so strange all evening. She was befuddled. His embrace had been warm as they waltzed, and there was the scene when he had brought her home. Desperately she wanted to believe that he was jealous, that he was attracted, at least a tiny bit, but the cold fact remained: Alex was not in his bedchamber next door, he was with Millicent. If he felt any jealousy, it was only because she was his wife, his property, not because he had any true feelings for her.

Sleep was impossible. Every nerve in Penelope's body was waiting for the sound of Alex's return. The hours crawled by. He did not come. Each chime of the quarter hour deepened her depression. She loved Alex. Penelope became more sure of that with each passing day. She loved him. She wanted him. As she lay there curled up on the bed, she toyed with the idea of seduction. Maybe if passion came, love would follow. It should not be too difficult. She was not well versed in womanly wiles, but surely if she went to his bedchamber and—no, that must not be! She would fight to win Alex, but not that way!

Her spirits revived. Tomorrow she would begin the contest again. She could not compete from Ashford. There must be some way she could devise to stay in London for the remaining days of the season. Maybe Amelia could help.

Penelope got out of the bed and went to the writing table. It was completely outfitted with crested stationery, quill pen, and ink. There was even a small folding travel desk. She gathered up everything she needed, and walked back to the bedchamber. All was quiet. Alex had not yet returned. She touched the door to his room. A few tears threatened to gather. She forced them back. No tears were going to stain Amelia's letter. Briefly she described the confrontation with Alex when she arrived, asked after the Thomas matter, then launched into a description of the Jerseys' rout. She wrote of Brummell's deception, and her offer for a waltz with the Prince of Wales. Amelia will enjoy hearing all of the amusing details, Penelope thought. She tried to keep the tone of the letter light and chatty. The dowager would fret if she thought things were going amiss in London. Still, she must know of Alex's ultimatum that she return to Ashford. The words were difficult to write. Finally, Penelope simply closed with "I shall see you in about a week," and signed it, "your 'spirited' daughter-in-law."

The dawn light was coming through the windows as Penelope dripped the last of the sealing wax on the back of the envelope. Hemnings could post it later. There was still silence in the chamber next door.

It was long past noon when Penelope awoke. She rang for hot chocolate. The maid was setting the tray before her when she heard Alex's muffled orders to his valet. He had returned at last, but obviously only to change. Soon his door slammed and all was quiet again. There was no message for her.

The sleep had helped restore Penelope's energy and her

determination. She had a light lunch in the morning room. Her step was firm as she went up to her bedchamber to change for her ride in the Row. The white velvet riding habit was pressed and hanging in one of the armoires. The scarlet silk blouse and red kid leather boots added the needed splash of color. Mademoiselle Geneviève had even found a red riding crop for her to carry. The masterpiece, though, was the little red hat. It was of twill and made to perch on the side of her head. There was a small black feather that would bounce saucily as she rode. Penelope picked up the trailing hem of her habit and started downstairs. She gave Hemmings the letter for Amelia and asked him to post it at once.

James was waiting for her in the study. He stood up as she entered. There was an appreciative gleam in his eyes. "Guess Brummell is not the only one with fashion ideas," he bragged proudly. "My idea for your riding habit passed off well."

"Indeed it did," Penelope reassured him. "I feel as though I am in the first stare of fashion. Were you able to find me a white stallion to ride?"

"Yes." James looked uncomfortable. "In fact, Ashford helped me pick him out."

"What! How did that happen?"

"Met him on the street in front of Weston's. Alex was in a devil of a bad mood that day," James remembered. "Looking at horses helped restore his spirits. Didn't last though. He was back into the black temper last night. You didn't have a fight with him on the way home, did you?"

"No." Her heart was beating faster. There was a gleam of hope. She had to know. "James, were you with Alex after the ball?"

"Certainly. Didn't Alex tell you?" he asked. "Lord Jersey invited several of us to stay and play faro with him. Wasn't much fun. Had no luck at all. Lost at least a monkey. Alex won, but it didn't seem to make him any happier. He walked out of there at dawn with as deep a scowl as when he entered. Can't figure him at all. Sure you two didn't quarrel?"

Penelope laughed. "We talked of violets, nothing else of importance." Alex was not with Millicent last night! She wanted to yell the words out loud. He had not gone to her arms. A radiant smile lighted up her face.

"Violets?" James croaked. "Both you and Alex are balmy! He was muttering about violets last night too. Said he hated them." He shook his head in confusion. "Seems like a deuced queer thing to hate."

The clock on the mantel chimed. "Brummell is meeting us at the entrance to the Row. We had best leave," suggested James.

"Are you sure Alex will be there?"

"Yes, he promised Prinny they would ride together and then go and look at some damned Chinese bronze dogs, or dragons, or some such nonsense. Wants Alex's opinion before he buys. He's got so much art stuff now he's having to build that monstrosity at Brighton to house it all. Can't think why he wants more."

The day seemed brighter and the air fresher, now that Penelope knew her husband had been with James last night. It was easier to fight if she knew the contest was not over. Alex's tiger was holding the two horses as they walked out of the house. The young boy looked lost between the two huge animals, but he had them firmly under control. James helped Penelope mount the white stallion. He smoothed out the hem of her velvet habit over the horse's rump and swung into his saddle. They cantered off across the square.

Her horse wanted to frisk and she let him have his head. James watched nervously. He feared it was a lot of horse for one rather small lady to handle. Penelope's hand was firm on the reins. He relaxed. As promised, Brummell was waiting at the entrance. They were an impressive sight as they entered the promenade. All three horses were enormous beasts, and the color contrast of Penelope in white, between the two men in black, was striking. No one could possibly miss noticing them.

As they rode slowly around the circuit, they nodded to friends. Penelope was scanning ahead for Alex, when Brummell observed, "Ah, I see a 'friend' there by the rail. We can scarce go on without paying our respects." Penelope glanced over and saw Millicent sitting in an open barouche with her mother-in-law.

Millicent gave the three an icy nod as they approached. She felt very much at a stand. She bit her lip in vexation. Penelope's unusual habit, and her daring in riding a prancing stallion, angered her. Lady Ashford had put her in the shade again.

Introductions were exchanged. Penelope smiled sweetly down at her rival and commented, "It is so nice to see you again, Lady Shellingham. Pray, how is Lord Shellingham? When we met at Buxley Manor, I recall he was not feeling at all the thing. I do hope he is better."

Millicent clenched her teeth. The country bumpkin has claws, she fumed, but no anger showed as she replied, "How thoughtful of you to be concerned, Lady Ashford. Chester is much improved and enjoying the grouse hunting in Scotland. I find London quite lonely. I must find something to help fill the empty hours."

Penelope ignored her sharp barb and politely invited, "You must come to tea. I am sure Lord Ashford would be most delighted to see you." She paused. "We both would enjoy having a cozy chat with you."

Millicent's eyes narrowed dangerously. She poked the coachman in the back with the tip of her sun parasol. "Drive on."

When the Shellingham barouche had moved off, James observed with amusement, "Lady Ashford, you really should not have said that. Chester's mother is the worst fussbudget in the ton. She will give Lady Shellingham no peace until she finds out what was ailing her darling Chester."

With an innocent look Penelope confessed, "Oh, dear, I really do feel quite bad about that. I would not wish to overset Lady Shellingham."

Brummell reached over and lifted Penelope's hand from the reins and carried it to his lips. "Lady Ashford," he complimented, "you are a little hellcat!"

Penelope smiled serenely. "So I have been told."

Alex was across the Row in the group around the Prince of Wales. Lady Jersey reached out, tapped him on the arm with her sun parasol, and pointed to the scene around Millicent's barouche. His eyes grew black. He did not like Penelope talking with Lady Shellingham, he did not like her riding between the two men, and he did not like Brummell nuzzling his wife's hand. Damnit, why did she have to keep intruding into his well-ordered life! A suspicion pestered him as he watched the three trotting toward them. Penelope's white stallion looked familiar. He would need to have a discussion with James.

The Prince of Wales noticed the three riders approaching and loudly commented, "Ashford, isn't that your wife? I say, she is a fetching creature! Doesn't seem to have any lack of gallants, does she?"

Alex's hands tightened on the reins. "No," he muttered harshly, "she does not!"

"George," the prince yelled, "come and join us. Want your opinion later on some bronzes I may purchase."

The three riders nudged their horses into a canter and joined the prince's party. Lady Jersey called from her barouche, "Lady Ashford, that is another most original outfit. I compliment you."

"Yes," Prinny agreed, "smashing, just smashing! I like that little feather bobbing about. Ashford, you ought to have Sir Lawrence paint your wife like this. It would make quite a picture."

Penelope smiled. "Your Highness, you are most flattering, but actually I prefer landscapes to portraits. I hear there is an exhibition of Turner's work at the Royal Academy which I hope to visit before I must leave London."

"You have excellent taste, Lady Ashford. Turner is one of my favorite artists as well. However, I fear you are in for a disappointment. There has been a small fire at the Royal Academy. It is temporarily closed."

"I hope none of the paintings were damaged."

"Luckily no," the prince reassured her, "but the place fairly reeks with smoke and the damage to the foyer must be repaired." He noticed her disappointment. "Lady Ashford, don't fall into the dismals. I've got a smashing idea. My collection of Turners is hung at Brighton. I am taking a few friends out there late next week to see the progress on the palace. I fear I cannot offer you a formal dinner. The dining room is not finished yet, so we must picnic. Your husband is coming. Will you join us?"

Penelope peeked at her husband and grinned. He did not look pleased. The invitation from the Prince would delay her return to Ashford. Gleefully she prepared to accept. Alex spoke first. "I am afraid, sir, that Lady Ashford must decline, because—"

"Yes, I know," interjected Lady Jersey, "she must decline because you are riding out with His Highness, and you do not wish her to travel to Brighton alone. You are a most thoughtful husband. Rest easy, milord, Lady Ashford may ride out in my carriage. I would welcome her company."

"Splendid," the prince said, "it is all settled. Brummell, I must tell you about these Chinese bronzes. They arrived from the imperial court at Peiping and . . ."

His enthusiastic description of the art pieces continued as Alex motioned for James to join him. They moved their horses a few paces away. "James, old boy, that white stallion Penelope is frisking about on looks like the one you bought the other day. Is it?"

James ran a finger under his starched neckcloth. He looked uncomfortable. How in the world did he ever get in the middle of Alex's and Penelope's marital problems? He liked Penelope and wanted to help her, but Alex was his best friend. What a coil! The thought of escaping to his country estate in Kent sounded vastly appealing. "Yes, it's the same horse," he mumbled.

"Well?" Alex demanded.

"Well, what? Never said the blasted thing was for my stables," James weakly defended himself. "Lady Ashford requested I find her a white stallion." He met Alex's stare. "You seemed preoccupied with other matters. Saw nothing wrong with helping her."

A hint of anger underlaid Alex's words. "I am glad you find such pleasure in doing favors for my wife!" He wheeled his horse around and rejoined the Prince of Wales.

The prince was preparing to depart. "Ashford, Brummell, we had best be off. I have one of those cursed dull meetings with the Prime Minister later this afternoon. I want you to view those bronzes before that."

"Sir," Alex requested, "I would like to escort Lady Ashford home before I join you."

"That is not necessary," Penelope protested. "The viscount of Harrington can see to it."

"I am sure Harrington has more important business to attend to," he answered curtly. "Don't you, James."

"What? Ah," he stammered as he cast around for an excuse. "Hmm, yes, I must meet, hmm, Lord Cowper at White's."

"I assume I have your permission, sir," Alex asked the Prince of Wales.

"Certainly," Prinny agreed. "I know how you new bridegrooms are. If Princess Caroline looked like Lady Ashford, I would want to escort her home too. For that matter, I would probably want to tarry a bit once I got there." He chuckled knowingly. "I am afraid my Chinese bronzes cannot compete with that!"

Alex did not respond to his joke. "I will meet you at Carlton House, sir, as soon as I see my wife safely home."

The two great stallions, one coal black and the other white, turned away from the group surrounding the prince. The Ashfords made an attractive couple as their horses pranced back down the promenade. Their exit together was not missed by Millicent. Her hand tightened around the crook of her parasol. Her eyes followed them until they turned out of the Row.

Her mother-in-law prodded her with a sharp finger. "Millicent, what is ailing you? Three gentlemen have tried to pay their respects and you refused to acknowledge their bows."

Millicent passed a shaky hand over her forehead. "I fear I have had too much sun. Do you suppose we might cut our ride short and return home? My headache is most distressing and I forgot to bring my vinaigrette."

Chester's mother moved cautiously away. She raised her linen handkerchief to her nose. "You are not coming down with a fever, are you?"

"No!" Millicent snapped when she noticed her mother-

167

in-law's heedful retreat. "I shall not give you a fit of the ague. I am merely fatigued."

Alex's mood was not much more pleasant than Lady Shellingham's as they trotted toward Grosvenor Square. Penelope tried to chat with him about the prince's art collection. He would not cooperate. Both fell silent. The young tiger was waiting to take their horses when they arrived. Penelope peeked up at her husband's thunderous scowl and decided a hasty withdrawal was in order. She gathered up the hem of her riding habit and, with head held high, swept into the entry hall. Briskly she ordered, "Hemnings, please have a maid bring tea up to my bed-chamber."

Her foot was on the first step of the sweeping staircase when Alex's voice stopped her. "Lady Ashford and I will take tea in the study." The authoritative note in his tone was not to be ignored.

Slowly she followed him into the study. The door closed and they were alone. Penelope seated herself demurely in a leather wing chair and folded her hands in her lap. "Milord, I would prefer to change before I take tea."

Alex was angrily pacing through the room. He halted and stared down at her. "Would you? That is an interesting idea. Maybe you would like me to assist you, milady. You seem to be asking for help from everyone else!" He took a step toward her. There was a rakish gleam in his eyes. "I assure you," he growled deeply, "it would be my pleasure."

Unconsciously Penelope's hand flew to the neck of her riding habit. Had she pushed Alex too far this time? Her heart beat frantically. He took another step nearer. His hand stretched out and touched one of the pearl buttons on the front of her jacket. A knock on the door forced him to jerk back his hand. Hemnings entered with the tea equipage. Alex turned away and threw himself down in the chair at his desk. His glittering eyes did not leave Penelope as the butler served the tea. An uneasy silence filled the room as they sipped the hot brew. The vibrations would not be stilled.

Finally, Alex dropped his cup back on the saucer. "You maneuvered that very nicely."

Penelope swallowed nervously, but she met his gaze. She tried to keep the quiver from her voice. "I do not take your meaning, Alex. Whatever do you mean?"

"I mean finagling that invitation from the prince to accompany his party to Brighton."

"I am hardly responsible for His Highness's generous offer," objected Penelope.

"No?" he asked with a curve of his lip. "I suppose it was an accident that you happened to be riding in the Row with Brummell and Harrington when the regent was there. Where else can I expect you to pop up and plague my life?" he demanded irritably. "I am surprised you have not stormed the door at White's."

Penelope pretended not to notice his anger. She patted a yawn. "All of this toing and froing has quite fatigued me. I believe I shall rest until the picnic at Brighton. I do so want to be at my best to view His Highness's paintings."

"Good!" he snapped. Alex walked to the door. "The invitation from the prince cannot be rejected. You may go to Brighton. However, you will leave for Ashford the very next day. There will be no further delays!" The door was shut firmly as he left for his meeting with the prince.

For the next few days Alex was scarcely ever in the house. He attended the sessions of the House of Lords, rode down to a horse fair at Newmarket, boxed often at Jackson's, and found other, often contrived activities to fill his time. Nothing he did, though, seemed to help ease his vague discontentment. He avoided both Millicent and his wife.

Penelope noticed that he was avoiding her and assumed he was still in a huff over the prince's invitation to Brighton. That couldn't be helped. She was more concerned that no news had come from Ashford. Mr. Carling had not returned, and there had been no letter from Amelia. She wondered if the Thomas family was all right. She worried about the matter all during her morning bath and decided she had best write her mother-in-law again. She was soaking in the warm water when the maid poured in the bath salts Lady Buxley had given her. The exotic fragrance floated up around her and brought back all of the shattering memories of her wedding night. Penelope pushed the thoughts away. If only she could pretend it had never happened. When she remembered her weakness at Alex's touch, she wanted to flee, not fight. Resolutely she forced her mind to think of other things.

Later, she was writing the letter to the dowager, telling her about riding in the Row and the prince's invitation to Brighton, when the maid came in and happened to mention that Alex had returned and was working in the study. Quickly Penelope called for her maid to help her change. A new morning dress in deep sapphire blue had been delivered from Mademoiselle Geneviève's. Fluttering satin ribbons in ice blue accented the empire waistline. The maid brushed out Penelope's long tawny hair and threaded a matching ribbon through it. Her hair hung loose, as on the night of the ball. Penelope rubbed the tiniest hint of color on her lips and descended the staircase.

Without knocking she entered the study. Alex was bent over his desk, writing. He glanced up when he heard the door open. No smile of welcome greeted her. "Shall I ring for tea or would you prefer a glass of claret, milord?" she inquired politely.

"I would prefer . . ." He paused as his eyes roamed over

170

her face. "I would prefer," he began again, "to be left in peace!"

"I am afraid that is not possible." Penelope walked over and pulled the bell pull. She was acutely conscious of his eyes on her back. She kept her voice calm as she insisted. "There is something we must discuss."

When Hemnings answered her summons, she ordered tea and a decanter of wine. "Alex, the cook baked some fresh apricot tarts this morning. Would you care for some?"

He studied her a long moment, then forced a grudging smile. "Did my mother tell you that apricot tarts were my favorite sweet as a child? Is that why you asked the cook to prepare them?"

"Naturally." Penelope returned his smile. "I was hoping they would tempt you to stay home."

Alex got up from his chair and walked toward her. His eyes held a devilish gleam. "I could think of some other ploys you might use to keep me home."

A scarlet blush slid over her face. She took his meaning perfectly, but would not let him see her embarrassment. "Oh?" she asked innocently. "Would you have preferred a raspberry custard?" She walked away from him toward the desk and touched the papers of his speech. "Or would you rather I act as your secretary, while Mr. Carling is absent? Would that be termed a ploy?"

"I had in mind something a bit more personal. You could . . ."

Alex's suggestion was interrupted by the butler bringing in the tea cart. His eyes flicked over Penelope, but he said no more. Instead, he ordered, "Hemnings, remove the claret. Lady Ashford tells me there are apricot tarts today. Please bring a pot of coffee and a tray of the sweets."

"Very good, milord."

Penelope busied herself pouring tea. Neither spoke until

171

the coffee and tarts arrived. Much to her surprise Alex had Hemnings place the large silver tray on the low table in front of the settee, then he sat down beside her. His nearness sent a wave of weakness through her body. Her hand was not quite steady as she handed him his cup of coffee.

As she leaned toward him, a whiff of her perfume reached him. He moved slightly away and threw his arm across the back of the small sofa. His action seemed casual. In truth, he was trying to escape the memories that perfume always invoked. Hell and damnation! he thought. Why does she have to taunt me with that scent? And why can't she leave her hair braided?

The temptation to reach out and stroke Penelope's hair was strong; he resisted. Instead, he coolly commented, "This domestic scene is quite charming; however, I have a speech that must be delivered tomorrow and it is not finished. What do you wish to discuss?"

"Have you had any word from Ashford? I am concerned about Dick Thomas and his family. Are you sure they will not be put off their farm?"

"If you are so concerned," he reasoned in a half-teasing voice, "you should go back to Ashford and check on the situation yourself. That would also get you out from under my feet. Do you wish me to send a note around to the Prince of Wales and tell him you will miss his cursed picnic?"

"Alex, be serious! I am concerned! I would go to Ashford, if I thought there was something I could do."

"I suppose you would," he conceded.

"Have you had any message from Mr. Carling?" she repeated. "What is happening out there?"

"All right, Penelope, I can see you really do care. No, I have had no word from my secretary, and I admit that is unusual. Normally, he is very prompt in his correspondence."

172

"What does the delay mean?" she asked in a worried voice.

"The delay may mean nothing, or it may mean there was more of a problem than we anticipated."

"Do you think your bailiff took action after I left? What is that family going to do if they are turned out of their home? Alex," she pleaded desperately, "they have a tiny baby and . . ."

He reached over and patted her hand. "Milady, your vicarage upbringing is showing. Don't fly into the boughs over this matter. Mr. Carling will attend to everything. There is no reason to be so terribly overset."

Penelope yanked her hand away from his warm touch. "I am sorry if I embarrass you by being different from your tonnish friends. Alex, I care! I cannot help that! I cannot be as uninvolved with people's problems as is proper in your circle."

She jumped to her feet to leave. Tears glistened on the ends of her lashes. Alex blocked her way. His hands went out, grasping her shoulders. She wrenched away and sped from the room.

Alex sat down at his desk and picked up the pen. The lines of his speech, protesting against child labor practices, made no sense. Penelope's words rang in his ears. He stared at the door and murmured to himself, "Yes, I guess you are different." With a shrug he dropped his pen in the ink and began to write.

CHAPTER TWELVE

Alex yanked the drapes closed with an angry tug. The sun was shining! It was a beautiful day for the Prince Regent's outing. The day before had been foggy and drizzly. He had hoped the foul weather would hold; it had not. His mood as he dressed was as gray as yesterday's weather. He was not sure why.

Penelope was in her bedchamber next door. She too was having mixed feelings about the day. Prinny's picnic should be a gay romp, no question of that. It would be fun to remember she had visited his oriental pleasure palace. On the other hand, the dawning of this day meant her time with Alex was almost over. He would not tolerate another delay in her return to Ashford. Maybe if she had had more time? The question would have to remain unanswered. Her time was gone.

There was only this one day left in London. She pulled out the newest walking dress from Mademoiselle Geneviève. The maid helped her slip it on. It was done in a deep shade of turquoise with ruffles at the neck and hem. A matching parasol nestled in the bottom of the box. She had found a delicately wrought turquoise, diamond, and silver necklace hidden among the larger, more impressive Ashford jewels. It, with the matching earbobs and a turquoise ribbon in her hair, completed her outfit. She looked vastly more festive than she felt.

Lady Jersey's ceaseless chatter of tonnish on-dits and acid comments about the members of polite society filled the time of the carriage ride to the seaside resort of Brigh-

175

ton. Penelope could not help but gasp in wonder as the Royal Pavilion came into view. Several oriental domes, with ornamental tracery, reached toward the sky. Here and there other domes of various sizes and shapes were under construction. Scaffolds, and other construction materials, were mixed with rich slabs of marble and pieces of gilt carving. The whole site was opulent bedlam. Things were made even more chaotic by the servants and guests milling about the green lawn in front of the building.

Lady Jersey's coachman maneuvered along the gravel drive as far as he dared. The ladies had to walk the rest of the way. The Prince Regent was waiting. He greeted them eagerly. He singled out Penelope for special attention. "Ashford," he yelled, "I am going to escort your wife through the pavilion to look at my Turner paintings. You had best come along and chaperon. She is such a fetching little thing"—he chuckled—"that there is bound to be talk if we go alone. You know Sir Chinningsworth is on one of his reforming crusades again. I do not want to hear any more rubbish about the raffish set of Carlton House."

The prince held out his arm. Penelope laid her fingers on it as they entered the main door and walked into the Octagon Hall. Prinny exchanged political gossip with Alex as Penelope looked around the oddly shaped room. There was an ornately ribbed dome over their heads, and everything was decorated with Chinese accents. Even the gaslights shone through Chinese lanterns. The oriental touches became even more exotic as they strolled through the vestibule and into the long gallery. The paintings by Turner that he wanted her to view were all hanging in this large room. They walked from painting to painting as she savored the misty landscapes and seascapes. They were incredibly beautiful. The prince talked knowledgeably about each piece of art, then observed, "Enjoy them while you can, Lady Ashford. They will soon all be moved to

Windsor. I have found a new architect, John Nash, and we are going to create a real oriental palace here. No place for the Turner's, I fear."

"It is a lovely palace now, sir."

"Too small," he fussed. "Can't even hold a decent-sized dinner party. Nash will remedy that. He has this smashing design for a banqueting hall, and then we plan to add a music room."

His boyish enthusiasm was endearing, but Penelope truly felt his palace was a bit much. The harsh colors, the grotesque Chinese dragons, the enameled pagodas, and the huge porcelain figures, all seemed too fanciful for her taste. They were walking through the salon when the prince spotted a couple of workmen carrying a black lacquer secrétaire toward the back of the pavilion. "Lady Ashford, I have enjoyed this tour mightly! It is nice to have a new acquaintance to share my pavilion with. I fear I must dash off, though. That secrétaire is for my bedchamber. I must direct its placement."

Penelope dropped a deep curtsy. "It was an honor, sir." He raised her hand to his lips and waddled off after the workmen.

Alex and Penelope exchanged glances. She saw that her husband shared her amusement at the prince's extravagant folly. He gave her a knowing smile and observed, "Yes, I know precisely how you feel, milady, and you have not even visited his glass-domed stables and riding house yet. They look like something out of an Indian raja's book of fantasy." He held out his arm. "Shall we rejoin the other guests?"

The servants had laid the picnic fare out on the seaward side of the pavilion. Alex and Penelope strolled by the glass-domed stables he had mentioned and joined the throng. Dozens of white linen tablecloths were spread on the sloping lawn for the guests to sit on. To one side was the prince's thronelike chair and a small table. There were two places set at his table, one with a gold service, and the other with silver. The food and drink was being unpacked from huge hampers.

No one could eat until the prince was served. He seemed in no hurry to appear. The Ashfords moved through the crowd until they met Lord and Lady Jersey. Penelope unfurled her sun parasol and sank down on the white cloth beside Sally. The two men remained standing.

"Have you heard the latest, Ashford?" asked Lord Jersey with a grimace. "Prinny wants us to stay and play that damned battledore with him. I cannot see why he fancies it so. His girth won't allow him to move about the court. He stands there in one place and expects us to dash around like demented dolts hitting that blasted shuttlecock back to him!"

Alex shrugged. He was used to Prinny's freakish whims. Since there was no graceful way to decline, they would have to play his foolish little game. "The exercise will do you good, George. Lately your girth has been expanding a bit also."

Lady Jersey laughed and motioned for the two men to sit down with them. "The prince seems to be in no haste to dine. You might as well be comfortable." Her eyes sparkled mischievously at Alex. "Speaking of men with expanding girths, I hear tell that Lord Shellingham has returned from his hunting in Scotland. It is as well, for Lady Shellingham has certainly been in the dismals lately." She commented in jest, "I am sure Chester's presence will cheer her."

Alex glared a warning at her. The prince's arrival stopped him from making any comment. He emerged from the pavilion with a lady on his arm. She was rather plump, had a gentle expression, and appeared somewhat older than the man at her side. Glittering jewels sparkled at her throat and wrist. Penelope leaned over and whispered to Lady Jersey, "Is that Princess Caroline?"

Sally burst out laughing. "I am truly sorry, Lady Ashford, I forgot for the moment that you have been sheltered in the country. The prince and his wife do not care for each other," she explained, "and are seldom together. The woman with him is Mrs. Fitzherbert a, hmm, shall we say, an intimate friend of his."

Penelope was spared further embarrassment when Alex helped her to her feet. They moved toward the food tables. Her naively blundering question bothered her. She acknowledged sadly that for all of her expensive finery, she did not truly fit in the ton. At the vicarage she was raised to believe husbands and wives loved only each other. She could not accept the casual arrangements of the quality. Alex noticed her pensive look and wondered.

The prince offered his guests an abundance of food. It was hard for Penelope to choose as she was handed her silver plate and ushered through the line. There were platters of smoked salmon and quail, roasted joints of chicken, slabs of roasted beef, heaping bowls of garden vegetables, and a bewildering variety of jellies, custards, and tarts for dessert.

After they had dined, acrobats and tumblers ran out to entertain them. Their antics were amusing, but Penelope found it hard to smile. Her thoughts were far away. Tomorrow she would return to Ashford. She opened her turquoise parasol to shade her from the sun.

Alex glanced at his wife. The deep bluish-green of the parasol's silk framed Penelope's delicate heart-shaped face. She looked so young, so vulnerable. He remembered her innocent question about Mrs. Fitzherbert. She had spirit, he grudgingly conceded, but she was just not suited to the tonnish life in London. Truly, she would be happier back in the country with Mother.

When the tumblers and acrobats had somersaulted from the lawn, Lady Jersey arose. "We will leave you gentlemen to your delightful game of battledore." She raised her cheek for her husband's kiss. "George, we are entertaining the Cowpers this evening. Try not to be too late. Tell Prinny you twisted an ankle, or some such tale. Come, Penelope, I see that the coachman is waiting."

Penelope turned to follow. Alex's hand on her arm detained her. "Aren't you going to bid farewell to your husband? I may fall and break a leg chasing that damn shuttlecock. Think how distressed you would be then, to know you had left me without a farewell kiss."

"Would I?" Penelope inquired with a bat of her eyelashes.

"Oh, do kiss the fellow, and let us be off," Lady Jersey urged. "I have had quite enough of this outdoor living."

Her heart was beating wildly as she faced her husband. She turned to accept his kiss on her cheek. He had other ideas. As Alex's warm hand encircled the back of her neck, she stiffened. His lips brushed hers gently at first, then more demandingly. Every instinct she possessed yearned to return his embrace, but Millicent stood between them. She forced herself to remain unyielding in his arms.

He raised his lips and stared down at her white face. "There was a time, milady," he whispered, "when you were more willing." He released her and bowed to Lady Jersey. "Thank you for sharing your carriage with my wife. George and I shall try not to be late."

On the return ride to London Lady Jersey regaled Penelope with the story of the Prince Regent's amorous adventures and marital woes. They were on the outskirts of the city when the trouble happened. It was the noise that first attracted Penelope's attention. Out of the coach window she saw a group of young ruffians yelling and throwing mud balls and stones at something in the gutter. One of the boys bent over to pick up another rock, and she caught a glimpse of the small form huddled down on the cobblestones. It was a puppy. Without thinking, Penelope rapped on the sliding panel to the coachman's box and shouted for him to stop.

When the carriage had halted, she opened the door and leaped out. Lady Jersey called her name. She did not answer. Quickly she marched to the group of boys. One of them was raising his hand to throw another rock. Penelope grabbed it and yanked it down. Her eyes were blazing. "How dare you!" she demanded as she shoved through the group. "Which one of you owns this dog?"

The boys fell silent. Most were stunned to find a lady of quality in their midst; a few others looked shamefaced at what they had done. Finally, one of the older hooligans answered, "Ain't no one's dog, lady. Just havin' sport. Ain't none of your business."

"It certainly is! It is everyone's business when an animal is being mistreated." She knelt down in the gutter and reached out a gentle hand toward the puppy. The little dog trembled, whimpered, and ducked its head, expecting another blow. "Are you proud of what you have done? This dog never hurt you. It asked only to be left alone."

The youth who had answered her before growled, "Ain't nothin' wrong with havin' a little sport."

Penelope glared up at him. "I suggest you find a less harmful sport. You had best go home now, or I will call the watch and let them deal with this!"

At the mention of the police, the boys scattered. She leaned over the puppy again and talked to it in a low soothing voice. This time it did not shiver when her hand went out to touch it. She stroked the matted fur and softly felt for broken bones. Blood from the bruises and cuts on the little dog stained her fingers. She found no serious damage. Her hands formed a cradle as she lifted the pup and nestled him into her arms.

As she approached the carriage, she noticed Lady Jersey was standing in the doorway. "Penelope," she cried, "you cannot bring that filthy mongrel in here. Think of the upholstery."

"Then I shall have to walk back to Grosvenor Square," she insisted. "I am not leaving this puppy here for those ruffians to torment."

Lady Jersey could easily have had her dignity offended by the situation. Luckily she chose to be diverted. "Oh, very well," she sighed, "but do be careful!"

Penelope smiled at her. "Do not fret. Your upholstery will be safe. I shall hold him."

"Your gown will be ruined!"

"Well," Penelope answered practically, "it already is. I fear the London gutters are none too clean. Besides, it does not matter."

Lady Jersey stared at the mangy pup on Penelope's lap and laughed. "When I said you were an original, I did not know how original! I would enjoy seeing the expression on Lord Ashford's face when he discovers that creature romping about his house."

Alex! Penelope gulped. She had not even thought of him. No doubt he would be angry! She did not care. She could not leave the puppy in the gutter. He could rage at will. What she had done was necessary.

"A rather pathetic little thing, is he not," Sally noted as she moved over to the seat next to Penelope. Gingerly she reached out her hand to touch the dog. When he tried to lick her fingers, the famous Lady Jersey actually giggled with pleasure. "Do you think he will survive?" she asked with concern. "There seems to be a frightful amount of blood."

"I hope so. I will bathe him when we arrive home, then

182

I should be able to tell more about his injuries. I am almost sure he will be all right," Penelope reassured her. "I do not believe there are any broken bones and the cuts do not seem too deep."

The Jersey carriage rattled to a stop in front of the Ashford mansion. The coachman helped her out. Sally poked her head out of the window and called, "Please let me know how our little friend is doing."

"I will send an under-footman round with a message tomorrow," Penelope promised.

Hemnings's normally unruffled expression cracked when he opened the door and found his mistress on the step holding a battered mutt in her arms. Penelope swept past him and requested, "Please have a maid bring up hot water and towels to my chamber without delay. We will need salve and possibly bandages." She started up the steps and called over her shoulder, "We will also need a pallet. Have one prepared, please."

Alex was happily unaware of his wife's unusual rescue as he batted the feathered shuttlecock back to the prince. Luckily His Highness soon tired of the game and the gentlemen were able to start for London. As they were riding in from Brighton, Penelope was inspecting the puppy's wounds. She dipped a cloth in the warm water and gently washed the matted fur. Once in a while the little pup whimpered when she touched a tender spot, but he did not try to run away. He recognized loving care when he felt it. When the worst of the filth and blood was cleaned, Penelope discovered his wounds were mostly superficial. His thick curly fur had protected him.

She left the pup warming by the fire and summoned the maid again. "Please have a footman bring up a washtub. We will also need more hot water and towels. I am going to give the dog a bath."

The maid bobbed a curtsy. Her look clearly indicated

that she felt Penelope had run mad. Nonetheless, she was too well trained to argue. A servant was not supposed to understand the strange ways of the aristocracy.

Surprisingly, the little puppy enjoyed the warm water. He wiggled and jumped and splashed until the whole front of Penelope's dress was soaking wet. The trouble came when she tried to take him out of the bath. He barked loudly, yelped, and growled when she tried to wrap him in the warm towel. She was kneeling on the floor, struggling with the unwieldy bundle, when her chamber door crashed open. She gave a startled gasp as Alex came stomping into the room. "Penelope," he roared, "what the deuce is going on here?"

The little dog wiggled free of the towel and darted across the room toward Alex. He stopped two paces off and shook himself all over. Droplets of water flew everywhere. Penelope sat on the floor and laughed as the elegant Lord Ashford got drenched. "You misbegotten cur!" Alex shouted angrily.

He snatched the little dog off the floor and held him out at arm's length. The puppy whined and whimpered in his hard grasp. Instantly, Alex's touch became more gentle. He carried the dog over and laid him by the fire. He looked at his wife. The damp dress clung to her figure, revealing again what he had seen through her tattered nightgown those many nights before. His voice was unsteady as he ordered, "You had best go and change. I will stay with your guest."

While Penelope dried off and changed her gown, Alex took a towel and began to rub the dog's damp fur. He soon found the knots and bruises where the stones had hit, and the cuts that were still a bit damp with blood. The more wounds he found, the angrier he got that anyone would do a thing like this. When the pup was dry, he picked him up and laid him across his lap. He stroked the curly fur

184

and muttered softly, "You really are a misbegotten cur, do you know that?" The dog wagged his tail and laid his head comfortably on Alex's knee. He let out a contented yelp when Penelope entered the room, but he did not move from her husband's side.

She stood there with her hands on her hips and commented, "You are an ungrateful dog," she teased. "I rescue you from a bunch of ruffians, and you will not even come over here to be petted." She walked to her husband and bent over the puppy. Her silken hair brushed over Alex's hands as she reached down to pat the dog. The faint scent of her perfume filled his senses. He shifted uneasily in the chair. The dog raised its head and looked at him questioningly. A scratch behind his ears settled the pup back down. Alex wished he could find contentment so easily.

It was less difficult to keep his voice level when Penelope moved back across the room. "May I ask," he inquired politely, "where you found this disgraceful mutt?"

The word mutt was greeted with a sharp bark from the dog laying on his lap. Both he and Penelope burst out laughing. "You did not take offense when I called you a misbegotten cur, why stand on formality now?" Alex asked as he patted the furry head. "You certainly cannot claim to be a purebred! Look at yourself," he teased the pup, "you are as motley a mixture as I have ever seen. In fact, Motley is the ideal name for you. We could call you Mott for short. Do you approve?" A wag of the bushy tail answered his question. "Motley it will be then." He glanced up at Penelope. "Now that the name business is settled, I would like to know where Mott came from." He ran a hand over the furry back and felt the lumps again. "Obviously, he has been ill used. Who did this?"

Penelope described what had happened. She noticed Alex's deep frown when she talked about breaking up the group of hooligans that were abusing the little dog. The lines became harder the longer she talked. Finally, he snapped, "Penelope, that was really a very hen-witted thing to do! Those young ruffians could have been dangerous."

"Lady Jersey's coachman was there with his blunderbuss," she argued.

"Still, it is hardly proper for the marchioness of Ashford to engage in such activities."

Penelope stared at him. "Hardly proper!" she retorted. "Is it proper to let some wicked boys torment a helpless dog? What was I supposed to do, ride by in my expensive carriage and pretend it was not happening? Would you have done that?"

The question she hurled at him made him look somewhat uncomfortable. He tried to explain. "Probably not, but then I am a man, and better equipped to handle rough situations. I do not expect my wife to be involved in such predicaments. If you will recall, this marriage took place to avoid an unpleasant scene. I do not want you to create new ones for the ton to gossip about. Your action must have embarrassed Lady Jersey."

She started to argue, but he raised his hand. "A truce, milady." His eyes were serious. "I am concerned for your safety, Penelope. Mixing with ruffians, even in the defense of a right cause, can be dangerous."

She wanted to ask if he truly cared whether she were hurt or not. The words almost came, but she forced them back. She was acutely aware that they were alone in her bedchamber. The touch of his lips, where he had kissed her earlier in the day, still sent a throb through her body. She dared not provoke his passion again. The tone of their polite conversation must be maintained. "I shall try, Alex, to do the socially proper thing. I do not want to shame you, but I will not give up my right to care deeply for what occurs around me."

"Nor should you," he agreed. "Do try to be a bit more discreet, though. I do not want my wife involved in any scandals, and I do not want you harmed."

She glowed when she heard his words. Maybe he was learning to care. A soft smile spread across her face as she looked at Alex. He was stroking Mott gently. The little dog stretched lazily and curled back up against his leg. The puppy's velvety brown eyes slowly closed and he dozed.

"It appears, Alex, that you have found a friend. I planned to take Mott back with me to Ashford when I am exiled, perhaps you would rather he remain here."

"Exiled?" he asked as he raised an eyebrow.

"A poor choice of words, I retract it. I do not wish to quarrel with you."

"Good, neither do I." His hand rested on the pup. "Mott would be happier in the country where he can run free and chase rabbits if he wishes. London is no place for a dog, unless it is one of those silly little pooches some of the ladies like to carry about with them." He looked down at the small sleeping mongrel. "I fear you would never convince anyone that Mott's ancestry is illustrious enough to make him a fashionable lap animal."

"He already has one friend in the ton," Penelope informed him. "Lady Jersey was quite taken with him. I must send a note around tomorrow to let her know he is going to be all right."

"I meant to ask how Lady Jersey reacted to sharing her elegant carriage with what must have been a very filthy creature."

Penelope smiled. "Once she was reassured that the upholstery would not be damaged, she made him most welcome." She went on to describe what had occurred after the rescue.

Alex laughed so hard when she told him how Mott had licked Lady Jersey's hand that he woke up the puppy. Mott looked up at him with sleepy eyes as if to question what the ruckus was about. "Don't give me that innocent look!" Alex scolded him in jest. "You are a shameless toadeater. Playing up to Lady Jersey, indeed! Lord Jersey will call you out if you continue to make sheep's eyes at his wife." Mott cocked his head, then yawned widely. "I can see you are terrified at the prospect!" Alex observed with a grin, as Mott settled back down on his lap.

He looked up, and his eyes met Penelope's. He cleared his throat. "You mentioned returning to Ashford. I assume that means you are prepared to go tomorrow."

"Do I have a choice in the matter?"

"No, you do not." Alex saw the flash in her eyes and hastily continued, "I agreed that you could have a brief visit in London to shop. That brief visit has been extended by the Jersey's rout and Prinny's blasted picnic. Your visit is over. I want you to return to Ashford. I am concerned about Mother and would feel better if you were there with her. I cannot go until this session of Parliament is complete."

"Has there been some news from Mr. Carling?" Penelope asked.

"His report came yesterday. Apparently," he confessed with an uneasy smile, "I have much to thank you for. Mr. Carling found things at Ashford in a deuce of a muddle." Alex shook his head. "When he got there, Earnest had disappeared. This quarter's revenues went with him. It is galling to admit I hired a damned scoundrel for my bailiff. That should teach me not to allow anyone else to attend to my business. I will keep a closer hold on things from now on. At least you uncovered his activities before anyone was seriously harmed. My pockets have admittedly been burned, but our tenants are all right."

"He was not able to force the Thomas family out of their house, was he?"

"Not exactly. They have had to leave their cottage, because Dick had to—"

"Why?" Penelope interrupted with a cry. "What happened? You said—"

"Don't overset yourself. You always leap to conclusions before I can explain. Mr. Carling discussed the situation with Vicar Wesley. He suggested that Dick Thomas would make a good bailiff for my lands. He has some education, and by all accounts he is an honest man. Naturally, he moved his family into the bailiff's more comfortable cottage. My secretary is staying awhile longer to untangle all of the problems. Seems things were also in a muddle in the great house. Mr. Carling knew I would not want Mother burdened with those problems, so he is remaining there for a few days."

"The house?" Penelope asked with a frown. "Earnest had nothing to do with the management of the house."

"No, but Mrs. Grayson did. She disappeared with her son. Her household accounts were as dishonest as his."

"Her son! Was Earnest her son?" Alex nodded his head. "That must be why she looked so startled when I announced why I was coming to London," mused Penelope. She looked up at him with a worried expression. "Is your mother all right? I pray all of this has not fatigued her."

Alex got slowly to his feet and eased Mott down onto the cushion. The little dog stretched out, but did not wake. He paced through the room. "That is what bothers me about Mr. Carling's report. He briefly mentions that Mother is well, but gives no details. He is concealing something and that is not like him. I am concerned." He stared down at her. "You have had your taste of the

London season and Bond Street shopping. I want you to go to Ashford tomorrow."

Penelope's heart thumped wildly. Why did his towering presence have to disturb her so much? She could not think straight when he was near. Resistance was difficult, or impossible. She did not want to leave him, to leave him free to seek Millicent's arms, but his appeal could not be denied. She, too, was concerned about her mother-in-law. Maybe it was time to go back. She had fought fairly with every weapon she possessed and had not won his love. She might as well return to her countrified existence. If only there were more time, but there wasn't.

With great effort she kept her voice steady. "Rusticating in the country a bit ought to be a delightful change from the season's whirl. Yes, Alex, I will go to Ashford. I am as concerned as you about Amelia; however, I do not intend to be buried there forever while you wind your raffish way through society."

His eyes met hers. A sardonic smile touched one corner of his mouth. He picked up her hand and lingeringly kissed the palm. "That, my dear, is a problem we shall deal with later."

Her breath came quicker. He seemed unaware of the turmoil his kiss created within her. He casually brushed off his coat. "Milady, your mutt sheds. Are you going to allow him to sleep on the velvet chair, or shall I have a bed prepared by the fire?" Without sparing a glance toward her, he decided, "I believe a pallet would be best. I shall inform Hemnings."

Later Alex sat in the study, sipping brandy and staring at the fire crackling in the grate. He swirled the amber liquid in the glass and took a drink. An unfinished speech lay on his desk. He had tried to work on it; it was useless. The vague discontent that had plagued him of late had returned. He was restless and irritable. Impatient fingers drummed on the arm of the leather chair as he puzzled over the matter. His temper had been so changeable lately, and for no reason. The seat in Parliament was secure, there had been no scandal, and yet his life seemed in a constant state of disruption.

Alex got up and paced across the room. He had actually been furious at James that day he saw him riding with Penelope in the Row, furious with his best friend. It was absurd! He scanned the book shelves, trying to find something to read. Possibly he was merely bored. No book looked appealing. Even the brandy in his glass held no attraction. His hand reached for the bell pull. It stopped. For the first time Alex noticed the tiny violets woven into the bell pull's tapestry design. "Damn violets!" he muttered savagely as he yanked on the pull. Penelope's look as he had crushed her violets in his hand came back to haunt him. What gallant had sent them? Had she been more willing to accept his kisses than her husband's? "Hell and damnation!" he cursed. He very deliberately lifted the brandy glass and sent it crashing into the fire.

A sharp rap at the door broke the chain of his angry questions. Hemnings entered. The butler's unruffled expression flickered to the glass in the fireplace and back to Alex. "Do you wish the 'accident' cleaned up, milord?"

"What?" Alex frowned, then he noticed the direction of Hemnings's glance. "No, leave it till morning. Please bring a pot of coffee."

"Very good, milord. Is there anything else?"

Alex resumed his pacing. "No, that is all." His frown deepened. "Wait, Hemnings. Get rid of that bell pull!"

"Sir?" the butler asked in confusion. "Did you say to get rid of the bell pull. Isn't it working, milord?"

"Just get rid of it!" Alex ordered. "Put up a new one, a plain one. I don't want any damned flowers in my study!"

"Yes, sir, I will attend to it." Hemnings backed quickly out of the room. He left the door ajar so he would not have to fumble with the knob when he returned with the coffee tray. He gave the cook Alex's order, then commented, "Ooh, his lordship is in a royally foul mood tonight. Best stay out of his way unless you want one of your roasted pigeons thrown at your head. Put a couple of those apricot tarts on the coffee tray. Maybe they will sweeten things a bit."

While the coffee was brewing, Alex stood at the windows, staring out at the darkened square. Occasionally a carriage rumbled by, but most people were at rest. Why couldn't he find peace? A yelp at his heels and two paws scratching at his boots caused him to turn around.

"No, Mott, down! I shall not allow you to ruin my boots any further. You have already spattered them with water. If you scratch them, you will have to answer to my valet. He uses expensive champagne, old boy, to get this shine. I don't care to have you panting all over it." The little dog barked and jumped up against his legs. "You have no manners, Motley. At least your paws are clean. All right, all right," he conceded as he lifted the puppy into his arms. "You can stay."

Hemnings gave the mutt a disapproving look when he entered with the coffee. "Shall I remove him, sir? Perhaps he will stay out of mischief if we put him in the silver pantry for the night."

Alex dismissed him. "Mott can stay. His barks would probably keep the whole house awake if we tried to lock him away."

The door closed. Alex settled Mott by the fire and poured his coffee. He sank down in the leather wing chair again. The puppy crawled over, laid his head across his master's ankles, and yawned. Alex stared down at the curly-haired mutt. "You are just one more disruption Penelope has thrust into my life!"

Mott looked up at him, then laid his head back down and closed his eyes. "Don't look so complacent. She risked her life to save you." His hand stroked the sleepy dog. "She is far too innocent for the ways of London. You will both be better off at Ashford. My life will be less complicated too! Yes, things ought to be much easier when she leaves for the country tomorrow." He fleetingly wondered why the thought did not make him any happier or more content. He took a sip of the coffee. It tasted bitter.

CHAPTER THIRTEEN

Packing for the trip back to Ashford was not a pleasant chore for Penelope. There was a dull ache as she supervised the maid's busy tucking of Mademoiselle Geneviève's lovely creations into the trunks for her removal from London—and from Alex. As each trunk lid was strapped down, she felt a bit more saddened. A wan smile came as Penelope watched the maid wrap the emerald-green ball gown in tissue and lay it away. At least the Jerseys' rout had been fun. The smile faded as the maid lifted the ruby satin ball gown and the sapphire taffeta from the armoire.

"Milady," she inquired, "should we send these to Ashford? You haven't a chance to wear them yet. Perhaps it would be best to leave them here. Surely you won't be needin' such finery in the country."

Nor will I again in London, Penelope silently conceded. They might as well go. "Please pack everything. Put those gowns in the portmanteau with the emerald one." She sadly surveyed the clutter of luggage. The time to depart had come. "Ring for the footmen to come up and start carrying down the trunks. We must not tarry. I wish to reach Ashford before nightfall."

Motley slipped through the door as the footmen were hefting the trunks onto their shoulders. He barked shrilly when he saw the confusion in Penelope's bedchamber. She tried to grab the little pup, but he darted away and ran between the legs of one of the hefty footmen. The footman's steps tangled with the dog. He stumbled forward. The heavy trunk, which was balanced on his shoulders, teetered unsteadily. The man tried to hold it, but it crashed to the floor. His blistering oath split the air. Suddenly he remembered Lady Ashford's presence. His ruddy face blanched. The other footmen cast sympathetic glances at the offender as they hurried from the chamber. The rules at Ashford house were precise; such language meant the boot.

Nervously the footman turned to face Penelope's wrath. Her face was stern, yet there was no shock or anger. "Please beg my pardon, milady. Them words came afore I thought. Ought not to 'ave said that."

"No, you certainly should not have. I do not expect ever to hear you utter such blasphemy again!"

The servant gaped. "Ye mean ye ain't goin' to tell Hemnings wot I did? Ye mean I won't get the boot?"

"It was partly Mott's fault," she conceded. "I shall not inform Hemnings this time. Guard your tongue more carefully in the future, though."

The footman could not believe his good fortune. It was rare that a lady of quality had the compassion to forgive such a lapse. Quickly he shouldered the trunk and hurried from the room.

The bedchamber seemed strangely empty when all of the trunks and cases were gone. Nothing was left to show that she had ever lived in the rooms. Her presence, she mused, had made no impact on the elegant surroundings any more than it had on Alex's life. When she was gone, he would not even bother to remember she had once visited.

Penelope walked through the rooms one last time. She shook her head sadly. Best to collect Motley and leave. It was useless to try to hold on to something that never was. She called the pup's name, softly at first, then louder. No wagging tail bounded into view. A frown creased her brow as she looked under the day chaise, the writing table, and behind the ornate screen. Motley was gone.

An upstairs maid was passing through the hallway outside Penelope's suite of rooms. She bobbed a curtsy when she saw her mistress standing in the doorway. "Have you seen my little dog?" Penelope asked. "He seems to have disappeared."

"Yes, milady, he ran into Lord Ashford's bedchamber."

Penelope pulled on her traveling gloves. How vexing! Motley would have to choose Alex's rooms to hide in. She certainly did not wish to go in there and get him. "Please retrieve him for me."

"Oh, no, milady!" the maid sputtered. "I dare not!"

"Stuff and nonsense! Please go in and get Motley. I must leave for Ashford."

Tears sprang up in the maid's frightened eyes. "Milady, I cannot!"

Penelope's nerves were taut with emotion. She did not need this type of problem. "This is ridiculous! Please do as I request."

"Milady," the maid pleaded. "I have my orders. I am not allowed to enter his lordship's rooms. Only Lord Ashford's valet and Mr. Hemnings may enter his chamber."

Penelope sighed. She could not fault the maid. It was the rigid Ashford organization that was causing the trouble. "Well, then, I suppose you will have to go and get one of them."

The flustered maid saw Penelope's irritation and tried to explain. "Milady, 'tis impossible. Mr. Hemnings is at the mews checking on the traveling carriage and Lord Ashford's valet is at Weston's."

Penelope stripped off her gloves and handed them to the maid. There was nothing to do but go and get Motley herself. Her hand touched the knob to Alex's suite. She did not turn it. What if Alex was inside? She did not wish to see him, especially in his bedchamber.

She rapped loudly. Her only answer was a faint bark from Motley. Foolishness, sheer foolishness, she fussed at herself; go ahead and turn the silly knob. With determination she quickly shoved open the door and entered her husband's suite.

The arrangement was a duplicate of hers: a sitting room, dressing room, and bedchamber. Yet there were vast differences. Alex's rooms had no ornate furniture or opulent hangings. Everything was stark, with an almost spartan simplicity. The only ornamentation she saw anywhere was the carved and gilded frame around the military medals Alex had been awarded during the Napoleonic wars.

Penelope searched quickly through the sitting room and dressing rooms. Then with lagging steps she entered Alex's bedchamber. There was Motley, contentedly nestled plump in the middle of Alex's bed. Penelope called his name sharply; he refused to budge. She shook a finger at him. "You look most comfortable, but it is time to go." She clapped her hands. "Come on, hop off the bed. The carriage will surely be ready by now."

Motley cocked his head at her, then laid it back down on his paws. He showed no inclination to move. Penelope sighed in exasperation. "I know you do not wish to leave Alex either, Mott, but we have no choice. Think of all the rabbits you can chase at Ashford." She approached the bed and stretched out her hand. Motley edged away. The bed was too wide. She could not quite reach him. He stayed just beyond her fingertips. Penelope leaned over farther; her hand brushed Mott's fur as he wiggled away. She made a grab for him and toppled onto the bed. Motley leaped off the bed and disappeared underneath.

Penelope rolled over onto her back and found Alex

standing there staring down at her. There was a sardonic gleam in his eyes. "I must say," he commented blandly, "that it is an unexpected pleasure to find you warming my bed. Did you wish to make a personal good-bye?"

A scarlet blush raged across her face as she stammered out the explanation about Mott. Alex raised an amused eyebrow, as he towered over her. "Tut, tut, Penelope, you really ought to be ashamed. It is bad ton to blame this indiscretion on that innocent animal." He smiled roguishly as he observed, "Although, I suppose society would hardly consider a visit to your husband's bed an indiscretion."

Penelope struggled to sit up. The soft feather bed seemed to pull her down. "Well," she stormed, "you could be a gentleman and help me!"

Alex glanced down at her with a devilish look. "Are you sure you wish to get up from my bed? You look quite comfortable there." A warm current flowed under his words.

Penelope managed to squirm to her feet. She challenged him. "I doubt if you would allow my departure to be delayed for a mere dalliance."

"Wouldn't I?" he asked softly.

There was an unfathomable expression in his eyes that made her breath come quicker. He took a step toward her. Penelope knew this was dangerous! She must fight against this attraction. Bravely she met his stare. "I fear such a frivolous waste of time might keep you from Lady Shellingham's side. Surely she knows I am to leave. Your *chérie amante* must be expecting you."

A thunderous scowl flashed across Alex's face. For an instant Penelope feared she had taunted him once too often. They stared at each other. His voice was harsh as he snapped angrily, "Mott, come here!"

The little dog crawled slowly out from under the bed.

199

His normally busy tail was tucked sheepishly between his legs. Alex reached down and grabbed him. He thrust Mott into Penelope's arms and savagely muttered, "Keep your mutt in your own rooms. If I find you in my bedchamber again, the dalliance you scorn will not be delayed!"

Penelope trembled as Alex slammed out of the room. Why must they always quarrel? A few tears splashed on Mott's curly fur. He looked up at her and yelped softly as if he understood her pain. With slow steps Penelope left Alex's room. The connecting door shut; she was back in her bedchamber. She laid Motley before the fire and went to splash cool water on her reddened eyes. The ravages of her tears must not show. She refused to leave London with despair plainly written on her face.

It was fury, not despair, that remained on Alex's face as he stomped down the curving staircase toward the entry hall. Penelope's taunt echoed in his mind. "Women!" he mumbled angrily to himself. "Why must they always be either goose-witted fools or hellcats?"

"Do you know, dear, that your father used to mumble to himself in just that same way when he was vexed with me?"

Alex abruptly stopped in mid-step. His mother was standing amid all of the scattered luggage in the hall. Amelia noticed his black frown and commented, "I vow you are a thoughtless son. I travel all the way from Ashford, over perfectly shocking roads, and am greeted with only a scowl. Perhaps I am not welcome," she teased lightly. She handed her traveling cloak to a hovering maid. "Dear, you really must give the Prince Regent a scold about the odious condition of the pikes. I was rattled and jolted into a fatigue."

Alex's frown lifted. He came quickly down the stairs and gave his mother an affectionate hug. There was a shadow of fatigue in her face, to be sure, but not enough

200

to mask completely her renewed spirit. She had not looked so well since his father's death. He wondered what had put the glint of enthusiasm back into her expression.

After greetings were exchanged, Amelia glanced around the cluttered hall and inquired. "Whom are all these trunks for? Are you departing?"

"No, Penelope is returning to Ashford."

"A wife belongs with her husband, Alex," his mother insisted. Shrewd eyes met his. "Why is she being sent to the country?" Amelia demanded softly, but insistently.

Alex was uncomfortable under her scrutiny. He had never been able to hide the truth from his mother. "We thought it best that she return and companion you for a space." He continued a bit lamely, "We were concerned about your health."

"How considerate of you, dear," his mother commented with a knowing smile. "However, as you can see, I am here and in good health. Penelope's trip is unnecessary. In fact, I fear I must insist that she not leave London. She is most urgently needed here."

"Mother, do not try and cozen me. What the deuce is all this nonsense about? Why are you in London?"

His mother regally ignored his question as the great knocker sounded. "I believe the answer has arrived. Do answer the door, Alex. The noise of the clapper quite makes me wish for my vinaigrette."

Without waiting for a footman to appear, Alex yanked open the door. A demurely dressed young miss was standing on the step. Her enormous pansy-brown eyes peeked up at him. Ebony ringlets bobbed out from under her straw poke bonnet as she dropped into a deep curtsy.

"Alex, for heaven's sake," his mother requested, "do let the child come in. Her carriage was separated from mine in this dreadful London traffic. I daresay she felt she would never arrive safely."

Alex stared at the young miss as she walked past him into the hall. Kate, Penelope's maid from Ashford, followed carrying three hatboxes and a beaver traveling coat. There was something vaguely familiar about the chit, but he could not place her. He gave his mother an inquiring glance.

"Alex, where are your manners? Surely, you remember your cousin Leticia. Bid her welcome."

Leticia, of course, he should have known. It had been five years since he had seen his Aunt Isabella's eldest daughter; still he ought not to have forgotten. He made an elegant bow over her hand. Her eyes shyly fluttered up to meet his for the briefest of moments, then she lowered her gaze. Her whispered greeting was so low he could hardly hear it. Lovely child, but no spirit, he decided. Already he felt slightly bored.

Amelia allowed time for the mumbled pleasantries to be exchanged, then ordered, "Kate, please show Leticia upstairs. Put her in the rose chamber. Also find Lady Ashford and tell her to stop this ridiculous packing." Her eyes met her son's. She smiled serenely. "She will not be leaving for Ashford after all."

Sharp questions were on the tip of Alex's tongue, but he restrained himself. "Mother, I am sure you must be weary. Why don't you join me for a glass of lemonade while all this mess is cleared away?" He turned to an under-footman and issued orders for all of Penelope's trunks to be returned upstairs and the traveling carriages to be unloaded. "Please have Hemnings come in with some iced lemonade when he arrives back from the mews." He offered his arm to his mother and escorted her into the study.

When she was comfortably seated on the settee, Alex demanded, "You know, Mother, that I am always delighted to see you, but may I ask why you have suddenly popped up in London? It does seem a bit unusual." A suspicion grew. "Did Penelope write and tell you I was sending her back to Ashford?"

"Were you sending her back, dear? I sincerely hope not. Bad ton, you know, to exile one's wife during the season. The old tabbies do love to gossip about such things." Alex began a strong denial. Amelia raised her hand to stop him. "You are so like your dear father. He used to get that same indignant look when I was twitting him. I know that Penelope was returning merely to keep me company. Alex, do be seated. Your pacing is making me dizzy."

Alex threw himself down in the armchair. He tried again. "Mother, why did you bring Leticia to London? I assume you did bring her, even though you arrived in separate coaches."

"Yes, of course I brought her. It would have been highly improper for her to travel here alone. It seems that the poor child gets ill from the swaying, no matter how well sprung the coach, so I thought it wise not to try and crowd into one carriage. Besides, mine was full of hampers from your Ashford tenants. They were most delighted to get ride of that odious bailiff and sent you some choice meats and vegetables as a thank you. To be honest, I expect they poached the salmon from Buxley's creek, but I did not inquire too closely into the matter."

There was a slight bite to Alex's words as he commented, "All of this is fascinating, Mother, however, you still have not told me why you are here."

"Alex dear, do not be a dullard. It should be obvious we are here so Leticia can enjoy the remainder of the season."

"What a hum!" he insisted. "That schoolroom miss does not look old enough to be out yet."

"She is almost eighteen. It is time for her to be presented."

Alex studied his mother's face. She looked back at him

with an innocent smile. The story sounded a bit too convenient. "The season is almost over. Why could the chit not wait until next year?"

"I fear that was not possible. You see, Squire Randall's son, Isabella and Jasper's neighbor to the north, was becoming most particular in his attentions to Leticia. The Randall estates are heavily encumbered, so they could not favor the match. They thought it best that Leticia be removed to London for a spell."

Alex got up and started pacing again. "Why were you saddled with the chit? Jasper has a London house, why did her parents not bring her?"

"Isabella is not feeling the thing."

"Mother." Alex's voice was stern. "My dear aunt has been moaning and groaning about her weak constitution since as long as I can remember. No doubt she will outlive us all. Why do you let her impose on you?"

"It is not an imposition on me," she reassured him. "I am quite well and will enjoy a brief romp in town. My beloved Robert would say it is time I put off my widow's weeds. Naturally, I cannot escort Leticia to all of the routs, but Penelope can act as her chaperon when I am not able to attend, and of course you will lend her your countenance at Almack's. I believe we will brush through nicely."

"Almack's! That insipid bore!" Alex scoffed. "I have not been there since my first season in London."

"It will do you good to get out of those gambling hells you favor and back into polite society. Surely you can not object to escorting your lovely bride and cousin to a few ton parties." Alex started to argue. His mother smiled sweetly and continued without pause. "Your impetuous marriage to Penelope obviously must mean yours is a love match. I would think you would enjoy squiring her. Isn't that true, dear. I would fret if things were not well between you."

Alex looked at his mother. She really was such a love. She must not worry about the state of his marriage. He and Penelope would simply have to pretend all was well while she was about. He gave her his assurance, then commented, "Your arrival does solve a mystery. I wondered what Mr. Carling was concealing. I shall have to have a word with my secretary when he returns."

"Alex, you must not roast him. He was only doing what I requested. I asked him not to tell you I was coming until all the plans were set. He was most helpful and—"

Amelia's defense of Mr. Carling was interrupted by a rap on the door. Hemnings entered with the iced lemonade. As the butler set the tray down on the table, Motley bounded in through the open door and jumped up against Alex's leg. He barked a shrill greeting.

The dowager laughed at his antics and asked, "Who is your friend?"

"Motley!" Alex growled as he gathered the barking pup into his arms and endeavored to keep him from licking his face.

"I can see that!" Amelia chuckled.

"No, his name is Motley," Alex explained. "Appropriate, is it not?"

"Perfect," his mother agreed.

Alex sat beside his mother on the settee and introduced, "We call him Mott for short. Mott, this is my mother."

The little dog cocked his head as he studied Amelia, then he laid a gentle paw on her knee and yelped. She laughed again and ruffled the short curly fur on his head. "He is a charmer. Where did he come from?"

She was greatly amused when Alex related the story of Mott's rescue. When the tale was complete, Amelia observed, "Always knew Penelope had a lot of spirit."

"Spirit!" Alex snapped. "What she did was goose-witted! She showed no sense whatsoever. Do you realize she had on that wacking big turquoise and diamond necklace when she forced her way among those ruffians?"

His mother calmly patted the dog. "Surely that is a small matter. I venture to say that Penelope would far rather lose the necklace and save the dog."

Alex threw up his hands. "You are both balmy!" He put Motley down on the floor and ordered him to stay. "You must be fatigued, Mother. Let me escort you up to your suite. I will have a word with Penelope, then I shall send her to you, so you two can plan what ton parties and musicales you wish Leticia to attend."

Kate brought Penelope the good news that she was not leaving for Ashford. She was delighted to have Kate's cheery face around her once more and glowed when she heard she would not have to leave Alex. Penelope's smiles were warm, yet the maid had no trouble detecting the telltale shadows under her mistress's eyes. Kate suspected things were still amiss between the Ashfords.

The maid was brushing out Penelope's long hair and telling her all the latest gossip from the country when Alex's knock came. Kate was dismissed and Penelope stood up to face her husband. She expected him to be furious that she was not to leave London, instead she saw concern on his face. Alex cleared his throat. "Penelope, we are in a damnable coil."

"We?" she asked with a tilt of her head.

"I said we and that is precisely what I meant!" he insisted. "You are my wife and we must deal with this particular problem together."

"Since when is a visit from your mother a problem? I thought you were fond of her, or is it Leticia? Do you object to introducing her to your tonnish friends?"

Alex ignored her barbed questions. "Mother insists she

206

is well, but I doubt she is as strong as she pretends. We must do nothing to overset her." He stared at his wife. His eyes were serious. He cleared his throat again. "She believes our marriage to be a love match. I realize only too well that you hold me in aversion, but I am asking you to pretend wifely affection as long as my mother is here. When she leaves, we can continue to go our separate ways."

Tears gathered behind Penelope's lashes. If only she did hold Alex in aversion, things would be so much easier. Instead of pretense, it could be real and . . . it was hopeless! She turned her back on him and walked to the bay window overlooking the back garden. He must not see her tears. She pretended to look at the rose garden until her eyes dried.

When Penelope was sure of her voice, she turned to confront her husband again. "I am very fond of your mother and do not want her hurt, or disillusioned. I will play the attentive spouse, as you ask." She raised her chin. "I expect you to do the same. Amelia is no fool. If she sees you flaunting your mistress in public, she is bound to suspect the truth. Lady Shellingham is a rather obvious flirt."

Alex's eyes narrowed dangerously. He, too, was wearying of Millicent's clinging attentions, but he resented Penelope always dragging his mistress into every conversation. Angrily he turned to leave. "Lady Shellingham is not the only one who is indiscreet. You had best tell your violet-giving gallant to be more circumspect as well!" He was at the door when he ordered, "My mother wishes to see you. Do not keep her waiting."

It took several moments for Penelope to compose herself. She did not want to give Amelia further cause for worry. When she finally went to her mother-in-law's chamber, their reunion was most pleasant. She filled Penelope in on all the details about Earnest's embezzlement and gave her the latests news about Dick Thomas and his family, and the doings at the vicarage. Penelope listened to her happy chatter, then asked, "Is this tale about Leticia's involvement with some squire's son merely an excuse to prolong my stay in London, or was there truly a romance between them? Kate made it sound as if they were ready to fly to Gretna Green at any moment."

Amelia's eyes twinkled. "Kate always did have an overly romantic soul."

"Do you mean there is no squire's son?"

The dowager laughed. "Squire Randall definitely has a son, but I must confess I stretched the truth a bit when I told Alex there was a romance. At least, I should say, Leticia is not romantically involved. The trouble, you see, is that she has a fatally tender heart and cannot bear to cast this young man down, so he sits in her pocket. His attentions were becoming quite a nuisance. I suggested to Jasper and Isabella that it might be wise for Leticia to be removed to London for a spell."

"I am sorry your sister was not able to accompany Leticia," Penelope commented sympathetically. "Kate tells me she is unwell. How sad to miss her daughter's bow."

"Phoo! The only thing that truly ails Isabella is her desire to be pampered and coddled! She takes to her couch more often than your pup wags his scruffy tail. But since my dear sister fancies herself an invalid, and would never make the trip to London, I felt it was my duty to chaperon Leticia." The dowager looked off innocently into space. "Naturally, I knew you would have to stay here to help me."

"Amelia, you are a fraud!" said Penelope with a laugh.

"Yes." She smiled contentedly. "I know. Alex has too much family loyalty to send you back to Ashford when his cousin needs your sponsorship. Have Kate fetch the *Gazette* and your pile of invitation cards; we must plan Leticia's social debut."

CHAPTER FOURTEEN

The last few weeks of the London season spun down in a merry round of balls, drums, musicales, and card parties. Leticia's first introduction to the ton came on Wednesday when Alex escorted them to Almack's. The few days before that important night were spent shopping. Mademoiselle Geneviève created a gown for Leticia in a soft rose damask. The square neckline, as befitting a marriageable girl, was demure. The only decorative accents were dainty bows that peeped out from the gathers on the Mameluke sleeves. A simple strand of pearls was the only jewelry they decided Leticia need wear.

Penelope was very pleased with her newfound cousin. Leticia was undoubtedly shy, but once at ease she had a wonderful sense of humor and a warm, caring nature. Her wide brown eyes would light at the sight of a child, and she adored Motley. Penelope knew it was going to be fun sharing the remaining days of the season with her. Alex's hovering attention also pleased her. As long as Amelia was present, he was the picture of the perfect husband. It was easy to forget it was only a sham.

Alex tried to resist escorting them to Almack's, but his mother insisted. He refused to endure what he knew would be an insipid evening alone. James was pressed to join them. The two friends met at White's the day before the party. James was sitting in the famous bow window, sipping a brandy, when Alex entered the club. "Aha, just the man I need to see. James, old boy, what are you doing tomorrow evening?"

211

"Thought I might visit Vauxhall Gardens to hear that new songbird, Madame Cecily. Brummell says she is an incomparable. Have no ear for music, you know, but always like to shop the new talent."

"Madame Cecily can wait. I need your support at Almack's."

James was appalled at the thought. "Alex, have you got bats in your cockloft? Haven't been caught for Almack's since my cousin Drusilla came out. Perfectly dreadful place! That Constance Buxley is sure to be there throwing lures at me. The girl is a born antidote! No, Alex, I won't risk it!"

Alex smiled at his friend's sputtering refusal. "James, have a bit of imagination. Almack's is the perfect place to cast off the persistent Miss Buxley. You can spend the evening dancing attendance to my cousin Leticia. She is a fetching little thing. That should convince Miss Buxley that her hopes are dashed."

"No, Alex!" He was adamant. "She'd think I was merely doing my duty as your friend. It would never work. She is the stubbornest of creatures! Not even one of Wellington's cannons would make an impact on her. Will just have to hide until the season is over." James shuddered. "Every time I set foot at any ton rout, she latches onto me like a leech." He wrinkled his nose in distaste. "Quite puts one off all women!"

"Surely not all women!" Alex laughed. "You like Penelope and I know you will like Leticia. She is as quiet and refined as Constance Buxley is odiously brash. Tell you what," Alex urged, "you come and help squire Leticia, and I will contrive to draw off the clinging Miss Buxley."

"How?" his friend asked skeptically.

Alex smiled. "It ought to be easy. I will introduce your antidote to Basil Gilroy. He is looking to increase his jointure. All I have to do is casually drop a word in his ear about Miss Buxley's expectations; that should prick his interest. They might even make a match of it. He will like her money; she will adore his title. They suit each other perfectly. Both of them are incredibly shocking bores!" He nodded. "They should get along fine. Will you come?"

"I suppose so," James agreed grudgingly. "But your cousin had best be as fetching as you claim!"

James was not disappointed; he was not disappointed at all with the gentle Leticia! Alex had invited him to dine with the family on Wednesday before the ball at Almack's. He had arrived early and found Leticia in the salon. She was a bit flustered at being alone with a strange man, but his elegant bow reassured her. Her soft brown eyes fluttered tentatively upward and she smiled. Leticia thought he was wondrously handsome with his high-point collar that brushed his cheeks, the velvet coat, and the black knee breeches. Alex's dark roguish looks always daunted her. She could never be at ease with him, but James was different. His friendly smile met hers. The tinge of her pink blush matched the rose of her gown. For once, she did not feel the least bit shy. When Alex and Penelope arrived, the two were busily chatting like old friends. The dinner, which featured the salmon that had been poached from Buxley's creek, was superb. It was a merry group that headed for the dance.

Almack's glittered with candles as they entered the famed marriage mart. After an introduction from Penelope Lady Jersey had issued the coveted voucher to Leticia. When her sponsor saw them enter, she rushed forward with a greeting. Lady Jersey took Alex's cousin around and made the appropriate introductions. Too soon for James's pleasure, Leticia's card was filled with partners. He was only able to secure one quadrille with her, and a promise to share the late-night buffet.

True to his word, when Alex spotted Basil Gilroy enter Almack's, he made his way across the floor and engaged him in conversation. James had valiently tried to avoid the Buxleys, but still Lady Buxley had managed to snare him for a dance with her daughter. All his thoughts, however, were with Leticia as he led Constance through the intricate steps.

Alex casually gestured toward the couple, as he commented to Gilroy, "I see Harrington has Miss Buxley on his arm again tonight. Heard it was on the betting books at White's that he will make an offer. Doesn't seem fair, does it, Gilroy, for him to wed such a tidy fortune? James is already comfortably plump in the pockets." He cast a quick glance at his prey. "Too bad her hand cannot go to someone in need of a wealthy wife."

Alex almost laughed at the speed with which Basil ended their conversation and plunged off through the crowd in search of the suddenly appealing Miss Buxley. He turned his attention back to the swirling dancers and frowned when he saw his wife in the arms of a young man dressed in a dashing military uniform. A flashing smile lighted Penelope's face as her partner bent nearer and whispered something to her. How different she looks, thought Alex, from the drab miss who confronted me in the Buxley alcove. Alex leaned against the wall and stared at his wife. Suddenly he felt angry that she was dancing with another man, that she was smiling at someone else. The music stopped, he made his way through the milling crowd toward her. A man Alex did not recognize claimed her hand for the next dance. As he turned, Alex saw the fob dangling from his watch chain. It was painted with violets. Was this Penelope's gallant? In a rage he stomped between them and muttered, "Sorry, old boy, but Lady Ashford has reserved this waltz for me." Without a second glance at the startled man, Alex took her in his arms and they whirled away.

"Alex, are you demented?" Penelope gasped. "That is Lady Jersey's cousin!"

"I don't care if he is the duke of York, he is not going to waltz with you!"

"But why? How can you be so stubborn, when you do not even know him? Lady Jersey said he has just arrived from a long tour in India. After the way you acted, he must think the ton has become quite mad while he was gone! What must he think?"

Nor did Alex know what to think. He said nothing, but his grasp became firmer as he pulled Penelope more tightly to him. Why does he persist in making a bloody fool of himself over such nonsense? These fits of unreasoning anger were ridiculous! It must be Millicent, he decided. Their increasingly frequent arguments had to be the cause of his ill temper and vague dissatisfaction with everything. Lady Shellingham's jealous tantrums in public were wearying, and the one time they had met since Chester's return had ended not with a kiss, but with another angry scene. He had slammed out and had not tried to see her again, even though Millicent's heavily perfumed notes had repeatedly begged him to come back to her. Yes, that must be it; he was out of patience with Millicent. What other possible explanation could there be?

Once Alex had solved the mystery to his satisfaction, he relaxed and enjoyed the feel of holding his wife close in his arms. Penelope saw his thoughtful frown. She did not attempt to speak until it lifted, then she observed in a light teasing tone, "I pray Lady Jersey's cousin does not call you out. He looked a trifle angry when you threw a spoke through his wheel."

Alex smiled down at her. "If he calls anyone out, it should be you. This was really all your fault, you know."

"What?" she sputtered.

"Yes, your fault! You should not have promised him one of my waltzes. The man was stepping on my prerogative." Penelope started to argue. Alex ignored her protest as he continued, "I assumed you had saved all of your waltzes for me, as you did at the Jersey's rout. I was merely claiming what was mine."

Penelope could not stop the small thrill that came with his words. He must care a little if he insisted on dancing every waltz with her. For the rest of the ball Alex was very attentive. He stayed near her side as they waltzed away the hours and joined James and Leticia for the buffet. Penelope savored every minute of his presence. There was an extra sparkle to her laughter that evening.

The days that followed were the happiest Penelope had had since her parents' death. Alex was always there, always charming, always devilish appealing. He seemed truly to enjoy her company as they toured the maze at Hampton Court, waltzed again at the Castlereaghs' ball, rode in the Row, and visited Vaux' 'l Gardens. Everything would have been perfect, had not a few small incidents ruffled the happiness of her days.

James had become as attentive as Alex, but his interest was Leticia, not Penelope. He was a constant visitor at Grosvenor Square, dropping by on the flimsiest of excuses, or often for no excuse at all. Alex was used to his friend's presence and did not notice that his visits had become much more frequent, but Penelope did, and she was pleased. James had started taking tea with them in the afternoon. Alex was seldom there at that time of the day; he was surprised when he returned home unexpectedly and found James sitting in the drawing room with Penelope. Leticia had gone up to her chamber to fetch her embroidery frame. Alex's eyebrows raised when he found the two were alone. He stayed and joined them for a cup of tea, but the atmosphere remained somewhat frosty. Only when Leticia returned did he unbend a bit.

Alex's temper was tried again when he returned to Grosvenor Square and found James dancing in the music room with Penelope. They were not alone this time. Leticia was playing the pianoforte, yet Alex still was irritated. He took one look at his wife in the arms of his best friend and commented, "James, old boy, have you been evicted from your dwellings? Every time I come home, I find you underfoot!"

He said the words in half jest, but Penelope could detect the thread of anger underneath. Quickly she intervened before James could answer. "Please come in, Alex. James is being kind enough to teach us the latest minuet pattern from the French court. Isn't that thoughtful of him?"

"Very! Pray continue."

Penelope noted the flash of resentment in Alex's eyes. She did not want a rift to develop between the two men. "Leticia, why don't you show Alex the step, while I play," she suggested as she moved away from James's embrace. "You dance so much more prettily than I."

Leticia blushed rosily as she moved toward James. His eyes softened as he drew her into his arms. Penelope's fingers touched the keys and she began to play. A sigh escaped from her as she watched the two move through the stately motions. They were so much in love. If only Alex would look at her like that.

Alex's quarrelsome temper finally exploded on the night they were to return for another Wednesday romp at Almack's. Alex was dressed in the traditional knee breeches and was waiting in the study for the ladies to descend. Mademoiselle Geneviève had designed a gown for Penelope that complemented the Ashford amethysts. Penelope swirled the skirt out as she turned before the mirror. It was the loveliest dress yet. The gown was done in a soft purple that matched perfectly the color of the jewels. The fabric itself was simple, but there were sprays of violets embroidered on it to add interest and texture. She gaily swept down the staircase and entered the study with a smile. She knew the gown was vastly becoming on her.

Alex took one glance at his wife. His fingers tightened harshly on the stem of his port glass. He remembered the gallant's bouquet of violets. Was Penelope deliberately wearing the gown as an unspoken token of this mysterious man? His voice was hoarse with anger as he ordered, "You will not appear in that dress! Take it off immediately!"

The smile died on Penelope's lips. "But why?" she cried.

"Penelope, either you take it off, or I will help you!" Alex took one menacing step toward her. Penelope turned and ran from the room.

Amelia was watching the scene from the doorway. "Have you run mad, Alex? The child looked perfectly lovely in the gown."

Alex walked across the room and poured himself a drop more of port. He refused to meet his mother's questioning eyes. When she demanded an answer, he muttered, "I can't abide violets!" Without another word he slammed down his port glass and stalked out of the room.

His mother stared after him with a perplexed frown, then she gathered up her skirt and went up to Penelope's bedchamber. Tears glittered on the ends of her daughter-in-law's lashes as she ordered Kate to unlace the gown. It crumpled to the floor in a discarded heap as Amelia entered the room. "Kate, I will help Lady Ashford change. Please go and attend Leticia."

When they were alone, she demanded, "What was that stuff and nonsense all about? All Alex would tell me is that he hates violets. I know there is more to the story than

218

that!" She looked at Penelope. "You have not been playing Alex false, have you, child?"

"Oh, no!" Penelope vowed. "How could you think that?" Tearfully she told her the story of the Jersey's ball, her bouquet of violets, and the hum she had told Alex about who gave her the flowers. She was stunned when Amelia burst out laughing.

"My child, why do you look so forlorn? This is absolutely delicious!"

"Do you think it is delicious that Alex is furious with me?" Penelope sniffled. "I think it is dreadful!"

"Penelope, you are being a slow top! Alex would only be angry if he were jealous. You have him guessing, and that is putting him into a spin. I know my son. He does not like insipid misses. I also know he was never the least bit jealous over any of his ladybirds. He may not know it yet, but he is attracted."

Amelia's words gave Penelope much to think about as she redressed for Almack's. For the first time in a long spell Penelope allowed herself to hope.

The last ball of the season was to be the Cowpers' masquerade in honor of the duke of Wellington. On the night before this final rout the Ashfords went to the opera to hear a new Italian diva. When they returned home, Alex suggested they play a few hands of whist. He was warm in his praise of Penelope's bidding and skilled play. The cards were with them. They thoroughly trounced Amelia and Leticia. It did not matter. Amelia was delighted that Alex and Penelope were enjoying each other's company, and all of Leticia's thoughts were with James. They hardly noticed or cared that the points were piling up against them.

When Penelope raked in the last trick, Amelia commented, "Do not deal another round, my dear. I am fatigued. The thought of my bed is most inviting. I do want to be rested enough to enjoy tomorrow night's party."

"Yes, Mother, I know," teased Alex. "You always did have a weakness for the duke. Father used to get quite miffed when you would rave on about Wellington's exploits."

"Alex, do be still!" His mother laughed. "Robert knew I loved no one else. You must confess that our national hero does cut a dashing figure. My old heart is not the only one that flutters when he marches into a room."

While Amelia and Leticia started upstairs, Alex helped Penelope fold away the gaming table and chairs. "Are you for White's tonight?" she politely asked.

Her husband stretched lazily. "No, I think not. Playing cards has held little appeal for me lately, although I must admit I enjoyed tonight's game."

"We did seem to have the devil's own luck, did we not?" admitted Penelope with a smile.

Alex stared at her with a roguish gleam. "What is the old adage: lucky at cards, unlucky at love. Maybe that is our problem," he jested.

Two hot splotches of color appeared high on Penelope's cheekbones. "Would you prefer it the other way, milord? I should think you would detest losing at faro."

He raised one dark eyebrow. "I do not intend to lose at either one," he paused, then added silkily, "Lady Ashford."

Penelope's heart raced as she heard the passion under his words. She did not want to leave his side, yet this conversation must cease! With apparent calm she walked to the sideboard. "Alex, would you care for a cup of coffee? I fancy a glass of ratafia, but I know you do not care for it." She poured a cup of coffee from the pot that had been warming on the brazier. Serenely she met his gaze. "Might we talk a spell? There is a bill up in Parliament that I wish to ask about."

A sardonic smile touched the corner of Alex's lips, as he settled himself in an armchair. Her businesslike prattle did not fool him for a moment. "Certainly, my dear, what is your bluestocking little mind interested in this time?"

She was too concerned with the issue to bristle at his tone. "One does not have to be a bluestocking to care about children. What chance does your bill, restricting the use of child labor, have of passing through the House of Lords?"

"How the deuce did you know about that?" he demanded.

With a glance toward his cluttered desk she admitted, "I read your speech on the issue."

For a moment his temper flared, then he was forced to laugh. "That ought to teach me to keep my comments under key until they are ready to be delivered. I am glad you are not a spy. I would not want the large factory owners to know of my bill until I can back up my allegations with some more evidence."

"Might I make a suggestion?" Penelope ventured. "Papa always said that one good example was of more value than all the words man can speak. Why not find one or two children who have truly suffered under the system's abuses, and show them to your fellow Lords? They could scarce ignore that type of evidence."

Alex pondered the notion. He held out his hand. "Why don't you tip a bit more coffee into my cup, and we can discuss your idea." He relaxed back in the chair and enjoyed the spirited interchange that developed. Never before had he argued politics with a woman. Women were for other, more personal moments. It was a novel evening's diversion, one, he was forced to admit, he could unexpectedly take pleasure in. He was impressed anew with Penelope's wit and deep caring.

The hours passed as the debate continued. Finally a scratching at the door told them Motley had come to find out why Penelope had not come up to bed. He frisked about their heels as they slowly walked up the curving staircase.

Outside the door to Penelope's suite they stopped. Alex's eyes were warm with a sensuous light. He picked up her hand and raised it to his lips. The soft kiss brushed her tingling skin. He turned her hand over and lingeringly nuzzled her palm. That familiar weakness flooded through her body at his touch. He raised his eyes and searched across her face. His voice was husky as he murmured, "Must you always deny my luck at love, fair lady?"

"Perhaps not . . . always," she whispered.

They stared at each other another long moment. He kissed her hand again and turned toward his own suite. The doubts pounded through her head as Kate helped her change for bed. What would she have done if he had entered the chamber with her? Did she have any resistance left? She dismissed the maid and climbed into bed. As the darkness enveloped her, she wondered if the connecting door would open. Her sleep was fitful that night, as if she were listening for the knob to turn. In the pale light of the morning Penelope did not know if she were relieved, or saddened, that she had remained undisturbed.

Alex had some business to transact with his barrister concerning Earnest's embezzlement, so he had asked Lord and Lady Jersey to escort the ladies to the Cowpers' ball. He promised to join the party later. At Grosvenor Square Leticia was in an excited fever over the preparations for the route. "Aren't masquerades the most thrilling thing?" she giggled as she tried on first one domino, and then another. She held a purple mask over her face and flut-

222

tered her eyelashes. "One can flirt outrageously and never feel the least bit shy."

In a teasing voice Penelope asked, "Might there be one special beau you wish to flirt with?"

Her cousin blushed rosily. "Indeed there might be! I shan't tell you who, though. He has not come up to scratch yet."

"I vow he will," Penelope reassured her. "I have never seen a more smitten case!"

They both laughed with delight and gave each other a quick hug. She tied the strings of Leticia's domino in place and went to fetch her own. Mademoiselle Geneviève had designed a mask out of the same material as her dress. Penelope fingered the raised palmette design woven into the sapphire brocade fabric. This was the last of the ball gowns the seamstress had made to match the Ashford jewels. Next season they would have to create a new idea to keep her in the first stare of fashion. Kate pinned the sapphire sunburst clip in her hair and fastened the necklace in place. There was a large sapphire ring to match the set, but Penelope preferred to wear only her wedding band. She stared down at the entwined lover's knots. They symbolized the bond of husband to wife. In their marriage Penelope knew only she was bound, not by the vows, but by love. She pushed the sad thought away and tied the blue domino in place. No regrets were going to mar this evening. She intended to enjoy the final ball of the season.

Motley romped down the marble staircase beside Penelope, as the great knocker thudded through the entry hall. Penelope picked him up and admonished, "I wish Lady Jersey to see that you are mended, but you must behave yourself." She shook a finger at him. "None of that yipping and jumping you do whenever Alex comes home."

The little dog pranced out to the Jerseys' carriage and issued a sharp bark when the footman was slow to open the door. Once the step was lowered, he bounded inside and hopped up on the seat beside Sally. She petted him and fussed over his recovery, while he acted like the perfect gentleman dog. Between strokes Lady Jersey introduced the mongrel pup to her husband. They all dissolved in laughter when Motley politely held out his paw and Lord Jersey solemnly shook it. Amelia and Leticia finally arrived. Penelope handed Mott out of the coach to the waiting Hemnings. They could hear his unhappy barks as the coachman snapped the whip, and they rumbled off toward the Cowpers' mansion.

The music was already playing as they made their way toward the ballroom. After an introduction and curtsy to the Duke of Wellington, they walked down the staircase and joined the swirling dancers. The moment they reached the floor James appeared at Leticia's side. They joined a country set that was forming. Penelope stayed with Amelia through that set, and got her comfortably settled among the other dowagers, before she accepted a dance with Beau Brummell.

Beau's witty chatter was entertaining as always. He caught her up on all of the latest gossip in the ton, then commented, "We must think of a new way for you to dazzle society." He nodded his head toward a woman in a green gown to match her emeralds. "Already your jewel-tone gowns are being copied. I always did say Lady Shellingham had no originality."

Penelope missed a step. Why did Millicent have to be here to make a muddle of things? She peeked over her shoulder to see if Alex had arrived and was at her rival's side. With relief she saw he was not. Beau noted her glance. He did so love to set things in a spin.

Lord Jersey was her next partner. When their cotillion was over, he and Penelope walked over to where Lady Jersey was holding court. Sally was regaling her admirers with the story of Motley's antics, when a deep voice at her elbow interrupted. "A most engaging dog to be sure, but a masquerade ball is a night for lovers, not for tales of mongrel pups. Might I beg an introduction to the lovely blue domino beside you."

At the sound of his voice Penelope's eyes flew upward. A black mask covered his eyes, but there was no mistaking Alex's voice or his broad shoulders. Lady Jersey giggled. She knew full well who the speaker was, but she played out the charade. "It seems you have a most impatient, as well as mysterious, beau, milady. Sir domino in black, may I present the lady in sapphire."

Alex bowed over Penelope's hand. As on the night before his kiss was warm and lingering as his lips moved over the back of her hand. Every nerve was aflutter as he pulled her into his arms and they waltzed off. His embrace was demanding as they whirled across the floor. Casting caution aside, Penelope snuggled closer in his arms and let her feelings rule. The waltz ended. Alex did not leave her side. A quadrille was next. He maintained the flirtatious banter as the pattern repeatedly brought them together, then pulled them apart. The interchanges were fun. Penelope found herself flirting outrageously with her own husband. The domino covering her face made it easy to play the coquette. Dance after dance followed. He never let another partner take her hand. The opening notes of a waltz began, and she was once more held tightly in his embrace. There was no conversation this time, just sensuous feeling, as his hand moved in possessive strokes across her back, and then down to caress her waist. Alex pulled her yet nearer. She came willingly. A light kiss brushed her hair as the music ceased. They were at the end of the ballroom. Without a word Alex drew her through the French doors and out onto the terrace.

A full moon softly lighted the flagstones as they walked

to the far stone balustrade. Penelope turned to face him. Climbing roses arched up over the railing. They scented the air around the couple with their heady fragrance. The moonlight, the roses, Alex's touch, it was all too much. Penelope could fight no longer. Alex's strong hands encircled her waist. The warmth pulsed through his fingers and sent tingling waves through her body. His voice was deep with desire. "You have the most enticing lips, my domino in sapphire." Dark eyes glittered through the slits in his mask. Slowly Alex reached up and untied the strings of Penelope's domino. It fell to the flagstones. His hand caressed her neck and moved up to touch her flushed cheeks. A finger softly caressed the line of her trembling lips. His eyes searched her face. As he lowered his head toward her, he murmured, "I do believe lady luck is smiling kindly on us tonight!"

The touch of his lips was gentle, almost teasing. Alex lightly brushed her lips with his, kissed a corner of her mouth, then nibbled on her ear. The pleasurable torment went on and on until he finally claimed her mouth again. His kiss demanded surrender. There were no defenses left. Penelope's hands came up to his chest, not to push him away, but to urge him closer. Her lips parted under his. His victory was complete.

Long moments later he released her. Penelope's head fell back against his shoulder. Her eyes were dark with desire. A satisfied smile curved one edge of his mouth, as he stared down at his wife.

"Shocking, absolutely shocking, or at least decidedly racy!" A familiar voice chuckled behind them. "What the deuce will Lady Ashford say?"

Penelope's voice called over her husband's shoulder, "Lady Ashford will say it is positively delightful."

"Knew it was you all the time, milady." The Prince Regent laughed. Alex moved slightly away from Penelope, but his arm remained around her waist, as Prinny continued to chatter on. "I heard a tale, Lady Ashford, that your trip back from our picnic at Brighton was most exciting. Please join me for dinner, and tell me all about this smashing rescue."

He held out his arm graciously to Penelope. As they re-entered the ballroom and started toward the buffet table, he commented, "I am quite awed by your bravery, Lady Ashford. Wellington could have used you at Waterloo! You must tell me how it all happened."

They were chatting together easily, as their path took them past Lady Shellingham. An angry frown distorted her face when she saw Penelope on the prince's arm. Millicent tapped her foot impatiently. She had not missed the attentions Alex was paying to his wife. She wanted an explanation. Disregarding discretion, she reached out and grabbed Alex's arm. In a fierce whisper she demanded, "I want a word with you!"

His mouth became a hard line as he towered over her. He glanced down at her clinging hand. "Not now, milady. I must join the prince for dinner."

Millicent's fingers plucked at his sleeve. "When, Alex, when? I must see you. I must talk with you!" There was a rising note of hysteria in her voice. "Why are you avoiding me? Alex, I—"

A thunderous scowl clouded his eyes. Rudely he yanked his arm from her grasp. "Millicent, you are acting like an ill-bred shrew." He turned to follow the prince and Penelope into the dining room.

Her hands reached out desperately and caught his arm again. Others around them were beginning to take notice of the scene. Alex's eyes blazed as he whirled around to face her. "Hell and damnation!" he cursed under his breath. "Will you leave me alone!"

"Alex, please," she pleaded. "You must see me!" Milli-

cent's green eyes flashed. "If you don't, I swear I will
. . ." Tears choked her words. "I swear I will . . ."

He refused to tolerate any more of her jealous tantrums.
"Millicent, stop making a cake of yourself! The whole ton
will be gossiping if you don't stop that ridiculous whining!" She started her pleading again. In exasperation he
muttered, "Oh, devil take it! If you will halt this infernal
fuss, I will meet you on the terrace after the dancing begins
again. Until then, show a little breeding. Try and be discreet!"

Luckily, Penelope was unaware of the meeting between
Millicent and her husband. The dinner for her was a
smashing success. Everyone was enchanted with her story
of Motley's rescue. She kept them entertained throughout
the many courses with humorous descriptions of her pup's
capers. The ton approved. Lady Ashford was rapidly
achieving a reputation for not only being in the first stare
of fashion, but also as a charming wit. After the music
began again, the prince honored her by dancing the first
cotillion with her. She was not aware Alex had disappeared.

A waltz began. Penelope looked around expectantly.
Alex did not claim her hand. With a shrug she accepted
Brummell's arm and they whirled out onto the floor. She
was a bit warm when the dance ended. She snapped open
her fan and fluttered it. Beau took the hint and went off
in search of a glass of iced lemonade for her. The breeze
from the open French doors was refreshing as she waited
for his return. Constance Buxley strolled by, sporting
Basil Gilroy on her arm. Her eyes narrowed spitefully
when she saw Penelope standing alone. "Basil," she ordered, "I am thirsty. Fetch me a glass of ratafia and make
sure it is cold!" He meekly scurried away to do her bidding.

Penelope smiled a welcome. She had noticed that Basil

was dancing attendance and was pleased that Constance had finally found a beau. No smile was returned. Instead, Constance sneered in a condescending voice, "Well, Lady Ashford, how are you enjoying being a lofty marchioness? I do hope your title is keeping you warm while your precious husband beds another." Her laugh was cruel. "But then, what more should a vicar's daughter expect?" Constance tossed her head toward the open French doors. "I see his lordship isn't even bothering to be discreet anymore. How the tongues must be wagging!" Constance laughed again and started to move off. "No wonder the marquis did not offer for me. He knew I would never tolerate his continued philandering."

An icy chill gripped Penelope. Surely Constance was only trying to set her in a spin. Surely her words could not be true. They do not warrant a second thought, Penelope weakly tried to reassure herself. Still, she could not stop her step from turning toward the French doors.

The cool breeze swept her face as she stepped out onto the flagstones. Her soft kid slippers made no sound. The moon was high. There were no shadows to conceal her husband. On the spot where Alex had kissed her so passionately earlier in the evening, he now stood beside Millicent. Lady Shellingham's arms were entwined possessively about his neck. Her body was pressed close against him. Penelope could stand no more.

Silently she fled back into the crowded ballroom. The truth pounded through her head. It was all so clear! Alex had set out on a deliberately calculated course of seduction. He wanted an heir and intended her to give him one. Penelope shuddered when she realized how willingly she had almost fallen into his bed. She should have known a rake would never change. Alex wanted to enjoy the favors of both his mistress and his wife!

Her head throbbed painfully as she walked aimlessly

through the crowd. Several people called her name. She did not hear them. Escape—she must escape! Penelope knew she could not bear to see Alex return with the gloating Millicent. A dance was ending. She saw James standing by Leticia on the far side of the ballroom. Quickly she made her way to them. Leticia noticed her white tear-stained face and asked with concern, "Penelope, are you all right? You do not look at all the thing." She searched in her reticule. "Do you need my vinaigrette?"

Penelope summoned up a wan smile. "I fear I have developed a most dreadful headache. James, do you suppose you could escort me home? I do not want Leticia to miss the rest of the ball."

Several questions pestered James. He held his peace. He had seen Alex slip out to follow Millicent and suspected Penelope had also discovered the tryst. Alex is a fool, he thought to himself once again as he offered his arm to his friend's wife. "Leticia, please inform your Aunt Amelia where we have gone. I will see Lady Ashford home, then I shall return." He smiled warmly at her. "When I come back, I hope I will find that you have convinced one of your partners to resign his dance in my favor."

CHAPTER FIFTEEN

Soon after his wife had left the ball, Alex returned from the terrace. The parting from Lady Shellingham had not been pleasant! She had cried, whined, and pleaded until he was quite out of patience with her. He had intended for their last good-byes to be civil. Millicent was not so easily cast off. Subtlety did not work. Finally, he told her bluntly that it was over and stomped away.

Alex was in a thoroughly foul mood as he glanced briefly over the country sets that were forming on the dance floor. He did not see Penelope. Constance and the still-attentive Basil Gilroy were about to join a group of the dancers. She saw Alex standing off to the side. "Come, Basil," she ordered, "we must pay our respects to the marquis of Ashford. He is a neighbor, you know," she bragged proudly. "Our land marches beside his."

Alex's nod was barely polite when Constance came up and greeted him. "Lady Ashford looked quite lovely tonight, milord. It is a pity she had to leave early. I wanted to introduce her to Lord Gilroy."

"Early?" Alex asked with a raised eyebrow.

Constance looked smug. "Yes, milord, she must have been taken ill rather suddenly. I saw her leave with the viscount of Harrington. From the way he was hovering solicitously about her, and from the way she was leaning on his arm, I assumed she was unwell. He seemed most concerned!" She noted his thunderous scowl with pleasure. It was high time the prim vicar's daughter paid for her theft of the marquis. "Pray, let us know how dear

231

Penelope is feeling. She must have been ailing dreadfully, to leave without your lordship." Constance smiled a snide little smile and left Alex to his own raging thoughts.

His wife and his best friend! The idea burned through his mind. Penelope and James taking tea together, dancing together, and now leaving the ball together. Was Penelope playing him false? Why else would she leave? An anger of chilling intensity swept through Alex. James and Penelope! The thought echoed in his head. He pushed roughly through the dancers to where his mother was sitting. His words were clipped, "Mother, we are leaving. Where is Leticia?"

During the ride back to Grosvenor Square James tried to make polite conversation with Penelope. She was too distracted to answer. He fell silent. After what seemed like a vast age, they arrived. Hemnings's face showed a faint trace of disapproval as he opened the door and found his mistress escorted by someone other than Alex. James squeezed her hand in understanding and was gone. She kept her head proudly erect and her eyes dry until Kate was dismissed and she was alone in her bedchamber. Her hands shook as she bolted the connecting door to Alex's room. She half expected him to arrive any moment in a thundering rage. Upon reflection Penelope realized she should never have left the ball with James. It was an indiscretion her husband, and the ton, would not easily forgive. Dejectedly, she sank down on the bed. One hand rubbed her aching forehead and the other wiped away a tear that threatened to fall. Her emotions were in such a muddle! Anger, sadness disillusionment, and fear all battered her heart. Nervously, she waited for Alex's pounding knock on her door. There was nothing, nothing but silence. Hour after hour she waited in the darkness. The silence was greater torture than any scold Alex could have delivered.

At dawn the next morning Penelope crept out of the house and walked to St. George's. The serene interior of the church soothed her. Long hours passed as she sat in the pew and thought about Alex, and their marriage. Did they have a future? She had hoped so many times, only to have those hopes shattered. She truly did not know if she could bear to hope again. Usually the cloistered atmosphere of a church helped her to solve her problems. It failed to help her this day.

Penelope left the church and started back toward the Ashford mansion. There seemed to be no satisfactory answers. Her walk took her down Bond Street. The window displays of fashionable merchandise did not catch her attention, nor did the tonnish crowd strutting up and down in front of the shops. She acknowledged the many bows with a vague nod of her head. She did not stop to chat. Nothing penetrated her misery until a coachman's rude shouts startled her.

She glanced across the street to where an elegant coach and four was standing. A fancy coat of arms was emblazoned on the door of the carriage. The coachman's shouted obscenities shocked her. The burly man was waving a long whip and yelling at a small boy.

"By gaw, wot the bloody 'ell are ye doin'! Sum tiger!" he yelled. "Ye almost let that lead 'oss take a header. Git away, I tell ye, git away!"

When the small boy failed to move fast enough, the man raised his whip and savagely snapped it across his back. The lad stumbled and fell against the horses. The four spirited animals began to shy nervously. The coachman yelled again and raised his whip. He snapped it in the air, barely missing the small boy. The crack of the whip, whistling over their heads, set the horses plunging against their traces. It was bedlam!

The lad bravely tried to grab the reins to calm the horses

down. He was not strong enough to control them. The angry man shouted, "Now see wot ye've done! Git back afore t'osses bolt."

He was raising his whip to strike again, when Penelope, who had hurried across the street, grabbed his arm. She moved protectively in front of the child. Her eyes blazed angrily. "Put that whip down and stop yelling!" she ordered.

The coachman's massive hands grabbed the leather reins. He pulled the plunging horses to a standstill, then turned to glare at her. "Git away from me tiger. All t'fool had to do was 'old the 'osses. Demmed brat!" The lad peeped his head out from behind Penelope's skirts. The man shook a fist at him. "Ye expect a thrashin' when we get back to t'mews!"

The wealthy shoppers gathered to gawk at the altercation. Penelope ignored their snickers, as she vowed, "You shall do nothing of the kind! No one is going to beat this child!"

Lady Jersey walked out of Worth's with two hatboxes in hand and strolled toward the crowd of people. The argument between Penelope and the husky coachman continued at full shout. Sally took one look at the embattled Lady Ashford and hurried to her side. She touched Penelope's arm and urged, "Please come away, Penelope. Everyone in the ton is on Bond Street today. The on-dits will surely fly, if you do not leave right now!"

"No, I shall not! I do not care a jot what the gossip-mongers say. I am not going to let that odious lout beat this child!"

Lady Jersey shook her head in exasperation. "The boy is in his employ. He has a right to discipline him."

"No one has a right to abuse another being. I will not let him take the boy."

Sally quickly assessed the situation. Penelope would not

yield. Any further quarreling would only fuel the talk. How the old tabbies were going to love to gossip about this incident! She turned to the outraged coachman. "Tell your master to settle this matter with Lord Ashford. Until then, the boy shall come with us." Before he could object, she swept regally by. "Come, Lady Ashford. Bring that lad with you. My carriage is waiting at the corner."

Lady Jersey noticed the pungent odor of the unwashed child as they started to climb into the coach. The horsey smell quite put her off. She put a scented handkerchief to her nose and suggested, "I do believe, little boy, that you would enjoy the ride far more if you hopped up there by the footman. Here, you may hold my hatboxes."

She sank down on the plush velvet seats and quizzed Penelope with her lorgnette. What an odd girl Lady Ashford was! Last night she had been a belle of the ton with all the appropriate social graces; today she had gotten involved in this deplorable debacle. One simply did not argue with menials. That was one of the fundamental rules of proper behavior. Lady Jersey frowned. Would Penelope ever learn what a lady could do and what a lady must not do? Motley's rescue was amusing, if somewhat eccentric. Today's behavior, played out in full view of everyone, was not. Alex was going to be furious! Words of advice came readily to her mind; she remained silent. The determined jut of Penelope's jaw meant they would have gone unheeded. Best let Alex handle it.

Alex, however, was in no mood to handle anything. Last night still rankled. After escorting his mother and Leticia back to the Ashford mansion, he had ridden to White's. He set off, with determination, to get completely foxed. It had not worked. The glasses of Burgundy gave him a shocking headache, but that was all. They could not dim the knowledge that his wife had played him for a fool. His appearance looked casual, as he sprawled lazily in an armchair with a wineglass lightly held in his fingers, but his close friends saw the brooding cast to his frown and knew better than to venture too near. The long hours of the night and the dawn crawled by. Alex did not join in the boisterous gambling or respond to any of the racy jokes that were being bantered about the room. He remained alone.

The chimes of St. George's struck the hour. Leisurely he arose, stretched, and straightened his cravat. His walking stick was in the small cloakroom by the entrance. He picked it up, shrugged with apparent unconcern, and turned toward the door. His fist tightened angrily on the head of the cane. James was standing in the doorway. The two men stared at each other. "Alex, I want to talk with you. You've been a—"

"Step aside, Harrington. We have nothing to say." His words were hard. "You can count yourself lucky, I will not call you out! We shared too much in the past for that. I warn you, though, if I find you with my wife again, there will be hell to pay!" He brushed rudely by him and left the club.

Outside on the steps he bumped into Brummell. "Ashford, I need to—"

Alex curtly nodded, but did not stop. Beau's idle chatter was the last thing he wanted to endure right now. "Can't stop, Beau, I must dash."

The other man put out a hand. "You can find time for this. It is about Lady Ashford."

Alex's eyes narrowed. If Beau knew of Penelope's and James's tryst last night, soon the whole ton would be aflutter with the news. Damn, damn, damn, he thought. "All right, George, what is it? I am a bit castaway this morning, so do be quick."

"You know I am quite fond of your wife, always have been. She is most lovely, but still, I fear, an innocent. You

236

had best have a word with her. Such behavior will soon set the ton in a spin. Making a cake of herself in public is most unaccep able!"

Alex was still somewhat foggy. It did not sound as if Beau were referring to the masquerade last night. He rubbed a hand across his throbbing forehead. What the deuce was he trying to say? "Sorry, George, guess I don't take your meaning."

"I thought you had heard, apparently not. Don't like to be the one to mention this, but I don't wish for Lady Ashford to put a foot wrong. Compassion is no doubt admirable, but not when it creates a public scandal for the duke of Wellington! You ought to—"

"Penelope and the duke! What the deuce has she done now?"

Beau briefly related the tale of Penelope, the little tiger, and the duke's blustering coachman. "Apparently the duke wasn't actually there," admitted Beau, "but you can see how this looks. It was his servant; it reflects badly on him. He is not going to like it! I advised her to be an original, but not this original! You had best speak with her. I fear she is still somewhat unversed in the ways of polite society."

"Never fear, I certainly shall!" growled Alex.

Beau nodded a bit uneasily and turned to mount the steps. This was bound to spark a nasty row. He flicked the folds of his cravat to make sure they were perfect and entered the club.

A cold rage built in Alex as he walked toward the Ashford mansion. His cane jabbed savagely at the pavement with each step. How the ton must be laughing at him for wedding a wife who so brazenly flaunted convention. "A convenient bride," Millicent had said. "A countrified miss who will cause you no trouble . . ." Hell and damnation! Penelope had caused him nothing but trouble since their wedding night. The memories of her rejection that night, the damned violets, James, and now this! The thoughts pounded through his head as he raised his hand and sent the knocker crashing down against the door.

While Alex was stomping home, Penelope was busy combing the tangles and knots out of the little boy's tousled hair. He had balked at the idea of a bath, but Kate, who had four younger brothers, knew how to handle grubby little boys. He was much more presentable now, and most talkative. Hemnings had escorted the lad on a brief tour of the Ashford stables. As Penelope tried to make him sit still so she could work on his hair, he jabbered on about the wonderful horses he had seen. He particularly liked her white stallion. His enthusiasm was engaging, even if his thick cockney accent made it difficult to understand every word. There, the last snarl was gone. She laid down the comb and gave the boy a hug. He squirmed, as little boys often do, but from his shy smile she knew he liked it.

A knock sounded on the door to her chamber. An upstairs maid entered, "Lord Ashford has returned. He wishes to see you in the study."

Penelope swallowed nervously. "Kate, take him down to the kitchen and have Cook fix some bread and jam. Be sure he gets plenty of milk."

She stopped outside the study. Her hand rested on the brass knob. The memory of her husband's kiss still burned across her lips—so did the pain of seeing Millicent in his arms. She did not want to see Alex, not after the torturous silence of last night. There was no choice. He had to know about the latest scrape she had gotten into. When the enraged employer arrived to claim the boy, he would need Alex's protection. Pushing her own feelings aside, she pulled a protective wall of dignity around her and entered the room.

"Alex, something has . . ." The intensity of the anger in his glare choked off her words. She bravely tried to meet his eyes. "I want to explain about—"

"I do not wish to hear it," he interrupted. "There is no explanation that can justify what you did. How dare you interfere!"

"The child was being beaten, beaten with a horse whip! That is why I interfered."

Her words were meaningless. He would not listen. "How dare you involve the duke of Wellington in such a shocking scandal!"

Penelope's hand flew to her mouth. The duke of Wellington, oh, no! "I did not know it was his carriage, Alex. I did not recognize his crest, but it would not have—"

"You do not recognize anything, do you? Least of all your own lack of discretion! Such a public scene is disgraceful enough, but you had to drag in England's greatest hero to share the scandal!"

"How can you call this a scandal? It would have been a scandal if I had done nothing!" Penelope tried to defend herself. "I do not care if the coachman was the duke of Wellington's servant. If the duke condones this type of behavior, then it deserves to be made public. You speak such noble words in Parliament, yet when I act, you rage at me."

"My speeches do not embarrass a great man!" All of Alex's pent-up frustration boiled out. "Will you never learn to behave properly? You are a disgrace to the Ashford name!"

Penelope tried to argue. He brushed her aside. "I should have known better than to marry a vicar's daughter." He laughed harshly. "I thought I could avoid a scandal by wedding you. This is my punishment for that monumental stupidity! Lord Shellingham's accusations would have

239

been nothing compared to this! Society must be laughing at the fate of the famous Lord Ashford!"

The anger and hurt were so deep he was beyond shouting. His words were so cold, hard, and precise that she did not detect the bitterness underneath. She almost wished he would yell. "Wasn't it enough that you played me false with James? How many others have there been, Penelope? How many? Are Lady Jersey's violet-loving cousin and that young military officer also particular friends of yours? Weren't they enough to keep you happy? Why did you also have to drag Wellington into a scandal?"

"Alex, no!" she cried. "I never cared—"

"I know you never cared for me. You have made that amply clear!" His bitter laugh rang out. "I actually thought you might be different. I wish to God I had never met you! Unfortunately, I did." A cynical smile curled his lip. He stalked purposefully closer. "Since I am trapped, I might as well get my share of the favors you give so willingly!"

He grabbed her by the shoulders and roughly pulled her into his arms. The tears streaming down Penelope's face mingled with his hard kiss. There was no tenderness, no love, only a determination to hurt, as he thought he had been hurt. Her small fists beat against his chest. He would not let her go. His arm tightened around her waist. She could not move. She could not stop his hand from roaming over her body.

Someone rapped loudly on the door. With a muffled oath he angrily pushed her away. She stumbled and fell back against the settee. Alex ignored her tears as he yanked open the door. "What is it?"

Hemnings took a step back when he saw his master's flashing anger. He's been in a deuced rage ever since he got married, the butler thought. Wonder why. "Milord, the duke of Wellington is here."

240

Alex's voice was harsh and grating as he muttered, "Put him in the red salon. I shall be there in a moment."

He slammed the door. His eyes were still blazing as he looked down at his wife. "Those innocent tears won't save you this time, as they did on our wedding night. Tonight I intend to take what is mine! Go to your bedchamber and pack. You will leave for Ashford in the morning. Take everything. You will not be returning to London!"

Alex's greeting to the famous hero was cordial and friendly, but the duke was not deceived. Something was seriously amiss. He studied Alex with concern. They had served together in the battles against Napoleon. They had gone through hell, faced tragedy and death for endless days, but he had never before seen the haunted look that filled Alex's eyes now. The duke tried to be jovial, but he was concerned about the younger man. "Came to fetch my young tiger. I assume the lad is all right."

"Sir, I cannot tell you how sorry I am that this happened."

"You are sorry it happened?" The duke chuckled. "Seems to me I am the one who should be sorry."

"Yes, I realize that, sir. I fear Lady Ashford is unversed in the ways of the ton . . ."

"Probably a damn good thing she is! Most of those high-bred ladies, flitting down Bond Street, would have ignored the whole thing. They would have been afraid something might soil their precious gowns. Your wife's got spirit. I like that. That young tiger is a favorite of mine. His father was my head groom for twenty years. The boy's an orphan now, so I take special care of him. Call your wife down. I want to thank her."

Alex was somewhat dazed by his reaction. He had expected anger, not gratitude. He yanked the bell pull and asked Hemnings to fetch Penelope from her chamber. "Will you have a glass of claret, sir?"

"Believe I will, Ashford." He sipped the wine, slowly savoring the mellow flavor, then commented, "Cutting off our supply of French wines was one of the most dastardly things that rascal Napoleon ever did." He smacked his lips appreciatively. "That alone justifies his exile! Anyway, best get back to my tiger. Can you believe some damned fool at White's said I ought to be angry with Lady Ashford for interfering? Rest assured, I told that dolt a thing or two. My servants' behavior reflects on me. I can't have them mucking about, can I? Sorry I missed it. That coachman tops thirty stones. Must have really been something to see, when Lady Ashford lighted into him!"

Hemnings knocked on the door and beckoned to Alex. The butler whispered something. The duke saw Alex frown. "Sir, I am sorry. Lady Ashford is resting. Could you pay your respects another time?"

"I can understand that. Masquerade balls by night and rescues by day, she must be quite fatigued. Tell her for me that the coachman has received a royal dressing down. He won't be snapping that whip at anything but horses ever again."

The duke spotted the cleanly scrubbed little boy waiting for him in the entry hall. "Come, lad, Cook has fixed some fresh jam tarts for you. Could use some of those myself. Best be off. I'd rather face Napoleon's cannons again, than her wrath if anyone is late to tea."

Alex politely waited for the duke to take his leave, then he stormed up to Penelope's bedchamber. The armoire was open, drawers were pulled out, a hatbox lay discarded on the floor. Penelope was gone.

CHAPTER SIXTEEN

Alex stared numbly at the evidence of Penelope's hurried packing. He walked slowly across the room, not wanting to believe what he saw. The armoire was gaping. The row of jewel-tone gowns were nestled securely inside. He frowned. Nothing appeared to be missing. The open drawers of the chiffonier caught his attention. He walked toward it. The discarded hatbox lay in his path. He kicked it angrily out of the way. The box skidded across the floor and jolted into the chest of drawers. The chiffonier teetered a bit. Something rattled across the top and fell to the floor. It bounced and landed on the carpet in front of him. Reluctantly Alex bent over to pick it up. It gleamed softly as it rested in the palm of his hand. Two lover's knots forever entwined; it was Penelope's wedding band.

She is gone. The words stabbed through his head. Penelope is gone. Alex's fist clenched tightly around the small ring. He turned. His mother was standing in the doorway. Amelia glanced quickly about the room. "Where is Penelope?" she demanded.

"I don't know." He tried to be calm. "Apparently she is gone."

"Alex, it is time we talked. Come to my sitting room."

When the door was firmly shut, Amelia observed, "I assume you and Penelope had a thundering row. Best tell me about it."

It was difficult for him to describe what had happened. The Wellington incident seemed so meaningless now.

"Alex, I am not goose-witted! Penelope would not have

left merely because you gave her a scold over helping that child. It is time for the complete truth." She eyed him sternly. "Does Lady Shellingham have anything to do with this muddle?"

"How did you . . . I mean . . ." He stopped. He looked decidedly uncomfortable.

"I have known the truth about your marriage since the beginning. I have tried to let you work this out on your own, but you have been a bigger slow-top than your cousin Percy! Are you still keeping company with Lady Shellingham? Is that what overset Penelope?"

"No, my affair with Millicent is over. It has been for a long time."

"Then why did she leave?"

Alex remembered the harsh accusations he had hurled at her. He remembered the salt of her tears when he had forced that kiss on her. He remembered his threat. The words were painful. "We had a nasty row over James," he confessed. "He had been sitting most attentively in her pocket. I suppose I deserved it, but . . ."

"Bosh!" his mother snapped. "Penelope cares nothing for James, except as a friend."

He stared sadly at his mother. "Don't try to protect her. I know it is so. He is always at her side and last night—"

"Last night he brought her home, because she said she had a dreadful headache. I suspect there is more to the story, though. I saw her when she came in from the terrace. She was deathly pale. Immediately after that she asked James to escort her home." Amelia's glance was questioning. "I searched for you, but you were nowhere about. Your friend had to be the one to help her."

A slow flush crept over Alex's face. Penelope had seen Millicent's clinging plea. She must have thought it was a lover's rendezvous. The remembrance of their own romantic interlude on that terrace forced its way into his mind. Her kiss had been so tentative at first, then as their desire grew, she had willingly . . . Abruptly he stood up. No! He did not want to remember. "It isn't just last night, Mother. Lately James has been here more than I have. I know—"

"You know nothing! Don't be mutton-headed, Alex. James came here to see Leticia, not Penelope. He has not come up to scratch yet, but he will. I have never seen a more besotted pair."

Alex whirled around and gaped at her. "James and Leticia?" he repeated, hardly daring to believe her words.

"Yes, your friend is in love with your cousin, not your wife." He opened his mouth to argue, but she ordered, "And I do not wish to hear any gibberish about violets. Penelope bought those flowers herself. She invented a mysterious gallant to make you jealous. There has never been anyone else but you. She loves you, Alex. She always has."

He sank dejectedly into a chair. His hands came up, and he rubbed his eyes. Amelia studied her son for a long moment. Her words were softly sad. "I prayed that you would come to love her too, but if you can't, let the child go. It would be kinder. You have hurt her enough."

Dear God, he thought, how could he have been such a dolt! His eyes were anguished as he confessed, "I can't let her go. We must find her. Where the devil could she have gone?"

"Maybe she went to a friend here in London. What did you say to her during your row? That might give us a clue."

"How the deuce am I supposed to remember. I was too angry to think!"

"Yes, your papa was just like that too. He would say the most frightful things to me when he was in a rage, and then vow he had never said them. But, dear, you must try and remember. It is most important."

He threw himself out of the chair and began to prowl through the room. "We quarreled over that brat of Wellington's. I threw James up to her . . . and . . . other things happened." He frowned as he remembered the punishing kiss he had forced on her. "Then Hemnings knocked and . . . Ashford! She has gone to Ashford, I am sure of it."

Amelia's face blanched. "Alex, you must go after her! Penelope has to ride through Finchley Common to get to Ashford. She does not know of the danger. Jack Tatum escaped from Newgate last month. If he waylays her, he'll . . . Oh, Alex, you must find her!"

It was not necessary for her to finish the thought. They both knew what would happen if that villainous highwayman captured Penelope. "Have my horse fetched. I cannot ride like this." He ran swiftly from the room. In his chamber he stripped off his evening wear and flung himself into a pair of leather breeches and a riding shirt. He rapidly loaded a pistol, jammed it into his belt, and donned his great coat.

The huge black stallion shied nervously as Alex came crashing out the front door. Amelia wrung her hands and begged, "Hurry, Alex! The groom said Penelope was riding that white horse of hers when she left. Find her. Bring her back!"

He wheeled his horse around and galloped out of the square. The ride toward Finchley Common was pure hell. It seemed as if every slow lorry in London barred his way. Once out on the post road he dug his heels into the stallion's flanks. The horse broke into a smooth, powerful gallop that rapidly ate up the miles. Dusk was falling as Alex approached the notorious common. He drew his pistol. All seemed quiet. He slowed the horse to a walk and searched the darkening woods for some sign of

Tatum's henchmen. He saw a shadowy figure slip through the trees, but he was not challenged. He prayed Penelope had made it through all right. "I hope Black Jack decided to take a holiday," he muttered as he urged his horse toward Ashford.

The great house was shrouded in darkness. Alex pounded furiously on the heavy oak door. After what seemed to him a vast age, a very sleepy Jenkins, with his nightcap atilt, opened the door a crack and peered out. Mi—milord," he sputtered, "what is amiss?"

"Has Lady Ashford arrived yet?" he demanded as he shoved through the door.

"No, milord. Was she expected? We had no notice that she would be arriving."

A cold chill swept through Alex. He had told himself over and over on the long ride from London that he would find Penelope safe at Ashford. She wasn't. Where did he look now? He rubbed a hand across his tired eyes. "Have Cook throw together a cold supper and call Jem-groom. I want him to rub down my horse, feed him, and fetch me another. I must ride for London."

"But, milord, 'tis the middle of the night. You mustn't —"

He did not even bother to argue. "I will be in the library when the food is ready."

Jenkins shrugged. "The quality get balmier every year!" he fussed as he set his nightcap back on straight and yanked the bell pull to summon one of the footmen.

On his way to Ashford Alex had ridden on the post roads in hopes of overtaking Penelope, now he cut through the fields to hasten his return to London. The moon was high to light his way. It reminded him of the soft glow that had lighted the terrace at the masquerade ball. His arms ached with emptiness. How could he have driven her away? How could he have driven away the woman he loved? That certainty had grown in him with each passing moment. He loved his wife! How could he not have seen that his jealousy was caused by his growing love? He should have known, but he had been blind, maybe deliberately blind. Alex had thought himself in love once and had been bitterly disillusioned. He swore he would never open his heart that way again. His feelings for Penelope had come so slowly, so softly, that he did not realize what was happening. He knew he wanted her in his arms for every waltz, her smile enticed him, the thought of her kiss warmed his blood, and still he had not realized what he felt was love.

As he rode through the awakening morning bustle of London, he tortured himself with the angry words he had yelled at her. No wonder she had fled from him. He had to find her! He had to tell her! Where the deuce could she have gone? Alex threw the reins to a waiting groom and wearily mounted the steps to the Ashford mansion.

Amelia was in the entry hall. One look at the despair in his face and she knew Penelope had not been at Ashford. She was aware of the servant's hovering presence. "Come, Alex, Cook has fixed a hot breakfast."

She watched him with concern as he ate the steak and kidney pie. It could have been cold gruel for all he tasted. There was a deep sadness in his eyes as he asked, "She hasn't returned, has she?"

"No, Alex, I fear there has been no word. I had Kate check through Penelope's bedchamber. The only things that are missing are her riding habit, those few dresses her mother made for her, and Motley. She left everything else." Tears gathered in her eyes. "I am so worried! Where could she be? You don't suppose Tatum—"

"If he had her, we would have received a ransom note by now. He would not let such a plump chicken escape. She must be somewhere here in London. She has no money. She could not have gone far. Help me think, Mother. God, I have been such a fool!"

"Yes, dear, you have!" Amelia agreed firmly. The silence lasted a long moment. "Lady Jersey. Maybe Penelope is with the Jerseys."

She rose quickly. "We do not want the whole ton to know of this. You go up and catch some sleep. I shall pay Lady Jersey a morning call." Alex tried to protest, but she was adamant. "You cannot search for your wife if you fall asleep in your saddle."

It was several hours later when his valet gently shook his shoulder and awakened him. He had not truly believed he could sleep, but he had. He sprang up and hurried to his mother's sitting room. Leticia was there. Amelia silently shook her head. He sank down on the chaise.

Leticia timidly ventured, "Cousin Alex, please do not rage at me, but I think Penelope might have gone to James. She knew he would be more discreet than Lady Jersey, and he was her friend."

There was a time when such a suggestion would have infuriated him. All that mattered now was finding his wife. The faint hope buoyed his spirits as he once more mounted his horse. The Harrington butler formally bowed him into James's dining room. His friend was slicing into a joint of roasted beef when Alex was announced. He laid down the knife. "Come to call me out, after all, huh. Well, what's it to be old boy—pistols or swords? Know it's tradition, but must we duel at dawn? I do so hate to get up early. Guess we could make a night of it at White's, and then meet. That might answer. Suppose Brummell will stand as my second? You could ask—"

"James, please stop the blather! Is Penelope here?"

James scanned his friend's face and quickly dismissed the servants. "See here, Alex, I have tried to tell you more than once that Penelope is only a friend. I am—"

249

"I know," he interrupted impatiently, "you are all in a basket over Leticia. I thought Penelope might have come here, because you have been her friend."

"Left in a miff over Lady Shellingham, did she? Can't say I'm surprised. Always thought you had a fair share of wits in your cockloft, but lately I haven't been so sure. Why the deuce have you been keeping company with Lady Shellingham when you are wed to Penelope? Any dullard should be able to see that your wife is an incomparable! I told Leticia—"

"There is no scold you can deliver that I have not already given myself. I fear Lady Shellingham is not the entire reason Penelope has run away."

James placed a heaping plate of food in front of Alex. "Best eat something while you give me all the details. Sounds like a deuce of a muddle!"

Alex's story was half done when James exploded, "Wellington! Why the devil did you scold her about that? You should have known she would save the brat. Good thing, too! Bad ton to have servants whipping lads on Bond Street. Bound to set the ladies up in a screech. You ought not to—"

"James!" Alex had to raise his voice to stop his chatter. "I fully realize how witless I was. I know now I was not truly angry with Penelope over that ridiculous fracas. It merely served to set off my damnable temper. Wellington was an excuse I used to punish her. I believed she was playing me false. That's why I raged at her, not because she saved that boy. I am proud of Penelope for what she did. Her caring is one of the reasons I have . . ." His voice trailed off.

"As I have discovered, it isn't some dread disease, old friend. Might as well say it."

The words came haltingly. "I—I love her, James. I have been a damned fool! The jealousy, the discontent, my

250

boredom with Millicent . . . I should have seen what it meant. But no, I was too deuced arrogant to admit it, or maybe," Alex conceded sadly, "I was afraid to let myself love again. I don't know. None of it matters now. Penelope is gone. You have to help me. Think where she might have gone."

"Ashford?"

"No, I have already checked there. And she is not with the Jerseys. Think, James, think!"

"How the deuce can I think if you keep shouting at me. If it were me, and I were in trouble, I would go home, but Penelope doesn't—"

Alex leaped to his feet. "James, that's it. It has to be. Thanks, old friend."

"What the deuce did I say?" James shouted at his retreating back. "Alex, wait. I'll—"

"No time." He rushed out and leaped onto his horse. "Go to Grosvenor Square and tell my mother and Leticia I know where Penelope is."

"Where is she?" he yelled as Alex slapped the horse's rump. The stallion broke into a gallop; he waved and was gone.

For the second time Alex rode through the fields toward Ashford. The Arabian strain in his horse gave his mount endurance to maintain the frantic pace he set. The stallion's coat was dripping wet and his sides were heaving when Alex finally reined him in. He swung out of the saddle and pounded on the door of the vicarage.

Vicar Wesley answered his knock. "Milord, is something wrong?"

Alex found it difficult to ask the question. "My wife? Is my wife here? I must see her!"

The vicar stepped aside and let him enter. They walked into the parlor where Harriet was sitting. She glanced up from her tatting. "Oh, dear!" she whispered.

251

His lordship briefly bowed over her hand, then turned with a questioning glance back toward the other man. "Well, sir, is she here?"

"You put me in an impossible situation, Lord Ashford. Lady Ashford is indeed with us, but she does not wish to see you. I must respect her wishes."

"Vicar Wesley, I demand . . ." The words died. Alex swallowed and began again. "I beg you to tell me where she is. I swear I shall cause her no more unhappiness!"

The vicar studied Alex for a long spell. Finally, he looked at his wife for help with the decision. "I think you had best tell him, Albert," Harriet declared. "I believe Lord Ashford speaks the truth when he says all he wants is her happiness."

The vicar still looked a bit doubtful, but he agreed. "Lady Ashford is at the far end of the rose garden under the apple tree."

Alex walked quickly through the tiny kitchen and out the back door of the cottage. The path wound through the rows of blooming rose bushes. He saw nothing but the spreading branches of the old apple tree at the garden's end. His steps slowed. There was Penelope. Motley was curled up contentedly on her lap. She was stroking the little dog, but obviously her thoughts were far away. He could tell from the despondent droop to her head that she was suffering as much as he.

He hesitantly took a step nearer. The gravel crunched under his boot. Motley raised his head, gave a joyous yelp, and flung himself toward Alex. The pup's paws clawed at Alex's breeches as he tried unsuccessfully to get his master's attention. Alex's gaze never wavered from Penelope's white face. "Mott, down!" he ordered. "Go chase a rabbit!" The dog cocked his head, looked from one to the other, barked once, and scampered off toward the stables.

Penelope rose nervously to her feet. Her hands were

tightly clasped in front of her. Before Alex could say a word, she said, "Milord, I know why you have come. I am aware that I should not have left as I did. No doubt this will cause another dreadful scandal, but I had to go. I had to!" She bravely met his eyes and hurried on, "We never should have married. I know that now. I can never be the type of tonnish wife you want. It is best we part. You can tell everyone I died, or I shall go away and you can get a quiet annulment. There will be no scandal, I promise." Tears glistened on the ends of her lashes. "I have caused you enough trouble. I will do anything you wish."

"Anything?"

Penelope could not bear to look at his beloved face. She must be brave! She lowered her eyes and whispered, "Yes."

"If you will do anything I want, then please come here. What I want is you . . . and your love, if you are still willing to give it to me."

She could scarce believe his words! Her eyes fluttered upward. She stared uncertainly at him. Alex opened his arms wide. "I love you, Penelope. Please tell me it is not too late." With a cry she ran straight toward his embrace.

His kiss was wondrously gentle at first, as if he were afraid he might frighten her. She was not frightened. Her arms went up around his neck. She pulled him closer. Alex felt her passionate response, and his kiss became more possessive. The longing of their separation made the desire sweeter. Finally, with a strength of will he did not know he possessed, he put her from him. His laugh was unsteady. "If you continue to be so enticing, we shall shock the good vicar."

"Would that be so awful?" she teased softly. Her pert reply called for another delightful exchange.

Alex raised his head and caressed her trembling lips

with soft strokes. "Still the little hellcat, I see. Do you suppose another kiss might tame you?"

Penelope batted her eyelashes provocatively, "You could try, milord."

It was a long spell before the two returned, arm in arm, to the vicarage. Both Harriet and Albert beamed with pleasure when they saw the love that radiated from the couple. Alex took Vicar Wesley aside and whispered something in his ear. The vicar smiled and nodded. "It will be done, milord."

Alex's arm never left Penelope's waist as they walked back outside into the warm sunshine. He swung her up on the back of the great stallion and mounted behind her. She snuggled back against him, secure in his embrace. Alex let the reins droop as the horse's tired gait took them toward Ashford. There was no hurry. He nuzzled the back of her neck lazily. His senses were filled once again with the exotic scent of her perfume. "Mmm," he murmured as he gently nibbled on her ear, "your perfume almost drove me mad. I would hold you in my arms as we waltzed, and remember that night you were almost mine. I hated myself for . . ."

Penelope turned in the saddle and laid a loving finger to still his lips. "No sad thoughts, no regrets, darling."

The stallion's walk halted as he felt Alex drop the reins. He lowered his head and contentedly munched on the tender green grass as his two riders shared yet another fully satisfying kiss.

Reluctantly, Alex released her. Penelope's smiling mouth beckoned him to linger a bit more, but he softly ordered, "Enough, vixen. Turn around. We must be off. I vow your wiles would tempt a saint."

She chuckled. "Hardly a proper comparison, milord. You are certainly no saint!"

There was a deep throb to his voice as he promised, "I

shall give you convincing proof of that very shortly, my beguiling little wife!" He picked up the reins and slapped them gently against the horse's neck.

Penelope laid her head back against his shoulder. His promise sent a tremor of longing through her body. They had been apart too long! His arm tightened possessively around her. She closed her eyes and savored the feelings that had so long been denied.

Alex kissed the back of her neck again. "We are here. Let me help you down."

Her eyes opened dreamily, she blinked once, then blinked again. They had not ridden to the great house. Instead Alex had brought her to the Ashford chapel. His hands were warm as he lifted her from the saddle and lowered her into his arms. Solemnly, he said, "Penelope, my one and true love, will you do me the honor of becoming my wife . . . again?"

Happy tears welled up in her eyes as she nodded. He reverently kissed her, then led her toward the waiting vicar. For the second time they knelt in the small chapel to receive the sacred marriage vows. The words were the same, but the beauty of their love made them so much more meaningful, so much more binding. Alex slipped the ring of entwined lover's knots onto her fourth finger. He raised her hand to his lips and kissed the wedding band. They shared a secret smile.

There was no elegant dinner and iced champagne waiting for them at Ashford this time. It did not matter in the least. Jenkins served them the simple shepherd's pie the cook had prepared and discreetly withdrew. A scratching and yelping at the door told them Motley had been returned. The door remained firmly closed. Between bites of the savory pie they kissed and talked and kissed some more. There was so much to say and so many misunderstandings to be explained. Alex tried to tell her about the scene she had witnessed on the Cowpers' terrace. All that was unimportant. Penelope stopped his words with a lingering caress. The pie grew cold as he pulled her more securely into his arms. Long moments later he confessed, "I never knew a kiss could be like that."

Penelope smiled at him. "You have never been in love before."

He stood up and lifted her high into his arms. Their desire flamed as he slowly climbed the great curving staircase. Each kiss was more deeply passionate than the last. Waves of pure delight ran through Penelope as she felt his rising need. She pressed her body deliciously closer, yet closer, to his hard chest.

The reached the door to her bedchamber. Motley was stretched out across the sill waiting for her. He arose lazily, stretched, and then scratched eagerly on the door to be let in. A slow smile spread over Alex's face. "Not tonight, Motley!" He gazed tenderly down at his wife. "I do believe we shall have to move that mutt's pallet to my chamber. I shall not be sleeping there again."

He kicked open the door and carried a very willing Penelope toward the great canopied bed. This wedding night would be different, oh, so very different, than the one before.